OLD SECRETS

OLD SECRETS

Rowena Summers

This first world edition published 2011
in Great Britain and in the USA by
SEVERN HOUSE PUBLISHERS LTD of
9–15 High Street, Sutton, Surrey, England, SM1 1DF.

British Library Cataloguing in Publication Data

Summers, Rowena,
    Old secrets.
    1. Aristocracy (Social class) – Fiction. 2. Orphans –
    Fiction. 3. Nephews – Fiction. 4. Family secrets – Fiction.
    5. Domestic fiction.
    I. Title
    823.9'14–dc22

ISBN-13: 978-0-7278-8099-4 (cased)

All Severn House titles are printed on acid-free paper.

Severn House Publishers support The Forest Stewardship Council [FSC],
the leading international forest certification organisation. All our titles that
are printed on Greenpeace-approved FSC-certified paper carry the FSC logo.

MIX
Paper from
responsible sources
FSC
www.fsc.org   FSC® C018575

Typeset by Palimpsest Book Production
Falkirk, Stirlingshire, Scotland.
Printed and bound in Great Britain by
MPG Books Ltd., Bodmin, Cornwall.

One

The splendid Melchoir House and estate sat high on top of the glorious Durdham Downs, overlooking the city of Bristol and its environs. To the right of it, above the snaking silvery Avon river far below, was the elegant expanse of Isambard Kingdom Brunel's suspension bridge, sadly not completed until after his death. If Cherry Melchoir could choose any place in the world to live, it would be here, she thought, a catch in her throat on that lovely summer's day as she and her best friend, Paula, watched their children at play on the Downs.

'Did you ever think we'd be doing this, Paula?' she said suddenly.

Her friend laughed, always able to follow the way her thoughts were going. Her eyes sparkled.

'Not on your Nelly,' she said, in the broad accent than contrasted so sharply with Cherry's modulated tones. 'In fact, when you and Lance were banished to Ireland after all the upset, I was convinced that we'd never blooming well see one another ever again.'

Cherry smiled, remembering. The 'upset', as Paula so delicately called it, was more in the nature of a holocaust as far as the Melchoir family had been concerned. A kitchen-maid becoming pregnant by the son of the house . . . and the son defying his father by declaring that he wanted to marry her! It was an outrage and a scandal that Sir Francis and Lady Elspeth simply wouldn't allow.

And even when Cherry had confessed in shame to Lance that it had all been a mischievous pretence, and she wasn't pregnant after all, the two of them had continued the deceit in order that they would still be allowed to marry, even though it meant banishment to Ireland. She had never believed that he would forgive her, but he had, loving her too much to let her go. She gave a small shiver, thinking what tenuous threads had held them together to become the happy family they were now, but they had come through it all.

'Do you think those two will grow up and fall in love like we once dreamed about when we were kids?' she heard Paula say idly, watching the ten-year-olds – her son Thomas, and Cherry's coppery-haired daughter Bella – screaming with laughter as they tossed the ball to one another, as Bella's small brother tottered between them, trying to catch it.

'Good Lord, no!' Cherry said without thinking. 'Lance has got far greater plans for Bella.'

She drew in her breath as she saw Paula's face. 'Oh God, you know I didn't mean that the way it sounded, Paula.'

'Well, you probably did, and quite right too. Why would the daughter of a Lord ever want to marry the son of a railway worker?'

'Harold's doing very nicely now, isn't he?' Cherry said awkwardly. 'A supervisor, no less, and your new house is lovely, Paula, and so much bigger than the old railway cottage near Temple Meads.'

Was she making it worse by going on so? How could any of it compare with the mansion across the Downs that they could see from here?

She heard Paula laughing, and her eyes were sparkling again.

'Gawd, kid, you sure know how to bite, don't you? We all know our place and I'm just glad your old man tolerates us coming to visit you such a lot, and even makes us welcome in his own toffee-nosed way.'

'Now I don't know if you're teasing me or not, and I'm not going to start defending Lance. He can't help the way he was born, and he will always welcome you, Paula. You know that. Remember your visit to Ireland?'

Paula snorted. 'Oh yes, when I was all fingers and thumbs and too afraid of dropping my Ps and Qs to relax. I just wanted to see that you were all right, Cherry, that was all.'

'Well, I was. I'd got what I always wanted, hadn't I?' she said softly.

The children came running back then, and Cherry marvelled again at the glowing face of her daughter. Bella was already shaping into a little beauty, with glorious flaming red hair like her mother's, a perfectly heart-shaped face, and large blue eyes that could melt a heart of stone, according to her father. And young Thomas treated her with all the rough and tumble of a pseudo older brother, even though they were only months apart in age.

There had been a time, she freely admitted, when she and Paula had been young, carefree kitchen-maids without two ha'pennies between them and did everything together, when they had dreamed of growing up and marrying their sweethearts and seeing their children play together, as close as they themselves had always been.

Well, it hadn't quite happened that way. After what Paula still called the 'upset', their lives couldn't have gone in more different directions, since Cherry had married the son of a Lord and had eventually assumed the title of Lady herself – a situation that had seemed impossible at the time, but a role that was perfectly natural to her now, ten years on.

And if she ever stopped to wonder where those two madcap girls had gone, it was with a sense of sweet nostalgia, the way you sometimes caught the sound of an old, half-remembered melody, and nothing more. Her life was happy and fulfilled, and she knew that Paula's was as well.

'Oh crikey, isn't that your posh friend among that group coming towards us?' Paula said, breaking into her thoughts. 'I swear she looks more blooming mannish every day.'

'She can't help that. She's always been sophisticated and fashionable, Paula, and it probably compensates for what people call a handsome face, rather than a pretty one,' Cherry told her generously.

'Well, I know which I'd rather have,' Paula muttered as the tall girl broke away from her companions for a moment to saunter over to them.

'Cherry, my dear, how are you? I haven't seen you in ages.'

'I'm very well, thank you, Cyn,' Cherry replied.

She had long overcome her feeling of awkwardness in front of the people who had once been Lance's friends, and never hers. Until, that was, the Honourable Cynthia Hetherington had taken her under her wing like a Good

Samaritan – or a guardian angel. Cherry had never quite decided which.

'You know my friend, Paula, don't you?' she went on, determined not to leave Paula out, and Cyn inclined her head with a smile.

'Nice to see you again, Miss – Ma'am – your Honouryship,' Paula said, just about resisting giving a little bob, and making Cynthia peal with laughter.

'You were always a bit of a card, weren't you, Paula?' She turned away from her. 'And how are the delightful Melchoir children? I see that Bella's living up to her name. Such a beautiful little girl, and a credit to you, Cherry. She'll break some young man's giddy heart one of these days.'

She waved airily at them as her friends called to her, and went on her way, leaving behind a waft of expensive perfume in her wake.

'Dyke,' Paula muttered.

'*What* did you say?' Cherry said, startled.

'Well, don't say you've never thought it. It's obvious, isn't it? She's not interested in men and she hangs around with that weird crowd all the time.'

'They're not that weird. They dress in that flamboyant way because they're theatricals and clothes designers, Paula, and Cyn spends a lot of time among that kind of people.'

'There you are, then,' Paula said, as if that explained all.

In the end, Cherry was laughing, seeing that nothing would sway her. But she had known Cyn all these years, and at one time she was sure she had wanted Lance for herself until he fell for Cherry against all the odds, so why on earth would she prefer the company of women, in the way Paula was implying? She shut the unsavoury thought out of her mind immediately.

'Anyway, I must go,' Paula said suddenly. 'Oh, and have you noticed that bloke skulking over there by the bushes? I don't like the look of him. You want to watch yourself on the way home, Cherry, in case he's after grabbing your purse or something. He could be a pickpocket or a ne'er-do-well.'

'I don't see anybody, and I think you've been reading too many penny dreadfuls,' Cherry said, still laughing. 'You never trust anybody, do you?'

'Please yourself, but don't say I didn't warn you. There are some odd characters about, and I don't just mean the Hon Cyn. Now I come to think of it, that's not a bad name for her, is it?'

'For pity's sake, Paula!'

'Oh, all right, I'm just teasing. Now, I'm going to buy a nice bit of fish for Harold's tea. He's partial to it on a Friday. Says it keeps the devil away. I'll see you next week, then, Cherry. Come on, Thomas,' she yelled out, and the next minute the two of them were gone, Paula tripping over the grass, as trim and slight as ever, and Thomas prancing along beside her.

Cherry watched her go for a minute, her eyes full of the affection she had always felt for her friend. How much a part of each other they had been all these years, and yet how differently their lives had turned out. They had been as close as clams once, sharing everything, their attic room at the Melchoir house, their dreams, their secrets . . . and now Paula was going home to cook fish for Harold to keep the devil away, and Cherry would take Bella and Georgie home to have afternoon tea served in the nursery by their nanny-cum-governess, while she and Lance would dine later on whatever delights Cook had made for them.

She gave a sudden shiver, thinking how small a turn of the dice could make all the difference in a person's life. It all depended so much on chance.

The children were already wandering over to her, disconsolate now that the boisterous Thomas had gone, and she stood up from the sunlit wooden bench and brushed the thoughts away.

'Why can't Thomas live nearer to us?' Bella complained, as she always did whenever they parted.

'It would be nice, wouldn't it?' Cherry countered diplomatically. 'But we can't always have what we want, darling. Now then, let's go home for tea. Perhaps it will be cherry cake today.'

That always got Georgie chortling with laughter at having cake with his mother's name. She caught his chubby hand in hers. At four, he hadn't yet lost his baby fat, and she found herself wishing momentarily that he never would. That children never had to grow out of their innocence, and could remain forever young and sweet, instead of turning into the monsters some of them became.

'Why has your face gone all funny?' she heard Bella say.

'Has it, darling?' She smiled down at her little daughter hastily, catching hold of her hand with her free one. 'I was just having a bad thought, that's all. But it's gone now – see?'

A bad thought about a relative that neither of you will ever see, nor ever know about, my darlings, she thought grimly.

The kitchens of Melchoir House had been the domain of both Cherry and Paula ever since they were young girls and first went into service for Lord Francis Melchoir and his frosty wife, Lady Elspeth, both now deceased. Few of the early staff still remained now that there were more work opportunities for girls in the nineteen-thirties, and they were no longer prepared to work in service. It was a situation that suited the young Lord and Lady Melchoir, since, among those working below stairs, only Cook and the ever-loyal Mr Gerard knew of the events that had led up to their marriage.

Gerard had been both butler and chauffeur until a few years ago, when his arthritis had begun to make it difficult for him to sit in the limousine for any length of time, and a new young chauffeur had been hired. Dawkins was a lively one with the housemaids and kitchen-maids, and constantly had to be kept in order, but it was as harmonious a household below stairs as it had ever been when Cherry and Paula were there.

Either that or she was viewing it through rose-coloured glasses, she thought with a wry smile. The work had certainly been hard. Scrubbing and polishing and cleaning grates, their hands forever red and rough. And, even worse, hanging out wet sheets in force-nine gales that could whip across the chilly Downs high above Bristol, and rip the linen out of their sore hands and send them screaming after it before it was dragged in the dirt and had to be washed all over again, and they incurred Cook's wrath for their carelessness.

Happy days, Cherry thought now, as she scooted her children

indoors to the nursery for their afternoon tea on a day that was so different from those other ones. But they *were* happy days, for all that. And the best day of all was when she and Paula had been escorted home in the limousine by the young Master Lance, slightly the worse for wear after an evening's dancing and drinking. The day that had been followed by the incredible moments when Lance had taken her to the stables, and in the soft, sweet-smelling hayloft she had succumbed for the first time to the thrill of a lover's warmth and tenderness and love . . . well, perhaps more lust than love on his part, but not on hers . . . never on hers. And there had been more than enough love between them since those first heady days. Love, and anger, and fright, and remorse, and ultimately triumph when he had defied his furious parents and told them he intended to marry a kitchen-maid.

'Mummy, your face has gone all funny again!' she heard her daughter say complainingly when the children had washed their hands in the newly attached nursery bathroom.

She gave a small laugh. 'It's nothing, darling. Probably a goose walking over my grave, that's all.'

Bella pulled a face. 'That's a horrible thing to say, and you're scaring Georgie when you talk like that. He thinks you're going to die.'

Cherry glanced down at the small face of her four-year-old son, so like Lance that it always made her heart turn over whenever she saw him sleeping. She held his hand tightly as he spoke, his eyes large with fear.

'You're not going to die, are you, Mummy?'

'Of course I'm not going to die, my love. Not for years and years and years, anyway, not until you're both very old.'

'Thomas says that people can die at any age, even babies,' Bella said importantly. 'Thomas knows such a lot of things. He's very clever for a railway worker's son, isn't he, Mummy?'

Cherry had to bite her lips hard to keep the anger inside her. How dare this chit, with everything that money could buy, be so condescending about Paula's son? Even if it was true, she thought, a touch guiltily. Young Thomas Farmer had a sharp brain and an easy way of absorbing facts. He would go far, given the chance, while Bella, she had to admit, was not the world's best scholar. But nor did she need to be, she reminded herself. A good marriage was all that was expected of her, and with her beautiful, heart-shaped face and sunny disposition, she would be assured of that. It would be left to Georgie to make something of himself, and Lance had every confidence that he would. Even at four, he was ready to question things, and that was the way that knowledge began.

'Thomas is growing into a very polite young boy,' she told Bella now, 'and I'm glad that you and he are such friends.'

Bella nodded. 'I like him a lot, but he's not really our sort, is he, Mummy? Auntie Paula talks sloppily too, doesn't she? It's sort of – well, common, really.'

This time Cherry had to turn away as the anger threatened to spill over. Thankfully, Nanny Green arrived to take over the tea ritual, or she might have snapped at her daughter that if she thought Paula was common, then so had Cherry been in those far-off days. If it hadn't been her ability to mimic the voices of anyone around her, and if she hadn't been able to develop the persona of a lady so easily, she too would have been deemed common by her so-superior little daughter.

It was time she had words with Lance about it, she vowed. Although she wasn't too sure that he would be sympathetic. With the full responsibilities of being Lord Melchoir, managing the estate and several business ventures and investments, he had become harder over the years and preferred to leave the children's upbringing in hers and Nanny's capable hands. Until Bella was old enough to be found a suitable beau, and Georgie had acquired the manner of a little gentleman, children weren't Lance's priority in life. He loved them all dearly, but he couldn't be concerned with what he called petty domestic details.

At that precise moment, Lord Melchoir was contemplating the wisdom of what he had completed that day. Cherry deserved a treat, but he wasn't sure how she was going to take the news of a sea voyage halfway around the world – or rather, the Atlantic crossing both ways, which was just as bad. She hadn't fared too well on the ferry to Ireland some years ago, he remembered. But that was long ago, and now they had the chance, at the invitation of some good friends, to join the magnificent *Queen*

Mary on her sixth round-trip voyage in August while she competed for the Blue Riband trophy against the French ship *Normandie*. It was too good a chance to miss. And if Cherry bleated about leaving the children behind for a couple of weeks, they would be left in the very capable hands of the buxom Nanny Green.

In any case, by the time he returned to the house in time to say goodnight to the children and join his wife for dinner, the plans had been made and the tickets were in place. All that remained now was to tell her.

When he entered the dining room, she was already waiting for him, wearing a gown of his favourite blue that suited her colouring so well. Her hair was coiffed to perfection and she oozed sophistication with the underlying sensuality that could never be denied. He adored her now as much as he always had. His sweet Cherry-ripe, who was so much a lady, despite everything.

He nuzzled his face into her neck, breathing in the scent of her. Woman and perfume mingling. Was there ever anything so provocative?

'I've got a surprise for you,' he murmured softly.

'Another one?' Cherry said, her eyes dancing. 'You spoil me, Lance.'

'Ah, but this is not just another piece of jewellery or anything tangible.'

'Don't keep me in suspense, then. What is it?'

He laughed at her impatience as the door opened and their meal was about to be served, the maids prepared to hover discreetly in the background.

'After dinner,' he said. 'I want to be able to see your face in private when I tell you.'

'Tell me *what*?' Cherry said. 'It's not something I can see or hold, then?'

'That's what I said,' Lance said, irritatingly complacent. 'I'm sure you can manage to wait an hour to learn about something very special, my love.'

She would rather not wait ten minutes, and an hour seemed an interminably long time to eat a meal, when she and Paula had once had to gobble everything down in-between duties,

and never mind the niceties. But that was long ago, and now
that she was a lady, she had to abide by the proprieties so as
not to outrage the servants. Since she had once been one of
the servants in the house, and one of the lowest at that, it
would be laughable if it wasn't so incredibly true.

But the beautifully served meal of best beef with carrots and
leeks fresh from the garden, followed by Cook's special trifle,
was finally over, and she and Lance could move to the drawing
room for a nightcap before retiring to bed. Surely he wasn't
going to wait until then to tell her his news, whatever it was.
She was almost bursting with impatience by the time he went
to a bureau drawer and pulled out a folder.

'Come and sit beside me on the sofa, Cherry,' he said with
a smile.

He was in such a buoyant mood that she obeyed without
question, knowing that if she complained any longer, he would
go on teasing her.

'I'm ready,' she said solemnly.

He burst out laughing, putting his arms around her and kissing
her soundly.

'There's no need to look so apprehensive, my
Cherry-ripe.'

'Well, when you call me that, I know it has to be something
good,' she said, feeling a glow just by his use of her
pet-name.

'And so it is. Take a look at these photographs and tell me
what you see.'

Cherry gazed down at the folder containing the photographs
of an enormous ship whose length seemed to go on for ever,
its three symmetrical red funnels pointing skywards. She gave
a sudden shiver.

'The only ship I've ever heard about that was anything like
as large as this was the *Titanic*, and I know what happened to
her.'

'It's not the *Titanic*, you ninny. It's the splendid *Queen Mary*,
and you and I will be passengers on her round-trip crossing
of the Atlantic in two months' time. What do you say to that?'

For a moment, the room seemed to spin in front of Cherry's
eyes. She wished to heaven she'd never mentioned the ill-fated

Titanic, the thought of drowning at sea threatening to choke her. For God's sake, when Lance banished her brother to Australia all those years ago, hateful though Brian had been, she had had nightmares of the ship sinking, and her brother gasping for breath with it. She had never even told Lance about those night terrors, knowing how he loathed Brian and the evil he could have done to the Melchoir family. It was so many years ago now, and yet, without warning, the memories were revived in an instant, and the idea of voyaging any distance on a ship, with nothing surrounding them but a vast ocean, had filled Cherry with dread ever since that day.

'*No*, Lance, *no*! Please don't make me!' she almost croaked when she could finally find enough breath to speak at all.

He frowned at her, his face darkening with anger and astonishment. As always at such times, prominent now was the thin white line on his cheek that was all that remained of the livid gash he had once received at the hands of Cherry's brutal brother, Brian 'Knuckles' O'Neill, bare-knuckle fighting expert.

'Well, what an extraordinary and provincial reaction! Don't you want to see the world, Cherry? It doesn't revolve around petty domesticity.'

He probably didn't mean the domestic life that Cherry and Paula had once led below stairs. She didn't know if his words were barbed or not, but it was all she could see in them at that moment, and her face became as flushed as his.

'I'm sorry I wasn't born with your adventurous streak,' she said stiffly. 'I'm sorry I was born the way I was.'

'I'm bloody sorry too. I'm offering you the trip of a lifetime in excellent company, and you throw it back in my face like a frightened puppy. I suppose you've been seeing that feeble friend of yours again. It's time you remembered who you are, my lady.'

This wasn't fair! She owed him everything, and she knew that, but she had never let him down in any way. He rarely mentioned anything of her working-class past or how they had come to be together, but he had no right to sneer at Paula in that way, however obscurely. Society tried to make people believe that the old class system was gone, but it wasn't, and never would be. In class, status and education, Lord Lance

Melchoir was streets above the humble Cherry O'Neill, kitchen-maid, that she had once been, and she would do well not to forget it if she was to be all that he expected of her. She swallowed hard.

'What about the children?' she said huskily.

'The children will be in good hands in the care of Miss Green,' he said coldly. 'It's only for two weeks, and they'll hardly know we've gone. Surely you can manage to curb your maternal instincts for that length of time?'

'So they won't be coming with us?' Cherry said, aghast.

Lance uttered a brief oath.

'They will not. Do you have any more objections?'

'Would it make any difference if I did?' she said bitterly.

'None at all, so I suggest we sleep on it, and tomorrow you can start to plan a suitable wardrobe for the voyage. I'll telephone Cynthia Hetherington tomorrow, who will be more than happy to advise you, I'm sure. I believe she has contacts in Bath for such formal occasions, and if that fails, I may even be persuaded to take you to London for a few days' shopping so that you'll be the belle of the ball.'

If this was meant to appease Cherry, it did little more than alarm her. She had learned all the necessary social skills required of her in the years of their marriage, and she could dance as well as anyone. But she wasn't completely comfortable in large groups of strangers, and as for the thought of so many of them on board . . .

'How many passengers does the *Queen Mary* carry?' she asked, trying to sound interested.

'Just over two thousand, I believe,' Lance said calmly, as if it was no more than a local hunt meeting.

Where her face had been so flushed, Cherry was sure it had blanched now. It was going to be hell on earth . . . and not even on terra firma, she thought in an attempt to be witty. She managed a brief smile.

'Can we talk more about it tomorrow, Lance? You've taken me so much by surprise, my head's in a spin right now.'

'Of course,' he said, visibly relieved. 'But I promise you, once you've had a taste of shipboard life, you're going to love it, Cherry.'

She doubted that very much. But she didn't dare dampen his enthusiasm any more by saying so. She just relied on the thought that it would be only two weeks out of her life, and she could surely manage to cope with that. There had been worse weeks, after all.

Two

Once the shock of Lance's announcement had sunk in properly, Cherry was beset alternately with nerves and excitement. Nerves because of the distance they would travel on board an enormous ship among people she didn't know, and the thought of missing her children . . . and excitement at such an opportunity, the like of which she would never have imagined.

'You're really going, then?' Paula echoed, when Cherry related the news to her a few days later.

Thomas was at school, and Bella and Georgie were at their lessons with Nanny Green. Cherry never chose to dwell on how different things were for their offspring, always looking forward to this chance to just be herself with Paula.

'I could hardly say no, could I?' she answered dryly. 'I'm sure it will be an experience to remember, Paula, though I must admit I'm scared too.'

'I'm not surprised. You wouldn't catch me going on a blooming great ship with a lot of stiff-necks and nothing to see but sea. Still, I suppose you'll be one of the nobs, won't you?'

'I suppose I will,' Cherry said, refusing to be rattled. 'Cyn's taking me to Bath next week to buy some new clothes. We're going there in what she calls her fast little motor.' She grinned, remembering.

'Blimey,' was all Paula said to that. 'So is she going on this wonderful ocean voyage as well, then? It sounds just up her street.'

'Oh, stop it, Paula. I like Cyn, despite her odd little ways, and, anyway, she's not going on the voyage. She told me that she and her chums will be in Berlin for most of August.'

She took a sip of tea, avoiding Paula's eyes as she spoke. Everyone was aware that the Olympic Games were being held in Berlin, and that Paula's husband Harold was quite militant about them, calling them, as did many others, the Nazi Games. Predictably, Paula spluttered over her tea.

'A fine set of friends you've got, I must say. As well as being the way they are, they're toadying up to that odious Adolf Hitler.'

'Honestly, Paula, you can be such an idiot sometimes. Cyn's friends are mad about sport, and they're going as a mixed bunch, anyway, not just women. She's no Nazi sympathizer, any more than I am, and Lance certainly isn't! With his military background, he'd be furious if such a thing was even whispered about him.'

'Well, plenty of countries threatened to boycott those Games, didn't they? Especially America,' Paula went on stubbornly. Considering she had never bothered her pretty head about such things in the past, she was clearly well informed by Harold now.

'Yes, and they all relented in the end. It's the spirit of sporting competition that matters, not any threat by Hitler to be master of the world.'

'Tell that to the Jews,' Paula muttered.

Cherry stared at her, amazed at how belligerent she had become about something that was unlikely to affect her in any way. That would be Harold's influence again, presumably.

'Look, I'm not going to talk about it any more, and if all you can do is argue and show your jealousy of Cyn—'

'Oh, don't let's quarrel, Cherry,' she said. 'Let's talk about something else. How's Georgie getting on with his letters?'

Cherry sighed. 'Not all that well. I fear he's not going to be the scholar his father would have liked, and it doesn't help when Bella giggles at his attempts at reading and he gets it all wrong. She can be a little madam when she likes.'

'I'm glad you said that and not me,' Paula said with a grin, her good humour restored.

'You think it, though, don't you?'

Paula shrugged. 'Don't put words in my mouth, kid. She's a gorgeous child, and who could blame her for knowing it when everyone makes such a fuss of her? She'd win any beauty contest already.'

Cherry laughed. 'And can't you just see Lance bursting a

blood vessel if entering his daughter in such a thing was ever suggested to him?'

'*So common, my dear!*' she added, in a fair imitation of her late mother-in-law's aristocratic tones.

Paula recognized them at once, which started them both giggling and reminiscing over how they had once cowered from the stuffy Lady Elspeth, and the many times in the past when Cherry had mimicked her for the entertainment of the kitchen staff, so that by the time they parted their brief tiff was forgotten.

A few days later, Cherry was sitting beside the Honourable Cynthia Hetherington in her 'fast little motor', speeding along the roads towards the city of Bath.

'When are you leaving for Berlin?' Cherry asked, mainly to keep her mind off how close to the ground they were in the car, and how fast Cyn liked to drive.

'A few days before the beginning of August,' she was told. 'My chums have got connections there, so we'll be staying in their *Schloss*, no less – that's a castle to you and me, Cherry. Such fun!'

'My goodness. It sounds very grand.'

'The Germans know how to enjoy themselves, and some of my chums plan to put on a small musical *soirée* to thank them for their generosity before we all go to the Games. It'll be a bit *risqué*, which I'm sure our hosts will enjoy. But you'll enjoy yourself on the *Queen Mary* too. You must tell me all about it when you return.'

Much of what she said passed over Cherry's head. Except for one thought.

'You're not worried about any – well, any controversy about the Games?' Cherry ventured to say.

Cyn glanced at her. 'Of course not. What on earth made you say that?'

'I've heard a few things, that's all. I think Paula's husband still thinks we should boycott them.'

Now why on earth had she said that? It was nothing to do with her what Harold Farmer thought, and the last thing she wanted was for Cyn to think he was some kind of troublemaker. To her relief, she heard Cyn's tinkling laugh.

'Oh, there will always be little people who think they can ruin things, but the Olympics are bigger than that, sweetie. Now, let's forget them and get on to the far more important matter of decking you out with suitable attire for your wonderful trip,' she added as they swept into the courtyard of what looked like a large country house built in the beautiful pale Bath stone, and which turned out to be a fine couture house where everyone knew Cyn and flitted around her and Cherry like attendant bees.

By the time they emerged several hours later, Cherry had been utterly bemused by the efficiency of the staff, if that's how you described such elegant creatures – and by Cyn knowing exactly what was needed for a long sea voyage, and refusing to be swayed by any other suggestions.

'Lady Melchoir has a such a lovely shape, doesn't she, Madame?' she said to the woman who could hardly be called a salesperson, and who was tweaking a bit of silk here and smoothing a bit there, aided by Cyn's willing hands.

'She does indeed,' Madame said with a twinkle in her eye. 'It's a pleasure to be dressing such a beautiful lady.'

Such flattery was all getting too much for Cherry, as was the rather too personal attention, but thank God for Cyn's help, she thought fervently by the time all the purchases had been made. She had expected to be carrying bags and boxes home, but all the garments would be delivered later, when any necessary alterations had been done to the day clothes and diaphanous evening gowns. And, despite her nerves, Cherry felt a definite stirring of excitement at the prospect of the voyage.

'You can tell Lance there's no need at all to drag you up to London now,' Cyn told her triumphantly as they were driving back, clearly pleased by the success of the shopping expedition. 'He'd be useless, anyway. It takes a woman to know what another woman needs, doesn't it, darling?'

For a second, she removed her hand from the steering wheel and put it over Cherry's knee to give it a little squeeze. It was no more than a gesture of affection, but because of the words she used, what Paula had said, and the undoubted way

Cyn's hands had lingered over the various silky garments against her skin, Cherry felt herself tense.

'What's wrong?' Cyn said, glancing at her.

'Nothing. It's nothing. Just nerves.'

That evening after dinner, she related to Lance more details of the clothes she had purchased with Cyn's help, far more in one shopping expedition than ever in her life before, and costing what almost amounted to a king's ransom in her eyes. But she could see the relief on his face that she was now so accepting of the coming trip.

'Of course, I'd hoped to model them all for you tonight, Lance, but it will have to wait until they're delivered.'

'Then I'll just have to be patient for the fashion show. But didn't I tell you Cyn would be the one to help?' he said expansively. 'And saving me the journey to London as well. What a girl!'

'She was wonderful,' Cherry agreed. 'I wonder why she's never got married. Any man would be honoured to have her as his wife. In fact, I was quite sure she was after you at one time, as you very well know,' she added teasingly, confident of his affections.

She didn't know whether or not she was being unconsciously provocative. She didn't mean to be. She sat beside him on the sofa, his arm loosely around her shoulders, and she heard him laugh.

'You're so beautifully naive, my Cherry-ripe, and I hope you'll always stay that way.'

'What does that mean? And why are you laughing at me? Just because I once thought of Cyn as a rival!'

'She would never have been that, never in a million years, and you were always the only one for me, so stop fishing for compliments,' he said, neatly skirting around the questions. 'Anyway, tomorrow will be soon enough for you show me the illustrations of the outfits you've bought, and you can describe the rest, and then we'll see if you've broken the bank.'

'I thought we didn't discuss money,' she threw back at him.

'We don't. But I like to know that I've got my money's worth.'

'Do you think you've always had that with me?' she teased him.

He ruffled her hair. 'Always, and with two beautiful children into the bargain. What more could I ever want?'

'Then you don't regret anything, Lance? Even when I'm at my most difficult and ready to argue with you?'

He laughed again. 'Do you think I'd have preferred some simpering society miss who agreed with everything I said, rather than my boisterous, spirited, beautiful girl?'

Oh, he could be so romantic when he chose, and she was so ready to fall for his charms just as she had always been. She could see the passion in his eyes now. She could feel it in the way his body hardened against her as he held her close, his fingers running gently up and down her arms, and it was more sensual than if he'd swept her into a tight embrace. After twelve years, since that first exquisite encounter in the hayloft, he could still make her blood race with one touch.

'I think it's time I showed you just how much you mean to me, don't you?' he said, his voice rich with seduction. 'There's a bed waiting for us upstairs, and the master of the house wants to tame the unruly kitchen-maid.'

'Then I think he should,' Cherry said unsteadily, revelling in the little game they sometimes played, and feeling her heart pound with the sweet knowledge of all that was to follow.

'But I don't want you to go away and leave us! Suppose you never come back? Who's going to look after us then?' Georgie wailed for the tenth time that morning, the ever-ready tears threatening to brim over.

Bella sniffed. 'Don't be silly, Georgie. They won't be gone for ever, and they're sure to bring us back some presents, won't you, Mummy?'

'Of course, my practical little miss,' Cherry said, smiling at her daughter. 'And when my new clothes arrive next week, you can tell me what you think. It will be a fashion parade for my three best people in the world.'

She'd have preferred it to be just for Lance's eyes alone, but with these two making such a fuss over it all in their different ways, it was far better to include them. Georgie was so little, and didn't really understand that two weeks was a very short time. To him, it was a lifetime.

'Will I still be able to see Thomas while you're away?' Bella said suddenly. 'You wouldn't object, would you? I don't think Nanny Green likes his mother all that much, but she could bring him here, couldn't she, Mummy?'

'I don't see why not,' Cherry said evenly, knowing that the stuffy Nanny Green considered Paula common, which made Cherry feel defensive on her account as always. 'Don't worry, I'll have words with her about it.'

And also with Cook, whom Paula would surely want to see if she came to the house. She would need to be careful, since it could cause a few raised eyebrows and curious whispers among the other kitchen staff who had no idea that Paula, like herself, had once thought of the Melchoir kitchens as her domain. She sighed, wondering why everything had to be so complicated. Why couldn't everyone be the same?

And when did Harold Farmer turn so militant? Her thoughts changed direction as she remembered what she had said to Cynthia about the one-time proposed boycotting of the Olympic Games. Being a railway supervisor, and a shop steward now, had made him much more aggressive than the cheeky house painter he had been when he'd set his sights on Paula. Everyone changed, whether you wanted it or not, Cherry thought with a small shiver.

'So are we going for a walk across the Downs today or not?' she said with an effort, as her thoughts became more gloomy. 'I think there's going to be a fair there while we're away, so I'm sure Nanny Green will take you to it, if you ask her nicely. That will be a real treat, won't it?'

It was sure to put a smile on their faces too. And what on earth was *wrong* with her today, Cherry asked herself? After last night, when Lance had been so tender towards her, she should be feeling on top of the world, but somehow she was feeling more and more edgy.

But Georgie was whooping now. 'I want Dawkins to take us.

He's more fun than Nanny Green, and he lets me sit on his shoulders.'

'We'll see,' Cherry promised, thankful that it took so little to put the joy back in a four-year-old's face.

'Dawkins has got a lady friend,' Bella announced as they left the house.

'Has he? And how do you know that?' Cherry said.

'I saw them. She's the new housemaid.'

'What do you mean? You saw them?'

Did she really want to know? But she felt obliged to ask, in case Bella had seen something she shouldn't. She hoped this wouldn't be too tricky. Some things should be kept private. The memory of herself and Captain Lance in a clandestine embrace in the hayloft all those years ago made her face go hot. Just what had Bella seen between their young chauffeur and the new housemaid?

Bella looked abashed. 'Well, I didn't really see them, but Nanny Green did, and when Georgie and I were giggling over something she read to us, she said there was nothing funny about two people liking each other. It was natural, like you and Daddy, and then she muttered that it was like Dawkins and Agnes too. I don't know anyone else by that name, so I guessed she meant our Agnes.'

'I see. Well, you should be careful about putting two and two together and making five, Bella.'

'They don't, do they? Make five, I mean.'

No, but when passions got heated, one and one could make three . . .

'One of the things you need to learn in this life, darling, is never to repeat gossip. What goes on between other people is no concern of ours.'

'Daddy says that what the servants do *is* our concern,' Bella said, full of importance now. 'Daddy says they're our responsibility, like looking after pets. We're their superiors, so they have to be looked after and protected.'

Good God Almighty! Cherry found it hard to hold her temper in check now. This child definitely needed taking in hand. She felt Georgie tugging at her hand and looked down into his frowning face.

'What's a reponsib?'

'It's nothing for you worry your head about, my love,' Cherry told him. 'Look, why don't we walk to the edge of the cliffs and see if there are any boats in the river today? I said walk, not run,' she called out, as he broke away from her with Bella skipping after him. They couldn't go too far, as this part of the cliff edge was safely fenced now after many horrific accidents in past years.

Bella's words had made her think, though. She hoped Lance hadn't really told her that servants were like pets to be looked after and protected. The thought made her squirm, even though she supposed it was only his way of explaining things to his enquiring little daughter. What would Bella think if she ever knew that her own mother had been one of those servants, and her father was one of the so-called superiors who had definitely protected her against all the odds?

The way their married life had begun was something neither of the children must ever know, she vowed, and she knew that Lance was in full agreement. How devastating it would be to see the shock and derision in her daughter's eyes if she ever knew the truth. There were so few people who knew it now, and yet, if she stopped to consider it, Cherry thought, there were far too many.

In the household, there was only Cook and Gerard, trusted loyal servants. There was Paula and Harold, both of whom she was sure would never betray a secret. Cynthia Hetherington and her parents had always been loyal friends too, as were the few close acquaintances of the Melchoirs who had closed ranks when the scandal had threatened to break.

Apart from those, there was one other on the opposite side of the world. Her evil brother Brian, who Cherry rarely thought about, and didn't want to think about now. He had almost brought the family down, and could have ruined everything. Because of his profession, he was physically very strong, but Lance was mentally stronger and had been the victor in the end. By now, if she ever thought about her brother at all, she was generous enough to hope that he had made good in

Australia, and that after all these years, they need never fear anything from Brian O'Neill again.

'Cyn tells me she and her chums are going to Berlin for the whole of August, and for a few days before that,' she said conversationally to Lance that evening when the children were in bed.

'Really?' he said, taking little notice of what she was saying, more intent on studying the pages of *The Times.* 'I hope they enjoy themselves and don't get into too much mischief.'

'What an odd thing to say. I should think they're adult enough to know what they're doing – and staying in a friend's *Schloss* too.'

'I see she's been educating you,' he said, glancing up now.

'It sounds terribly exciting and a little daring too. She says some of the chums are going to put on a musical *soirée* for their hosts that's going to be quite *risqué.* Apparently, the Germans like that sort of thing.'

Lance put down the newspaper, frowning a little. 'What else has she been telling you?' he said.

Cherry stared at him. 'Well, nothing more that I can think of. I thought you'd be pleased that we're friends. It was your idea in the first place, I remember, and you were the one who suggested she should take me shopping. What's so *risqué* about a *soirée,* anyway? I thought it was just a sing-song.'

'That's a very *bourgeois* way of referring to a sophisticated evening, my dear girl. But some sections of the German elite can be very *louche,* and I'm sure Cyn will be in her element in such an environment, and that's all I'm going to say about it.'

'Good. Because with you spouting all these French words at me, I'm starting to wonder if I'm in England any more,' she said, nettled.

'You started it,' Lance snapped, and he ruffled his newspaper pages loudly as an indication that the conversation was over. Cherry felt snubbed, and more than a little upset. She had just been trying to show some interest in what Cyn was doing, but Lance's head was obviously elsewhere.

It wasn't until they were in bed that night, when she lay

sleepless and fully aware that Lance was the same, that he referred to it again.

'I'm not sure that Cyn is the best companion for you after all, Cherry.'

She turned her head in astonishment, seeing his set profile in the semi-darkness. 'Why ever not? I don't see her much, anyway.'

'Has she ever suggested you joining her and her friends for an evening?'

'Of course not. I like Cyn, but Paula's my best friend, not Cyn and her cronies. I'm not their sort, am I?' she said, full of sarcasm now. 'I wasn't born with a silver spoon in my mouth, and we both know I'm only tolerated because of you. It was your idea to send me off to Bath for my new clothes, remember.'

He turned to her now, genuinely astonished. 'Good God, have you still got a chip on your shoulder about that? Those things should have been forgotten long ago, and anyone who vaguely knows of it would never connect my lady with those early days.'

'Well, I remember it, and so do you,' Cherry said bitterly.

'Only when it suits me,' he said, his voice more seductive than before.

'Like now?' she said huskily, yielding to him as always.

Paula had been invited to Melchoir House on Saturday afternoon to be shown all the finery Cherry had acquired for the sea voyage, and was suitably impressed. They were now having tea by themselves in the drawing room, while the children were in the capable hands of Nanny Green in the nursery.

'Cyn's got pretty good taste, I'll give her that,' Paula remarked, knowing she would never get the chance to wear a quarter of the garments Cherry had displayed that day with such obvious pleasure.

'Yes, she has. But I'm starting to wonder if there's any truth in what you implied the other day.'

'Blimey, that's a first,' Paula said with a grin. 'Which of my words of wisdom was that, then?'

'About Cyn Hetherington being, well – you know . . .'

'A dyke?'

Cherry flinched. 'Must you use that ugly word?'

'It's what Harold calls it,' Paula said with a snigger and a wink now.

Cherry was fast going off Harold and his forthright ideas.

'I wish I'd never said anything now. I just meant perhaps she prefers women's company to men, that's all,' she said awkwardly.

'Why does it bother you? She's never made a pass at you, has she?'

'Good Lord, no!'

'Oh, blimey, I didn't mean anything by that, and I know you're not that way inclined. But live and let live, Cherry. If they want to get all lovey-dovey over one another, it's their business, as long as they do it in private and don't frighten the horses, as they say.'

'I just never thought about it before, that's all,' Cherry said, seemingly unable to leave the subject alone, despite what she had said.

'Well, you and me shared our attic room for long enough, and there was never any hanky-panky going on between us, was there, kid?' Paula said quickly, seeing how uneasy and defensive she had become. 'We talked about everything under the sun, sharing girly secrets that didn't involve men, and I daresay Cyn and her mates just natter all night long about their lah-de-dah pursuits.'

'I expect you're right,' Cherry said.

It didn't explain why Lance had called her naive, though, and at her age she didn't care for the word. But she didn't feel inclined to ask anything more of Paula as the children came hurtling into the drawing room, and her friend was saying decisively that it was time for her and Thomas to go home.

It stuck in Paula's craw, though, that Cherry could be so unaware of the goings-on of those society dames. Paula had always thought herself one of life's innocents compared with Cherry, but over the years it seemed as though their roles had reversed. It was what came of Cherry being married to a toff and having every little thing done for her, Harold always said. After all this time, it had become the natural thing for Cherry to live in a kind of expensive bubble and forget where her roots lay.

'One of these days she'll get her comeuppance, you'll see,' he had once told Paula, a remark that had culminated in an almighty row in defence of her dearest friend, a row which she knew very well neither of them could win.

Three

A month later, the man who had been hovering on the edge of the Downs on the day Paula had warned Cherry about pickpockets and ne'er-do-wells was blowing smoke rings into the air with all the expertise of a professional. In the cluttered room of the dingy lodging house in a Bristol lane, the smell of tobacco mingled with the unsavoury smells of the nearby river, and was threatening to make the young woman puke. She sat by the grimy window, pointless though it was, and wishing to God it would open if it hadn't been glued fast with lashings of paint over the years.

'So was it her?' she said, with an accent that was far removed from anything the man had heard before.

'Definite and for certain sure,' he said broadly. 'And a fine-looking bit of skirt she be. Any bloke would be glad to get in there!'

He made a gesture that had her smiling faintly, even while it disgusted her. She had seen plenty like him in her thirty-odd years. *He* disgusted her, but at least he had done what she asked of him, and found who she was looking for. When she said nothing for a few moments, he looked at her cynically, and then spoke in what he liked to call a professional voice. At best it came out with a menacing, guttural growl, due to too many years of inhaling tobacco and prowling among the underclass of society.

'So what's the next move, missus? You know my credentials. Putting on the frighteners. A touch of honest blackmail. Roughing up where necessary. A bit of kidnapping. Rape. Murder . . . though I'm only joshing about the last two, o' course. I have me standards,' he added with a throaty chuckle that ended in a gigantic coughing fit.

With ever-growing disgust, the woman waited for the fit to pass, doubting that he had any standards at all. She wouldn't put anything past him. How she had come to pick his name out of a book she couldn't imagine. But that was all he had been, just a name in a book, and when you were a stranger, knew no one, and had even less idea of where to start looking, you had to take what was on offer. And this lout had ticked all the answers to her questions. If she hadn't been so hardened herself, used to plenty of knock-backs, and seen more of life than most of the fancy folk in this airy-fairy town, he would have scared her shitless.

'I needn't trouble you for any more of your services, thank you, Mr Carey. Me and my son can manage fine from now on. So if you'll just give me your bill and final report, we'll call it a day.'

He was intrigued by the way her voice curled up at the end of every sentence as if she was still asking a question. He wasn't educated enough to think of it in any other way than that. But it didn't matter a damn to him who she was or where she came from, as long as she paid up. He could do what he did, and do it well, but that was about all. He thought with his instinct, and his fists when necessary.

From the start, when she had come to him, instinct told him that this woman was here on a mission, whatever the hell it was, and God help any bugger who got in her way. That it had turned out to be stalking a woman in a grand house had taken him by surprise. He'd have thought she was after a bastard who had done her wrong and left her with a kid, and now he had to pay. In his spare time, Will Carey liked watching Hollywood films, and fancied himself as a Western hero . . . though anyone less like one of the good guys was hard to imagine.

'Where you from, then, missus?' he said now, simply for something to say as he fished in his grubby satchel for the report he'd written up so far, and wondering how much he could add on to the bill for services rendered.

'That's no concern of yours,' she said briskly.

He shrugged again. Her boy was playing in the lane outside, kicking a ball with several other street urchins. If he cared enough, he'd ask him on his way out. If not, to hell with the pair of them.

The woman scanned the report quickly. It told her all she

wanted to know. That he was charging over the odds didn't matter. She could pay. She handed over the money and didn't bother asking for a receipt. She doubted very much that this oaf paid any taxes, anyway, and if she never had to see him again, it would be too soon.

'Well, if you need me for anything else, you know where to find me,' he said at last. At least she had paid up, and she didn't seem short of a bob or two, despite the dingy lodgings and the scurfy kid she had in tow.

She inclined her head, wanting to be shot of him, desperate to leave the door open and fumigate the place once he had gone, so she could breathe a bit more easily. But first she wanted to study the report in detail, to see just how much he had found out about Lord and Lady bloody Melchoir.

In the lane, where the mean little houses crowded together so much that they almost obliterated the sky, Will Carey watched the boy thoughtfully for a few moments. He was a well-built, muscly child, probably nearing puberty, towering above the urchins he played with, and lording over them. There was always a leader in any game or battle, and it was easy to see that this one took the lead. The rest of them kowtowed towards him, undoubtedly finding his accent, with that upward tilt at the end of sentences like his mother's, something to be curious about. Kids would always be curious about a new arrival. If he was weaker, they bullied him. If he was stronger, they acknowledged a leader. Like this one.

The ball they were playing with suddenly came flying towards him, catching him in the midriff. He wasn't winded, but he played up to it for the moment, holding the ball tight to his gut until the boy came running over to him.

'Sorry, Mister. You ain't hurt, are you?'

'It would take more'n that to hurt me, kid. So before I give you the ball back, tell me where you got such a funny way of talking.'

'It ain't funny!' the boy said, scowling. 'Not like yours.'

'So where'd it come from, then? Outer space, maybe? You tell me, and I'll think about giving you back your ball,' Carey said, holding it high above him.

The boy's scowl got blacker. 'Don't be bloody daft. Nobody comes from outer space. Me and my mum are from Australia. Now give us the ball!'

Australia, eh? Will Carey had never met anybody from so far away before. He hardly knew where it was, but he might look it up on an atlas just to extend his knowledge. He tossed the ball to the boy and went on his way.

As he did so, Sara O'Neill finally threw open the door of the lodging house, breathing in the comparatively fresh air of the lane. Not that it deserved such a term, with the varying smells of the rank river nearby, old vegetables and dogs' mess and other unmentionables in the lane. But the man's tobacco smoke had been sour and was making her chest tighten up painfully, and she was in time to see him slink away to continue his unsavoury job. But she shouldn't condemn him for that, she reminded herself. Not when she had come from the other side of the world and sought him out – or anyone of his ilk – to give her a helping hand. And so he had, and she settled down to read through his report, ill-written though it was.

By the time her son came indoors wanting food, she had to agree that, for such an uncouth exterior and unlikely sleuth, Will Carey had done a bonzer job of recording much of the Melchoirs' life over the past years. More than she had expected, in fact, including their time in Ireland, which Brian had never told her about, even if he had known it, or cared. Why would he care, since the bastards had banished him to a life Down Under so that they could be rid of him for good?

They had confidently never expected to hear of him again. They would never have expected him to make good – well, in his own sweet way, whether it was in the back-breaking work of cutting cane, or sweating his cobs off in the shearing sheds, in-between his own speciality of bare-knuckle fighting bouts, of course, whenever he could get the work. And leaving behind him a little package of his own, namely in the shape of his son, the spit of his father in every way. Sara looked at him fondly now, wondering just how much good fortune Will Carey's report was about to bring this little thug.

'Where's the grub, Ma?' he yelled now, never able to keep

his voice down after years of competing with wind and dust in the Outback.

Her answer was to give him a swipe around the ear.

'You just mind your manners, Ethan. It's bread and scrape today, mate, but if we play our cards right, we'll soon be dining on caviar.'

'What the bloody hell's that? Sounds like dog's meat,' he scowled, at which she laughed until her sides ached. Finally, she spoke with a gasp.

'You'll find out in good time if you're lucky.'

The time was drawing near when Cynthia Hetherington and her friends would be leaving for Germany. They would be abroad for more than a month, and as Lance and Cherry would also be away for half of August, the Hetherington parents decided to throw a small dinner party for their old friends, and Cynthia's cronies would assuredly be invited too.

'I'm sorry, my darlings, but it's for grown-ups only,' Cherry told her daughter, when Bella wailed noisily at not being invited.

'But I'm nearly grown-up!' the girl complained. 'Georgie's still a baby, but I could come, couldn't I, Mummy?'

'I'm not a baby!' her brother howled, kicking out at her shin and making her screech with pain.

'Well, if we were going to be subjected to this kind of nonsense, I'm quite sure the Hetheringtons wouldn't want you two reprobates at their dinner table!' Cherry said severely.

'What's a repro—?' Georgie began.

'Shut up, Georgie,' Bella snapped. 'She won't let us go, and that's that.'

'Who's *she*? The cat's mother?' Cherry said absent-mindedly, using an expression from her childhood.

Both children looked astonished for a moment and then Bella giggled.

'I've heard Auntie Paula say that,' she said. 'I thought it was something that only common people said.' She darted a look at her mother that made Cherry's heart skip a beat for a moment.

'Paula's not common.'

'Well, she talks common.'

'What, common like this, you dozy duckie dewdrop?' Cherry snapped back, reverting to a broad Bristol accent she hadn't used in years, just to stop the little madam condemning anyone who didn't conform to her own prissy ways.

Bella stared at her for a moment, her mouth wide open, and then she shrieked with laughter.

'Gosh, Mummy, if you hadn't been born such a lady, you could have been on the stage – couldn't she, Georgie? I shall tell Daddy when he comes in, and you must say something common for him as well.'

Georgie's eyes were welling with uncertain tears.

'I don't like it. I want you to talk like my mummy, not somebody else.'

Bella hadn't finished with him yet. 'Oh, don't be so wet, Georgie. That's what actresses do on the stage. They pretend they're somebody else, and make everybody else believe them as well. It's very clever. We should put on a little play one evening, Mummy, for some of our friends. Daddy could be the king, and you could be one of his servants.'

Dear God, this couldn't be happening . . .

Cherry began to feel light-headed as her daughter prattled on and on about creating a little play, her annoyance about not being invited to the dinner party temporarily forgotten.

'Let's not talk about it now,' she said, when her daughter finally paused for breath. 'It's time for your lessons, and you know Nanny Green doesn't like to be kept waiting.'

'All right,' Bella said pouting. 'But I never knew you could talk like a street person so easily, Mummy. It's what Nanny Green calls a gift!'

No, it's not, my love. It's actually the accent I was born with. And how outraged you would be, my snobby little daughter, if you ever knew it!

She needed some fresh air, and once the children had gone to the nursery to be educated, she slipped out of the house, praying that by evening, when Lance came back, Bella would have forgotten all about putting on a little play for their friends' amusement. She knew the suggestion wouldn't make Lance laugh, any more than it did herself. It was one thing for them to play out in private the roles they had both been born with, but it wasn't for public amusement.

Without thinking where she was going, her footsteps had taken her around the side of the house, beyond the kitchen gardens and towards the stables. The warm, pungent smells of hay and straw and horseflesh drifted into her nostrils, making her stand transfixed for a moment as the memories came flooding back.

'Can I help you, my lady?' she heard a voice say, and she started as she realized one of the stable-lads was leaning on his pitchfork for a moment as he mucked out the horses' stalls, clearly wondering what she was dong there.

'No, thank you. Please don't let me stop you getting on with your work.'

God, she sounded so patronizing, though probably not to him, only to herself, knowing that once she would never have spoken in such a high-handed way to a stable-lad.

More restless than she had been in ages, and hardly knowing the reason why, she gave the lad a quick nod and walked on towards the Downs. Perhaps a quick burst of country air would restore her sense of calm about where she was, and who she was. Perhaps the coming voyage across the Atlantic would revive her even more. Sea air was supposed to be good for the health. If only the very thought of it didn't make her feel queasy. Perhaps she was pregnant . . .

She almost missed a step on a tussock of grass as the thought occurred to her. But no. Thinking back, she knew it wasn't so. Even though Lance would welcome the idea of another child, it hadn't happened yet. For a moment, she let the thought of it play around her senses. Georgie would be over the moon at the idea of another little playmate, but somehow Cherry didn't think Bella would be so pleased. As if they had to let their lives be ruled according to a ten-year-old's needs!

At that moment, she caught sight of several young children riding their ponies across the Downs in the care of their grooms, reminding her that Bella too had been badgering her father to let her have a pony. It was something that Cherry was completely against. The thought of her daughter careering about on an animal, no matter how small, horrified her.

'She'd come to no harm under my tuition, Cherry, and you're just being myopic about it,' Lance had told her with a frown.

Since she had no idea what myopic meant, and had no intention of asking him, she resorted to feminine fears.

'I can't help worrying about her falling off and hurting herself, perhaps even breaking her neck,' she added wildly.

'Now you're being ridiculous. She would be trained properly on the gentlest of ponies, and it would do her good. She would get plenty of fresh air and learn to control an animal at the same time.'

'I still say no,' Cherry said stubbornly, 'but no doubt you'll get your way in the end. You and she usually do.'

Remembering that conversation now, she realized it was true. Bella could always wheedle her way around her father in a way that she could never do with Cherry. A man and his daughter, she thought, almost resentfully. But such indulgence was not helping Bella to grow out of the wilful and imperious little miss she usually was.

Cherry had reached the fencing around the top of the Downs now, and found herself gazing down into the silvery river, snaking far below in the Avon Gorge as it meandered into the city. How many tales it could tell, of pirates and smugglers, and the shameful slave trade, with its constant reminders in the city street names of Whiteladies Road and Blackboy Hill. And the more personal tale of her own brother's banishment to Australia, she thought with a shiver, when Lance had arranged for his working passage and told him never to return. She rarely thought of him now, but she couldn't help hoping that he had made some good out of his rotten life.

A dog's barking made her turn idly to watch a thickset, scruffy boy hurling a stick at a mongrel. The dog continued his excited yapping as the boy chased after it. It was coming Cherry's way, and the boy raced in its wake, almost bumping into her as he swerved in time to follow the dog's path.

'Sorry, missus,' he gasped, and charged on his way.

For a moment, Cherry felt as though the world was spinning in front of her. She thought she was seeing a ghost, the ghost of the way her young brother had looked at about twelve years old, his hair lank and unkempt, his skin and clothes unwashed, but with the cheeky grin on his face that could charm the birds from the trees, according to those who were taken in by him.

But it couldn't be. Brian was half a world away, and this boy was just a street urchin. She realized there was no sign of him any more, nor the dog. They had vanished over the Downs, and she must have been having hallucinations.

In any case, she told herself shakily, Brian was a man now . . . but, for a horrified moment, Cherry prayed that it wasn't some kind of apparition she had seen, telling her that Brian had died, and that this really was his ghost, reminding her that he hadn't always been bad. That he had once been her brother . . .

'Mummy, Mummy!'

She heard two familiar voices, and turned to see Bella running over the Downs towards her, with Georgie's fat little legs struggling to keep up. At a sedate distance behind them came the sturdy shape of Nanny Green, calling to Bella that little ladies shouldn't run. And with the words, Cherry's world seemed to turn upright again.

'So you've been let out, have you?' she said, smiling at the pair of them as Georgie caught up.

'We persuaded Nanny Green that we needed some fresh air,' Bella said with a giggle. 'We told her it would be good for us.'

'Good for us,' echoed Georgie once he had got his breath back.

Good grief, is my daughter manipulating the governess as well now? Cherry thought. Ten years old, and she was already capable of womanly wiles.

'Well, I hope you're not going to be any trouble to her while Daddy and I are away,' she said in mock severity.

'We're never any trouble, are we, Georgie?' Bella said innocently, poking him in the ribs and making him howl.

'I'm sorry, Lady Melchoir, they just wanted to get out of the nursery for a while,' the governess said when she finally reached them.

'It's quite all right, Miss Green. We can all walk back to the house together.'

'Perhaps it's as well,' the woman said in an aside. 'There are some rough characters about on the Downs today.'

'Really?

Don't ask. Don't sound in the least curious. Don't probe into things you really don't want to know.

Miss Green looked down her nose. 'They're putting up the tents for the summer fair over yonder, and the sort of people who work in such places are always dubious characters.'

'I don't think you can generalize. They're only doing an honest day's work, and they give a lot of pleasure to local folk.'

Why the dickens she should be defending them she didn't know. There had been plenty of times when Brian 'Knuckles' O'Neill would have been part of the show, pitting his wits and his strength and his bare fists against all-comers, and usually winning. And sometimes sneaking back to the obliging kitchen-maids at Melchoir House to lick his wounds, or, more likely, to get around Cook for a piece of pie and a drink of cider. But this sniffy matron wouldn't know anything about that. Thank God.

'I think it's time we were getting back home now,' Cherry said briskly, still glancing around her for another sight of the strange boy, but he had truly vanished, and she decided that the likeness between him and her brother had just been in her imagination after all.

Besides, there was so much else to think about between now and the sea voyage. There was the party at the Hetheringtons' for a start. She liked Cynthia enormously, but her flamboyant friends were a bit off-putting, and although she hardly knew them, they always made her tongue-tied.

'You shouldn't let them bother you, Cherry,' Lance said, on the evening of the party as they were getting ready in their bedroom.

'Why not? They're weird,' she said without thinking.

Lance laughed. 'That's one way of putting it, but I'm sure they'll all be in their element in Berlin.'

'Why Berlin, particularly? I don't understand.'

He leaned forward and kissed her forehead, breathing in the

fragrant perfume she always wore. His hands caressed her shoulders over her silky bronze-coloured gown.

'That's because you're one of the world's innocents, my darling.'

If it was meant to be a light-hearted compliment, Cherry didn't see it so.

'I really wish you wouldn't call me that, Lance,' she said. 'You've said it before, and it makes me sound like such an idiot.'

He dropped his hands from her shoulders, and in the mirror she could see a hint of annoyance in his eyes.

'You're anything but that. But there are all sorts in the world, Cherry, and I much prefer you the way you are.'

'To the way I *was* — Sir?' she flashed at him.

'Being my wife,' he said steadily, refusing to be either goaded or amused. 'Now, if you've finished titivating, shall we go? Dawkins has already brought the car round to the front of the house, so it's time to face the music. Let's put on a good show tonight, Cherry-ripe.'

His eyes challenged her, and she bit back the retort she almost made. Wasn't she still putting on a show, even after all these years? Wasn't she still play-acting at being Lady Melchoir instead of Cherry O'Neill, kitchen-maid? Seconds later, the arrival of the children, hammering on the door to be let in so that they could admire their parents in all their finery, cleared her mind.

Georgie hung back a fraction, seeing the elegant picture the two of them made, while Bella cocked her head on one side, considering, and then nodded approvingly.

'You look really beautiful, Mummy, and you look a proper gentleman too, Daddy.'

'Well, thank you, Isabella, dear,' he said solemnly, giving her name its full weight. 'So may the prince take Cinderella to the ball?'

Bells laughed and clapped her hands in delight as Cherry twirled around to allow the silky folds of her skirts to flare out.

'Mummy's far too glamorous to be Cinderella, and her hands are too soft and white to be scraping out fireplaces. She looks like a princess tonight!'

Cherry kept the smile fixed on her face as Georgie forgot his inhibitions and rushed towards her, to hide his face in her skirt as he wailed that he didn't want his mummy to be a princess, just mummy.

'For heaven's sake, child, stop that snivelling, you're not a baby any more,' Lance said in irritation. 'And let go of your mother's gown. She doesn't want it marked before we even leave the house.'

Poor Lance, thought Cherry, wishing his son could be a man already, when she wanted to keep him a baby as long as possible.

'It's not marked at all, is it, darling?' she said easily to Georgie. 'But you must let us go now, or we shall we late, and that would be very bad manners.'

As they left in the limousine, Cherry wondered idly what delights they would be given to eat that evening. It would be something tasty and exotic, she had no doubt, since the Hetheringtons liked to flaunt the fact that they were well travelled and had eaten dishes from all over the world. It would be nothing like the hearty dinners and mouth-watering puddings that Cook made. Nor anything like the juicy rabbit pies that she and Paula had always been so partial to.

She wondered what Paula was cooking for Harold and Thomas tonight. As it was Friday, it would probably be fish and chips, a bit of fresh cod bought from the local fishmongers and Paula's fat chips made from the spuds Harold grew in the garden, cooked in dripping saved and strained from the meat dish.

Cherry's mouth suddenly watered. Whatever fare the Hetheringtons were serving them tonight, she'd have given anything to be sitting down in a cosy kitchen with a plate of good old fish and chips right now, and sloshing a bottle of vinegar over them . . .

Four

'I tell you, it looked just like him,' Paula was saying excitedly.

'Well, so you say, but common sense tells you it couldn't have been, woman,' Harold said mildly, immersed in his newspaper while the tantalizing smell of battered fish and fried potatoes wafted all over the house.

'I know that, but it was uncanny, that's all I'm saying,' Paula went on stubbornly. 'You never saw the bloke as many times as I did, but that kid was the spitting image, I swear.'

Harold folded up his newspaper as she slapped a plate of dinner down on the kitchen table, and yelled out to Thomas to come indoors.

'It's just coincidence, Paula. Everybody's supposed to have a double somewhere, even though I don't hold with it myself, and the chances of this kid turning out to be the spit of some bloke that's on the other side of the world is just plain daft.'

'If you'd seen what I saw, you wouldn't say that,' she said, refusing to be put off. 'I just hope Cherry don't see him, that's all. It'd turn her stomach all over again, that's for sure.'

'Well, since she's not likely to be buying fish down by the wharf, I'd say there's not much likelihood of that.'

'Is Auntie Cherry sick?' Thomas said, clattering indoors and catching her last words.

'No,' his father said. 'Never mind the likes of them, boy. Get on with your dinner before it gets cold.'

He was a practical man who had no truck with anything odd or unusual, and a person having a double was totally unnatural to him. He didn't care for the thought of another chap looking just like himself, thanks very much. It was spooky, and a kid appearing out of nowhere looking just like the bastard brother of Cherry Melchoir, née O'Neill, made him more than uncomfortable, knowing what they all knew about the bugger. He didn't want Paula filling his son's head with it, either. He tried to think of something to take her mind off it.

'She'll be off soon, won't she?' he said. 'Going on this sea trip to America?'

'Not for a couple of weeks yet,' Paula said, her heart sinking at the thought. They may not see one another as much as they once had, when they had been closer than clams, but the thought of Cherry all those thousands of miles away, and with an ocean between them, was enough to turn her own stomach.

'We'll see them before they go, won't we?' Thomas said.

Harold honked. 'What's this? Don't tell me you're getting soft over the stuck-up little Melchoir girl, are you? She's out of your class, boy, and you've got about as much chance there as pigs flying.'

'Stranger things have happened,' Paula snapped, in the mood to be contrary. At Harold's frown, she felt her heartbeats quicken and she shook the vinegar bottle over her meal so vigorously the top threatened to come off.

'What things?' Thomas asked her.

'Never you mind. And don't talk so daft about our Thomas getting soft over a girl, Harold. The boy's far too young to be thinking about such things – and you'll need to be giving him a proper talking-to before that day comes,' she added meaningly.

'No, he won't. I know it, anyway,' Thomas bragged. 'The boys at school told me all about it.'

He got an oath from his father in response, followed by a swift clip around the ear.

'Well, whatever you know, you'd better be sure to keep your tackle inside your breeches and don't go bringing no bloody female trouble home here, you understand?'

Paula sighed. 'Can't we have our dinner in peace for once? I'm sure Thomas didn't mean anything, Harold. He's far too young for any of that malarkey, and it was just talk.'

She hoped to God it was, but there had to come a time when boys wanted to know all there was to know, and you couldn't keep them children for ever. It was Harold's duty to let him know the ins and outs . . . and she found herself smiling faintly at the thought. Ins and outs described pretty well what went on in the bedroom upstairs, and always on Friday nights . . .

And of course she'd be seeing Cherry again before she left for America. It was unthinkable that they wouldn't want to say goodbye. They had always had so much to say to one another, and that hadn't changed, no matter how different their circumstances were now.

They were still the same inside, despite Cherry being Lady Melchoir, and Paula herself being the wife of a militant shop steward who was so much harder than the free and easy Harold she had first known. She still loved him madly, though, she thought fiercely, and she was proud of him for pulling himself up by his bootstraps from the lowly job he'd once had.

But if he hadn't had it, painting and decorating the Melchoir house while the nobs had been away in London, he'd never have met the shy, pasty kitchen-maid she had been then, and courted her and made her fall so wildly in love with him, when they had always thought it would be the vivacious Cherry who would be married first. And if none of it had happened, they wouldn't be sitting here now with their bolshie son bragging over how he knew it all.

Actually, you know nothing, my son . . . not when it comes to what goes on beneath the sheets between two randy lovers . . .

'Mum's gone all red in the face,' Thomas said with a hoot. 'That comes from putting too much vinegar on your chips. They say it dries your blood or summat.'

'Is that so, clever clogs? Is that something else your friends at school have told you?' Paula said smartly.

'You leave your mother alone,' Harold said with a wink at her now. 'She's probably thinking about half a dozen things at once. That's what women do. They've got brains like bees, always busy and in a right old muddle, but they get there in the end.'

Paula let him get on with his idea of what women's brains were like. *They are cannier than yours, Harold sweetie,* she thought, *with your brain only on one thing of a Friday night.* Not that she objected. She was a red-blooded woman with a red-blooded man, and she pitied those high-class trouts like old Lady Elspeth, who probably only ever dropped her knickers that one time to produce Captain Lance . . .

And she didn't envy Cherry one bit tonight, she thought cheerfully a bit later on as she cleared the plates away and got on with the washing-up in the big stone sink. Sitting around with Cyn and her dyke friends and making daft small talk wasn't Paula's idea of the way to spend an evening.

If she had but known it, Cherry was thinking exactly the same thing. Not that she would have given the upper-class girls the same tag that Paula did, and she chose not even to think of them in the same way. They were just close friends, and if they seemed to share little jokes and asides that the rest of the company didn't quite join in, well, that was what close friends did. And contrary to what Lance might think of her naivety, she wasn't that simple. It was just that she chose to close her eyes to anything that was unsavoury. If she didn't acknowledge it, it didn't exist. Like the boy she had seen on the Downs. He didn't exist, either.

'Are you getting cold feet about the voyage, darling?' she heard Cynthia say smoothly a while later when the gentlemen had gone for their smokes, and the ladies were drinking coffee, a ritual that Cherry absolutely hated.

Was this what Emmeline Pankhurst and her daughters had fought for, this separating of the sexes, as if they were different species and unable to enjoy mutual conversation? Where was all the supposed equality and respect?

Before she could answer the question, one of Cyn's flamboyantly garbed friends had dropped down beside her on the sofa and curled an arm around her shoulders, her long fingernails pressing gently into her. Cherry had a hard job trying not to flinch away.

'You shouldn't be afraid to try anything new, Cherry baby,' the girl called Monica said lightly. 'All of life's an adventure to be enjoyed to the full. Isn't that right, Cyn?'

'Absolutely,' Cyn said with a laugh.

Cynthia's mother took pity on the look of desperation that Cherry was sure she was displaying right then.

'Come along now, girls. Cherry has enough on her mind

without you two badgering her. It's not always easy to adapt to new things, and you'll need to find your sea legs as well as everything else, Cherry dear.'

Several of the older matrons in the room nodded in agreement. Cherry was sure none of them meant to be patronizing, and Cynthia's mother had always been kind to her. But right then all she could see was the simpering, red-lipped faces of these high-class girls and their secret ways, and the indulgence of their mamas for whichever way life took them.

And it was too much. *Abso-bloody-lutely* too much.

Into her mind flashed the memory of that wonderful day, long ago now, when she had been summoned from the Melchoir kitchens to the presence of Lord and Lady Melchoir, to hear Lance declare his intention of marrying her.

She could still picture the fury on their faces that their precious son could consort with a kitchen-maid, and then their absolute shock when she had put in her own twopenn'orth in the crystal clear tones of a lady, instead of the rough servant they had expected. It had been a moment to treasure, and her ability to mimic her betters had never stood her in better stead.

She remembered it now as she gazed around at the roomful of ladies waiting to hear her say something, knowing they were expecting anything but what she was actually about to say. Her smile was cool and serene, belying the rapid beating of her heart, her voice never more aristocratic.

'Oh, I'm sure I shall manage perfectly well. Having already made several sea voyages across the Irish Sea with my husband in the past, I'm quite used to the motion of the sea. In fact, I rather relish it. Although, knowing how you all enjoy new adventures, if any of you have travelled across the Atlantic Ocean on a great liner like the *Queen Mary* before, I would be delighted to have a few pointers.'

She left the sentence up in the air as if it was a question, knowing damn well that none of them had, because Cynthia had told her so. It was another moment to treasure, knowing she would be doing something none of these fancy fillies had done.

Later, when the evening had finally come to an end, and she and Lance had discarded their finery and were settling down for the night, she relayed all that had been said with some relish.

'It was such a sweet moment, Lance, and you should have seen their faces,' she said, recalling it with a giggle. 'They wore the same expressions as your dear mama when she suddenly discovered I could talk posh whenever I chose. Of course, apart from Cyn, they didn't know anything else, and I must admit I laid it on a bit heavier than usual!'

'I can just imagine it,' Lance said in amusement. 'I always said you should have been an actress, my love. You could mimic anyone and get away with it.'

'But it wasn't just my voice, it was what I said, letting them know that they weren't damn superior to me, and that this was going to be the adventure of a lifetime. None of them had been on an ocean voyage with an adoring husband, or were likely to, so who was the lucky one!'

'You're a wicked witch,' Lance said, his voice thick with laughter now as he gathered her in his arms in the darkness. 'God, I wish I'd been there to hear it. So does this mean you're looking forward to it now, then?' he asked teasingly.

She thought for all of two seconds, feeling her heart swell with an excitement she hadn't expected. Her voice changed to that of the wench.

'Yes, I bleedin' well am, Sir, and I'm ever so grateful to you for giving me the chance, Sir. I don't know what I can do to thank you enough.'

Whatever else she might have said in that servile manner was lost as he smothered her face with kisses. She could taste the whisky on his breath, but none of it mattered. She was safe where she belonged, and nothing could touch her as long as they had each other.

The days passed so quickly now. July was quickly merging into August, and Cynthia and her friends had departed for Berlin and their *Schloss*, and to enjoy the Olympic Games in due course.

'They're welcome to 'em,' Paula said with a sniff. 'All them sweaty chaps running round the tracks, and the Germans hollering and cheering them on, and only wanting their own kind to win, according to Harold. He says it's all for show, to prove how marvellous they think they bloomin' well are.'

Cherry laughed. Paula and Thomas had come for tea, and the children were playing in the nursery under Nanny Green's supervision, although Paula guessed that Thomas was probably already bored to tears by the prissy nature of it all. He may be a bit sweet on Bella Melchoir in his own juvenile way, but he'd still rather be out in the road kicking a ball about, or fishing in the stream, rather than joining in girls' pursuits. And Georgie was too small to be bothered about.

'Harold seems to know a lot about a lot of things,' Cherry commented.

'He does,' Paula said proudly. 'He takes an interest in everything, not just his job. I reckon he could have been on the council if he'd wanted.'

'I bet he could too,' Cherry said, trying not to laugh at her friend's loyalty.

Harold was a solid bloke, and he could argue the toss with most folks, but a town councillor, sitting and arguing with the nobs? Never in a million years.

'So you'll be off soon, then,' Paula said at last.

'Next week,' Cherry said, feeling her heart give a little lurch as she said it. The enormity of it all still hit her now and then, even though she was determined to enjoy it. 'I can hardly believe it's come so soon. Dawkins will drive us down to Southampton and help us with the embarkation.'

'How very grand! A bit different from gettin' on a ferry across the Irish Sea, then,' Paula said sarcastically.

'Don't be mean, Paula. It's just the way we do things. You know that.'

'I do know it. I remember it from Lord and Lady Muck's days. Harold and me have just been wondering if we can manage a day out with Thomas at the seaside this month. That's a bit different too, ain't it?'

'Well, you'll still see the sea, won't you?'

'What, the boring old Bristol Channel? Thanks for nothing.'

'It's not *my* fault, Paula. And why are we arguing? You don't begrudge me this chance, do you?'

Paula's face softened at once, seeing how defensive Cherry
was becoming.

'O' course I don't, girl. Take no notice of me. I'm glad for
you. I just hope things will always be as right for you as they
are now.'

'What the devil does that mean?' Cherry said, frowning.
'Why shouldn't things always be right for me and Lance?'

Paula hesitated. It was on the tip of her tongue to mention
the boy she had seen at the wharf. But it had been one brief
sighting, that was all, and she hadn't seen him since. When
Cherry was feeling so chipper, it would be bloody awful to
upset her by stirring things up all over again when there was
probably no need.

She forced a grin. 'Oh, don't mind me. I'm just green, that's
all.'

'Well, don't be. We both got what we wanted, didn't we?
And since we won't be seeing each other again before I leave,
I don't want us to part on bad terms, Paula.'

'Nor do I,' Paula said stoutly. 'And it's only for two weeks,
after all. I'll want to see you the minute you get back, to hear
all about it, mind.'

'I promise.'

Paula giggled suddenly. 'I suppose you wouldn't care to take
me along as your maid? You'll need somebody to help with
your hair and to fasten all those buttons on your fancy new
frocks.'

Cherry laughed, her good humour restored. 'I can manage
perfectly well by myself, and both Lance and I decided we
didn't want any staff with us. It will be just the two of us —
and a hairdressing and beauty salon if I need it!'

At the time, it had surprised her that he didn't want any
staff accompanying them, but she was also very glad. Why take
other people along who they would ultimately be responsible
for? It wasn't only the servants who were responsible for *their*
well-being. They had to look after the servants' welfare too.

Paula's words had reminded her again of how very different
their lives were now, though. They had grown up together,
always worked and played together, sharing their hopes and

secrets and disasters. Until that magical day when Captain Lance Melchoir had seduced the oh-so-willing kitchen-maid she had been then, Cherry had had every reason to believe that she and Paula would continue together for ever. Always the best of friends, courting their boys together, marrying and bringing up their children together. But fate had changed everything. Fate could do that. It could move mountains . . . or was that faith? Cherry was never quite sure.

'All right, darling? You're very quiet,' Lance said, leaning towards her as the limousine sped them smoothly southwards towards Southampton where the great liner would be awaiting them. She felt his hand clasp hers when she waited a moment before replying.

'I'm fine. A little sad at saying goodbye to the children, that's all.'

'It will do them good to know they can't have their parents around them all the time,' Lance said briskly. 'Children must learn to be independent.'

Cherry smiled faintly. 'There speaks the army captain,' she murmured.

Though she couldn't imagine for a moment that Lady Elspeth would have had a qualm at sending her boy off to boarding school and then university before Sandhurst. She and Lance came from different worlds, as she had thought so many times, and the miracle was that they had ever become so compatible at all.

She was determined not to think of any of that now. They were starting out on a great adventure, and she was going to enjoy it. But as though Lance too wasn't averse to remembering how they had arrived at such a point in their lives, she heard him give a low laugh that had more than a hit of seduction in it.

'I think our stateroom will be a bit more opulent than the mean little space we once had on an Irish ferry, Cherry-ripe. But I'm sure we can make it our own cosy nest, and I imagine that retiring for the night on an ocean liner will be an excitement in itself. It will be a second honeymoon, no less.'

'I'm sure it will,' she said with an answering smile, feeling her face flush at what he was saying.

And why not? They were young and rich and alive, and about to spend two pampered weeks without the encumbrance of two children, however loved. Why not consider this a second honeymoon, the luxury of which Cherry had never dreamed? At that moment her nerves seemed to disappear, and as the sprawling port of Southampton came ever nearer, her spirits rose with it.

The sight of the ship itself nearly took her breath away. It dwarfed any other vessel in the vicinity, the three symmetrical red funnels towering high above its splendid girth, solid and reassuring. Any lingering thoughts of the fate of the *Titanic*, all those years ago, faded from Cherry's mind. Time had moved on, and with it, thankfully, had come insistence on safety at sea.

In any case, there was no time to ponder on anything else as they joined the melee of passengers and assistants all attempting to get trunks and other baggage on to the ship and to be shown to their staterooms by efficient white-clad stewards. They left them to it and went up on deck to watch the final preparations for leaving port, joining their fellow passengers to wave to the teeming, excited folk on shore, all waiting to see the great ship leave port.

With her wild imagination, Cherry found it a strangely emotional time, almost as if the ship was being wrenched from its moorings to start its long, lonely voyage on a vast ocean all alone. Which was absurd, considering there were about two thousand passengers on board, and many crew members looking after them and catering for their every whim.

'Why, bless my soul, if it isn't Lord Melchoir! It's a small world, and all that blah-blah nonsense. Heard you'd inherited the title some years ago when your old fellow popped it,' they heard a booming and ill-cultured voice say crudely alongside them.

Cherry groaned inside as Lance turned at once, and after a startled moment he took the portly man's outstretched hand. She didn't recall ever seeing him before, but Lance knew far more people than she did. Naively, perhaps, she had never considered meeting anyone they knew on the voyage. But how unlikely was that, on a ship of this size, and with those with money to spare wanting to see and be seen on one of the *Queen Mary*'s epic Atlantic crossings? And, presumably, anyone who could pay the fare was welcome . . .

'Good God, man, you're an unexpected sight. I haven't seen you for years, and I thought you were dead,' Lance said with a forced laugh, prompting Cherry to think that he must know the man very well to be so jovial.

'Oh, they can't kill me off just yet,' the man replied with a throaty chuckle, 'but the little lady thought a sea voyage would do me good. Makes you laugh, since I've always had the stomach of an ox, and she's already gone to the stateroom with a touch of the collywobbles, even before we've properly left port.'

So presumably he was married. And one of the loudest men Cherry had ever encountered, the kind whose voice would be heard for some distance all around him. She felt a stab of unease, wondering just how far back his association with Lance went. The man had barely looked at her until Lance spoke to him quickly.

'Phipps, this is my wife, Lady Melchoir.'

He looked her over in a way that made her want to squirm. But the fact that Lance called him by his surname encouraged her merely to incline her head towards him in a way that would have made Lady Elspeth proud.

'Well,' the man said, beaming, 'looks like we've both done well for ourselves, doesn't it? Me marrying money, and you getting the looker.'

'If you'll excuse us now, Phipps, we need to go down to our stateroom and oversee the unpacking,' Lance said, his voice considerably colder.

'Oh, of course, of course. We'll get plenty of chances to chat again during the voyage.' He swept aside with an elaborate flourish.

'Not if I can help it, we won't,' Lance muttered aggressively, as he thrust a way for them through the passengers still on deck.

Cherry knew him well enough to know that he was upset by the encounter, but as yet she felt more bewildered than anything else. She could understand that Lance didn't want the company of this oafish man for the next two weeks, but a sixth sense told her there was more behind it than simply a clash of backgrounds.

Once they were alone in their stateroom, she faced him squarely, trying not to notice that her heart was beating faster than usual.

'So who was that man?'

'He's someone I preferred never to see again.'

'But why? You have to tell me, Lance. If we're going to come up against him during the next two weeks, I need to know why you dislike him so much. It was perfectly obvious, and not that I blame you,' she added. 'He seemed like an odious man.'

'He is. He was. It goes back to my army days. He was my batman then, and he was accused of theft in the regiment. Nothing could be proved, but I was called in as a character witness, and since, to my knowledge, nothing had ever been taken, I had to defend him, even though I was highly suspicious. He got off, but he left the army soon afterwards. Some months later, I got a brief note of thanks from him, which made me feel like a bloody conspirator, and the whole affair left a very nasty taste in my mouth.'

'I see. And you've never seen him from that day to this?'

'Never. And never wanted to, either. He always struck me as a scrounger.'

'Well, not any more, from the look of the expensive clothes he was wearing, and that valuable pocket watch and chain. So I wonder who he married.'

They looked at one another, and Cherry knew that Lance was thinking exactly the same thing. She felt a small shudder run through her. The lady had to be someone with money, and there were always those among the upper classes and the large aristocratic families who liked a bit of rough and ready. But whoever it was, it couldn't make any difference to them – could it?

Five

The breathtaking and elegant craftsmanship of the *Queen Mary* was almost understated when compared to the opulence of the ladies and gentlemen in first class who all seemed determined to outdo each other in terms of costly jewels and dress. There was a time when Cherry would have been completely overwhelmed by them all, but thanks to twelve years of marriage to Lance, and the recent shopping trip with Cyn, she knew very well she could more than hold her own. And she not only needed to. She wanted to look her very best, to make Lance proud of her.

That first evening on board as they dressed for dinner, she wore one of the new evening gowns, in soft, subtle shades of aquamarine with a low décolleté neckline. The delicacy of the colour showed off her glowing hair to perfection, and it was set off by a glittering chandelier necklace of diamonds at her throat and a matching bracelet high on her arm.

'You look absolutely radiant, like a shining star,' Lance told her as he took her in his arms. 'You're more beautiful than any princess could ever be. In fact,' he added with an almost lecherous chuckle that only needed a twirling moustache to make it complete, 'why don't we just skip dinner and stay here all night?'

Cherry caught her breath, glorying in the undeniable lust in his eyes. It thrilled her now as it had always done, and the thought of this being a second honeymoon was ever more enticing. He might be teasing, but she had the feeling that she only had to say the word and all their finery would be discarded in a trice for the pleasures of the double bed.

At that moment, as if in protest at the words he had just said, there was an undoubted rumble from somewhere in the pit of her stomach. It was enough to make them both laugh and the heightened moment was broken.

'I think, Sir, that having taken so long to achieve this effect, if I don't have something to eat before you think about ravishing me, I shall probably expire from hunger,' she said daintily.

'Then allow me to escort you to the dining room, my lady, and the ravishing will be all the sweeter for keeping until later,' Lance said, in great good humour now, and all his earlier annoyance at seeing his old batman temporarily forgotten.

The excitement of it all was rubbing off on both of them. For Cherry, the sheer sensual feel of the expensive silk gown against her skin, and Lance's reaction to it, was an added pleasure she hadn't anticipated. Lance had travelled extensively over the years, but never before had he had the joy of showing off his beautiful wife to such a large company, and it was an unexpectedly heady experience.

By now, he had decided it would be simple enough to avoid any contact with the man Phipps. He had the raucous and coarse voice of the nouveau riche that was difficult to miss, and they could easily slip away when he was in the vicinity. It didn't concern Lance at all that it could be thought somewhat demeaning to have to do such a thing.

What he hadn't considered was that Phipps would be just as keen to seek him out, to hang on to the coat-tails of a lord of the realm and brag about having once known him well.

The first-class lounge was almost full when Lance and Cherry walked down the curving staircase towards it, prior to entering the dining room, and neither of them missed the admiring glances they received. They were a stunningly attractive couple, and the faint, jagged scar on Lance's cheek only added to the allure and mystique of the man. More than one lady present could attest to that, and eyed Cherry with more than simple envy of her exquisite appearance. Almost before they could merge into the crowd for a pre-dinner aperitif, they found themselves accosted by a white-coated steward.

'A gentleman requests that you join him and his party for champagne cocktails before dinner, Lord and Lady Melchoir,' he said, with the amazing ability of all ships' crews to remember passengers' names almost instantly.

'That's very kind,' Lance said, suppressing a sigh, and knowing they must be sociable for the next few hours at least. In any case,

Cherry deserved to be shown off to the best advantage, and to enjoy the experience.

They followed the steward across the floor and arrived at a table where half a dozen people were chatting and laughing. The host stood up, and Cherry smothered a groan at seeing the batman Phipps. But there was no help for it but to join the party now, other than appearing excruciatingly rude, which she knew Lance would never do.

'Sit you down, sit you down, Lord Melchoir and my lady,' he boomed with an exaggerated bow, 'and allow me to introduce my wife and some of our shipmates.'

The shipmates were obviously all new acquaintances, and Cherry wondered how many of them had been coerced into joining the man because of his persistence. Or perhaps she was the only one being extra-sensitive, since they all seemed to be having a jolly time. She barely took account of their names and was sure she would soon forget them, unlike the ship's crew members! No, it was Phipps' wife who startled her the most.

She didn't know what she had expected. Perhaps some brassy-haired dimwit who had inherited all Daddy's ill-gotten money and been seduced by the oaf. Or perhaps it would be some young foreign girl he had met on his travels or even had imported, since she had heard about such things. But such a girl wouldn't have had money, and she had been certain that this was the way Phipps had acquired what wealth he had. The reality of it was nothing like that at all.

'I'm pleased to meet you, Mrs Phipps,' she murmured, taking the woman's stringy hand in hers for a moment. She must have been at least twenty years older than Phipps, and her face was a crêpey parchment white. Cherry had a hard job not to glance at Lance and make her surprise obvious.

'The old girl's taking this sea voyage for her health, but we're not thinking about that tonight, so drink up, everybody. There's plenty more where this came from,' Phipps continued to boom, letting the people at adjoining tables overhear.

Cherry cringed for her, but she seemed not to notice, or, if she did, not to care. Whatever held them together was unfathomable to Cherry, but other people's marriages were always something of a mystery. You could say the same about theirs.

It was unavoidable that when dinner was announced, the party in the lounge should share the same dining table, however much Cherry would have wished otherwise. She found herself seated opposite Mrs Phipps, and several times she caught a curious look in the lady's eyes. She didn't say a lot, leaving it all to her verbose husband, but eventually she leaned forward slightly and spoke directly to Cherry.

'Have we met somewhere before, Lady Melchoir? You look somewhat familiar to me, but I can't place any occasion it might have been.'

Cherry's heart lurched painfully at the cultured voice, so different from her husband's. How on earth had these two ever come together?

'I don't recall any occasion, Mrs Phipps,' she said, more coolly than she felt. For if it had been anywhere, it would surely have been at one of Lady Elspeth's soirées, when Cherry was a kitchen-maid in the Melchoirs' employ. Though how she would have come in contact with the lady even then, she couldn't imagine – except that for some of them, it was a bit of sport to creep down to the kitchens during an evening to see how the other half lived. The lower half, of course, that had included Cherry O'Neill.

'Perhaps not, but I rarely forget a face. It's one of the quirks of old age. Names and places I can forget in an instant, but not faces. No matter, my dear.'

Phipps chuckled, and to Cherry's horror, he put a finger to his forehead and waggled it slightly. 'We often have a game trying to decide who's one of her old cronies, and who she's just invented, don't we, ducks?'

'So we do, and some of the invented ones can be preferable to the real ones,' his wife said smartly.

'Touché, my dear,' he said, blowing kisses across the table from his revoltingly fleshy mouth.

Whatever Phipps might think about his wife, to Cherry it was certain that she still had all her marbles and wasn't going to let him have all his own way. But the others at the table seemed to find him hilarious, and his wife was obviously prepared to indulge him. So far, Lance hadn't joined in the extraordinary conversation, but he clearly thought it was time to take the wind out of the buffoon's sails.

'Yes, real acquaintances can often be hard to bear, especially those from times past whom we would choose to forget,' he commented.

Phipps wasn't going to let this pass. His button eyes sparkled with something between delight and malice.

'Lord Melchoir refers to our time together in the army,' he said boastfully, putting them on an equal footing.

The arrogance of the man astounded Cherry, knowing what she did about him now. But if some of these well-heeled folk knew about her own past, perhaps they wouldn't be so keen to make her acquaintance, either. The next minute, her opinion of Mrs Phipps was confirmed.

'Come, come now, my dear Arnold, everyone in their right place. I hardly think Lord Melchoir would consider his batman as one who was his confidant in the army. You held the rank of captain, I believe, Lord Melchoir?' she added sweetly.

'That I did, Ma'am,' Lance said, just as smoothly, as several of the other ladies smothered a small giggle at the other man's discomfiture.

But then she turned to Cherry, and her next words made her hold her breath. 'I do believe I have an inkling of where I may have seen you before, Lady Melchoir, but it was so long ago that I'm probably mistaken. You and a friend were in the process of having your hair bobbed in one of the salons in the centre of Bristol. I was there on a brief visit to the West Country and thought how fresh and lovely the two girls looked with their new bobs, and you were both so excited by it. It was probably no more than your dramatic colouring that made me think you looked familiar.'

'Good heavens, what a memory you must have, Mrs Phipps!' Cherry exclaimed. 'If it was me, I'm afraid I don't remember the occasion at all.'

Oh, but she did. She remembered only too well how sophis-ticated and grown-up the new bobs had made her and Paula feel that day of their spur-of-the-moment decision to have their long hair cut off. And how astounded Captain Lance had been

to catch sight of her later, still the workaday Cherry O'Neill,
and yet not resembling the old Cherry at all. She remembered
how he had looked at her as if he wanted her there and then.
The way he was looking at her now.

Dear God, couldn't everybody see it?

And even though she knew how Paula would have relished
a good old ding-dong with Mr and Mrs Phipps, she was unut-
terably glad that Paula wasn't here now. She would surely have
rushed in at the end of Mrs Phipps' chatter, and opened the
lady's eyes still more as to what kind of girls those two had
been on that long-ago day. As it was, Cherry prayed that her
memory never went any farther back.

She lowered her eyes now, thankful that the mood at the
dining table had changed, since it seemed that everyone had
finally tired of listening to Phipps' boasting and his wife's
reminiscences. They moved on to other topics, including the
Olympic Games now being held in Berlin. And at last Cherry
could add something productive to the conversation.

'Some friends of ours have gone to Berlin to see the Games.
In fact, they're staying in Germany for the entire month of
August, staying in a friend's *Schloss*.'

'How very grand,' one of the other ladies said, clearly needing
no explanation of what a *Schloss* meant. 'I hope they enjoy
the spectacle. It's said that the Germans have spared no expense
on these Games.'

Phipps wasn't going to let this go. He snorted and drew a
long draught of his dinner wine. 'Oh, they're good at spectacle
all right. Next thing you know, they'll be polishing up their
jackboots and leading us into war again.'

'That's the last thing we want, and not the subject for a
civilized dinner table, I think,' Lance said coldly.

'Maybe not, but nor is it civilized to punish an entire race
on account of their faith and background, is it – Sir? And it's
everywhere. Think Oswald Mosley if you want an example of
how these people infiltrate.'

One of the other gentlemen intervened firmly. 'Lord
Melchoir is right, Mr Phipps. Can we not leave such a discussion until a more appropriate time? We've all come on this
splendid ship to enjoy ourselves and to leave our everyday

world behind, not to spend the time descending into a political debate.'

Cherry flashed him a look of gratitude as several of the others murmured assent. She didn't miss the glare that Phipps' wife gave her husband, either, and he finally quietened down.

After dinner, she and Lance managed at last to be rid of them, and had a late-night drink in one of the elegant lounges before retiring to their stateroom. But she couldn't quite forget the evening's encounter.

'I thought it was going to be a little tricky earlier,' she murmured. 'What with you meeting up with the ghastly Phipps again, and then his wife thinking she had seen me somewhere before, it could have been very uncomfortable, Lance.'

'They're nothing to us, Cherry, and nothing they say can affect us. They can surmise all they like, and so can we, if we could be bothered to wonder how two ill-matched folk ever got together. I can't say it's of any interest to me.'

'Well, I must say you're taking it all much more casually than I'd have thought. I know you don't like the man, but I never expected his wife to have any idea of who I was.'

'She doesn't, and she's not likely to, either. So just forget them.'

'It's not going to be easy to do that over the next two weeks, and there will be little chance of avoiding them,' she persisted.

He laughed, and contrary to the way *she* was feeling, she realized he was now looking surprisingly relaxed. He leaned across the small table they occupied and caressed her hand, regardless of other people in the lounge.

'But also rather exciting, wouldn't you say, Cherry-ripe? The risk of being found out after some misdemeanour reminds me of the bad old days at university and some of the scrapes I was involved in. Danger and excitement go hand in hand, my darling, and keeps the blood flowing.'

His words diverted her, and she found herself smiling at last.

'Good Lord, I would never have imagined you getting into scrapes. I always thought you were far too posh for that, and I was always far too much in awe of you to think of you doing normal things like normal people. That was before I knew you properly, of course,' she added.

He laughed again, his eyes sparkling at her assessment of him.

'And now that you know me better than any other person on earth, you'll know that my tastes are very normal indeed. And if we don't get back to our stateroom very soon, I shall probably disgrace myself by making love to you here and now, and shocking the entire ship's company.'

'Well, we certainly wouldn't want to do that, would we?' Cherry said, standing up simultaneously with him and letting him lead her out of the lounge.

Long into the night, when the unfamiliar stateroom had taken on a special and intimate familiarity that was to see them through the next two glorious weeks, Cherry lay half-dreaming. Lulled by the rhythm of the ship's engines far below, and the softly hypnotic movement of the ship, she thought she had never been so happy. Through the uncurtained porthole, she could see the soft indigo night, lit by moonlight and studded with a million stars, the stuff of fairyland. They were in a gossamer cocoon of their own choosing, where nothing and no one could touch them.

Lance was right. People could surmise all they liked, and it was something of a spectator sport that she and Paula had frequently indulged in anyway, but unless they had positive proof, it was never more than guesswork. Besides, she thought that Mrs Phipps, with her uncouth Arnold, had more than enough to put up with, to worry too much about her.

She felt Lance stir beside her, and his arm rolled over her, causing her to make a small sound. He murmured gently.

'Are you still awake?'

'Only just,' she murmured back.

'Would you like something to help you sleep?'

She couldn't miss the sweet seduction in his voice, and she revelled in the fact that she was still so desirable to him after twelve years of marriage, and he to her. She gloried still more in his virility, his ability to give her pleasure, and her own willing and eager response whenever he wanted her.

'Yes, please – Sir,' she whispered.

★　★　★

The voyage continued without any more unwelcome incidents. In the end, they found it surprisingly easy to avoid any contact with Mr and Mrs Phipps. There were so many beautiful places on the enormous ship where they could steal away and be alone if they chose, or join in a large company of fellow passengers for stimulating conversations. If, once or twice, Cherry caught sight of the unlikely couple, and found Mrs Phipps looking at her a little speculatively, she merely smiled and turned away, leaving the lady to ponder on her own haphazard memory or lack of it.

'That lady came into money when her late husband died,' one of Cherry's new acquaintances remarked a week or so later as they were taking a breather on one of the deck loungers, watching the mesmerizing wake of the ship.

'Who did?' she said, the words taking her off guard.

'Mrs Phipps. I was a bit puzzled about the two of them, being such unlikely bedfellows, if you'll excuse such a vulgar expression, Lady Melchoir. Then I remembered reading about her in one of the society newspapers about five years ago. There was a photograph of the pair of them, and the one she's with now was their gardener who'd been landscaping their property. Funny how things work out, isn't it?'

'It certainly is,' Cherry said without expression. 'And how fortunate that he was there to give her some comfort.'

The other lady chuckled. 'Why, Lady Melchoir, if I didn't think it unworthy of you, I'd think that was almost mocking!'

'Almost,' Cherry said, unable to resist her lips twitching, and more than ready to report to Lance what she had heard. It explained a lot.

But she didn't really care what circumstances had brought Lance's batman and an obviously cultured lady together. Still, it tied up a few loose ends, and Cherry always liked the ends to tie up neatly. And, as Paula would have said, plenty of upper-crust ladies like a bit of rough. It worked the other way too. Plenty of titled gents liked the lower orders . . . not that Lance had been a titled gent when Cherry had fancied him so madly. She hadn't even considered the possibility that one day he would inherit his father's title. And if she had, her chances of becoming Lady Melchoir had been as laughably remote as flying to the moon. But it had all come true, just as the most romantic fairytales sometimes said it did.

'What's tickled your fancy now?' Lance asked her, coming to find her later that afternoon and relieving her of a spell in the other lady's company for a stroll around the deck.

'What a common expression, my lord,' Cherry said with a teasing sideways glance.

'Never mind that. What did the well-upholstered one have to say to you that got you smiling?'

She laughed out loud now, hugging his arm as they took their afternoon constitutional.

'Just the interesting bit of gossip that Mrs Phipps came into money when her late husband died, and that Phipps had been their gardener, landscaping their grounds for them. I commented that it was fortunate he was there to give her some comfort, that's all.'

'So that's how he wormed his way into her life.'

'And her bed. And never mind the wrinkles.'

'And you're a wicked witch, aren't you?' Lance said, laughing back.

The round-trip voyage was nearly over now, and as Southampton eventually came into view once more, Cherry thought how wonderful it had all been. There were moments best forgotten, and others that she would always cherish. There were sights that she would always remember, not least the spectacular cruise into New York's sensational harbour. And now the news had already come through that the *Queen Mary* had won the coveted Blue Riband for the fastest crossings of the Atlantic Ocean, an added bonus to give everyone on board a feeling of personal pride that they had been a part of it.

'It's only now that I realize how much I've been missing the children,' Cherry said with a catch in her breath, just before they left their stateroom for the last time. 'And also how little I've thought about them while we've been away. Isn't that terrible of me?'

'Not at all,' Lance replied with a grin. 'It just meant you had more time to think about me, and that's how it should be. So tell me, Lady Melchoir, did your second honeymoon meet all your expectations?'

'More than I ever dreamed it could,' she said honestly, holding him close.

But there was no more time to linger. The stateroom was bare of their possessions now, and some other couple would be enjoying its luxury soon. Cherry hoped they would have as much pleasure from it as she had done. Everyone's luggage was packed and ready to be unloaded by the stewards, and as the great ship reached port to a similar mass of welcoming onlookers as before, there was little time for anything but the pleasure of disembarking and, for some, the relief of being on terra firma again, for hurried goodbyes and kisses for the few, and waves to those less favoured. Of Mr and Mrs Phipps there was no sign, for which Cherry was eternally grateful.

Farther down on the quayside, the Melchoir limousine, with Dawkins standing stalwartly beside it, was the most welcome sight of all now. By the time they disembarked, their luggage had already been delivered to it by the shoreside baggage porters, and after exchanging a few pleasantries with Dawkins on the success of the voyage, all they had to do now was sink into the car's luxurious soft leather interior and be taken home. *Home.* Never had a word sounded so good.

The children were overcome with excitement at seeing their parents again. Georgie immediately wet himself, causing Nanny Green to tut-tut in annoyance after dressing him up so smartly to greet his mother again, but Cherry didn't care as she gathered him up in her arms. He was still her sweet baby, and one little accident couldn't detract from her joy at being with him again. As for Bella, who seemed to have grown an inch for every week they had been away, all she wanted to know was what presents they had brought her.

'You're a mercenary little wretch, aren't you?' Lance said indulgently. 'What makes you think we've brought you anything?'

'Because Mummy said you would!' she almost howled.

Cherry soothed her. 'Of course we have, my love, and your father shouldn't tease you so. As soon as our unpacking has been done, we'll show you what we've brought back for you. But I'm sure you've had a good time while we've been away. Did you go to the fair on the Downs?'

'Nanny Green took us, but she didn't like it much,' Georgie shouted as he jumped up and down, knowing he was going to be dragged away at any minute to have his breeches changed.

'Nanny Green never likes anything we do,' Bella grumbled after he was taken off, kicking and yelling. 'She's such an old fuddy-duddy.'

Cherry hid a smile, ignoring the echo of her own opinion of the governess.

'And did you see anything of Paula and Thomas while we were away?'

Even saying her name, she felt a huge longing to see Paula for herself, to share all the wonderful experiences she had known on the voyage with her old friend. Well, nearly everything. Some things were too precious and private to share with anyone.

'We saw them a couple of times.'

Cherry detected a decided coolness in her voice. Was Thomas Farmer already losing favour with her pernickety little daughter? And would Lance mind too much if he was? She pushed the thought out of her mind, knowing full well that Lance would have far greater fish to fry for his daughter than the son of a railway employee.

By the time Nanny Green brought Georgie back to the nursery, clean and fresh, Lance had already tired of childish chatter and gone to the stables to check on the horses. His old favourite, Noble, had long gone now. His new favourite was a bay called Prince, and Cherry knew he would be itching to ride him again.

Georgie picked up the conversation where he had left it.

'So where are our presents, Mummy?' he said, his bottom lip quivering.

'We'll go along to my bedroom and see if they've been unpacked yet,' she said with a smile, knowing his impatience couldn't be curbed for much longer without descending into a tantrum of major proportions.

'I still like Thomas the best,' he said unexpectedly.

'Do you, sweetheart?' Cherry said. 'Better than who?'

Nanny Green sniffed. 'He means that new friend Bella was talking to at the fair. Not a good choice, if you ask me, Madam, and best kept well away.'

'You would say that,' Bella put in rudely. 'I liked him, and I can talk to whoever I want to, anyway. You're not my keeper!'

'Bella, really! Apologize to Nanny Green at once,' Cherry said, appalled at her rudeness. What on earth had been going on while she had been away?

'Well, not if she's going to be mean about Ethan.'

'*Bella!*' Cherry snapped. 'Oh, all right, I'm sorry, Nanny Green,' the girl said sullenly. 'Anyway, we liked him at first, but we don't any more, do we, Georgie?'

Georgie was stamping about now, not taking any notice of her, and Cherry began to wonder what she had come home to, after all. But the decision to take them both to her bedroom to search for presents managed to change their mood, and she breathed a sigh of relief. As for a new friend called Ethan, well, what kind of a name was that? It sounded more like a *heathen* name than a boy's.

Six

It was Paula's pride and joy that Harold had had the telephone installed in their house. It was mostly for his own purposes, of course, and his precious union business, but it lifted up their status by a country mile, she thought gleefully, and it meant that she and Cherry could have instant communication whenever they wanted it. Not that she ever telephoned Cherry, since she knew it would be the stuffy Gerard who would answer, and she could imagine him holding the receiver at arm's length when he realized it was one of their old kitchen-maids at the other end. It would affront his starchy nature to have to inform her ladyship that a Mrs Farmer was on the line, when he knew perfectly well her name was Paula. He had reprimanded her with it enough in the past . . . but, of course, she too had a different status now. She was a married woman.

In any case, she should stick her nose in the air and not give a toss about who answered her call . . . but she wasn't quite brave enough for that. And even before she was put through to Melchoir House, she would have to give the number to some supercilious operator who would intimidate her just as much as Gerard. No, she preferred to wait for Cherry to call her, and she had checked off the days on the calendar with eager anticipation until Cherry arrived home from the great adventure. But she must have been back for nearly a week now, and she still hadn't heard from her.

'I don't want to go up there again in that soppy nursery with those stupid kids,' her son grunted from the depths of the comic he was skimming.

'Why on earth not?' Paula said, startled. 'I thought you liked seeing Bella. You didn't worry about running into her last week when the fair was on, or so you said.'

He scowled. 'She's all right for a girl, but Dad thinks I'm a cissy for liking her, so I won't. And my mates thought she was stuck-up as well.'

'Don't be so daft,' Paula said, ignoring his last remark. 'All boys like girls eventually. It's human nature. Your dad was just playing with you, that's all. And you can't turn off your likes and dislikes just like that.'

'Yes, I can,' Thomas said stubbornly, burying his head in his comic again.

She gave up worrying about how different boys were from girls, and got on with her polishing and her pleasure in keeping her house shining like a new pin. After all those years of being in service and under Cook's thumb at Melchoir House, it was ironic that Paula's pride and joy now was cleaning and dusting and cooking meals for her two lovely boys.

Anyway, she should be thankful that Thomas hadn't started all that adolescent malarkey yet. It had to start some time, and it was up to Harold to put him straight. She hadn't gone to the funfair on the Downs when Thomas had gone there with a group of his pals, so she had no idea why he seemed to have turned against Bella. She shrugged. It wouldn't last, anyway. He could be as contrary as his father when it came to changing his mind, but she couldn't imagine anyone taking against pretty little Isabella Melchoir for long.

He was getting on her nerves lately, though. She was glad when he went out of the house, banging the door behind him, and she sighed, counting the days to when school started again after the summer holidays. She lovingly polished the telephone for the umpteenth time as it sat, black and gleaming, on the sideboard, and she willed it to ring. When it did, half an hour later, she nearly jumped out of her skin and ran to pick up the receiver, flustered as always, fearful that if she didn't answer it immediately, the caller would ring off, and she'd never know who it had been.

'Yes? Hello, please. Who is it? I mean, this is the Farmer household.'

'Paula, where's the fire? Slow down for pity's sake!'

She heard Cherry's laughing tones with a rush of relief, and almost squeaked a reply.

'You're back! Oh, I'm so glad to hear you.'

'Well, I'm glad to hear you too, though for a minute I

thought you were going to have a fit at having to answer the telephone.'

'Oh well, you know how it always ruddy well scares me. There should be some kind of a signal to let me know it's you before I pick it up, and then I wouldn't nearly pee myself with nerves.'

'Still as daft as a brush, I see,' Cherry said, laughing. 'But it's so good to hear you, Paula, and I've got such a lot to tell you.'

'Go on, then,' Paula said, settling down in the chair beside the sideboard now. 'Was it marvellous? And did you have to mind your Ps and Qs every minute of the day and night?'

She didn't know why she asked. Getting poshed up and spending time with the toffs wouldn't be any hardship to Cherry now. She could pass for the Queen of Sheba, no bother.

'It was wonderful, and if you want to come up here for tea this afternoon, I'll tell you all about it. Just the two of us, Paula. What do you say? I could really do with your company. Nanny Green has taken the children out somewhere and Lance has gone riding, and I'm *bored*!'

'Good God, what have you got to be bored about, having everything done for you!'

'Well, perhaps that's it,' Cherry said, and then added hastily, 'No, not really. I'm just being stupid. It's probably the after-effects of having such a lovely time with lots of different people on the ship, and now it's all gone a bit flat. I'm an ungrateful bitch, aren't I?' she said ruefully.

'I should say so,' Paula said with a laugh. 'All right, I'll be there this afternoon – and without Thomas, don't worry, since he's taken the huff over anything and everything. He's behaving like a right little brat these days and driving me crackers.'

'Good, so it will just be the two of us.'

Cherry was thankful that Thomas wouldn't be accompanying her, even though he had always seemed to be tacked on to her skirts at one time. That probably came from Paula babying him as long as possible, despite Harold always wanting to toughen him up, according to Paula. It would be good to be free of children for a couple of hours, though, and to have some adult conversation with an old friend, even though she had been achingly glad to see Bella and Georgie again, of course. Thomas was a nice enough boy, but a bit rough around the edges, and, as Lance would say, *not really their sort* . . . and as the words entered her head, she was instantly appalled at herself. But they were there now, and she couldn't blessed well unthink them.

But she wasn't going to think about it any longer, and nothing on earth was going to stop her friendship with Paula, whether or not her husband might look down his nose at it and wish that she would cut off all those earlier ties. Why should she – and *how* could she?

For God's sake, she only had to go down the stairs to the kitchens in her own house to be transported instantly back to the life she had once had. The bustle and gossip and chatter were the same. The smells were the same. The buxom shape of Cook was the same, if not even larger. And, between them, she and Gerard ruled the roost in exactly the same way as they had done when she and Paula were scurrying, snot-nosed kitchen-maids, at their beck and call, practically every hour of the day and night.

They had had a certain amount of time off, of course . . . and while Cherry was arranging for tea to be sent up to her sitting room the minute Mrs Farmer arrived, and to be sure that they weren't disturbed, she couldn't help thinking of a certain night long ago when their evening off had changed her life.

She hadn't known it was going to do so at the time, of course. She hadn't known that one madcap evening when they had run away from the dance hall down in the town, laughing and skittish and escaping the clutches of the louts who had wanted to pursue them, that a knight in shining armour . . . well, the Melchoir limousine . . . would recognize them, cruise along beside them and urge them to get inside. And with Paula so tipsy and falling asleep as she was enveloped in the softness of the lush interior, and herself catching the eye of their handsome driver and being enticed to the stables by Captain Lance . . . well, without all that, she wouldn't be here now, and Bella and Georgie wouldn't have such a privileged life, while Paula's Thomas larked about with the street kids in the lower part of town. Life was strange, all right, and you never knew in which direction it would take you.

'So what was it really like? Were the other people horribly stuck-up and snobby?' Paula said, when they had got over the first awkward moments of being together again, like any two people did.

'Some of them,' Cherry said. 'But none of that bothered us. You know Lance – he can always rise above anything like that, and you know I can hold my own with them too.'

Paula chuckled. 'I do know it. Lady Elspeth knew it too, didn't she? You could always put on a cut-glass accent to rival anybody's, kid.'

Cherry laughed. 'Do you know, you're the only person in the world who calls me kid now?'

'Should I stop doing it, then – my lady?'

'Good God, *no*! Sometimes I still think you're the only person I can really be myself with.'

'Bloody hell, Cherry. There's no trouble in paradise, I hope?'

'No, not at all. Far from it. Lance and I are as close as ever. We do have different ideas about things at times, though.'

'Well, so do Harold and me. He's a man and I'm a woman, and I'm not arguing with that,' she said with a chuckle.

'Yes, but – oh, take no notice of me. Like I said, it's just reaction from the voyage, I expect.'

Paula put down her dainty china cup in her saucer, and folded her arms.

'Cherry, I know you better than that, and I know when you've got something on your mind as well. So come on, out with it. I'm not leaving here until you tell me, even if I have to stop and have dinner with you and the ruddy toff tonight.'

Cherry smiled faintly. She could never fool Paula for long.

'All right. Your Thomas isn't the only one feeling his feet,' she said. 'Bella's been simply impossible since we came back. I don't know whether it's resentment at us for going off without her and Georgie for the first time in their lives, or something else. Whatever it is, she's driving Nanny Green wild too, and I fear she may threaten to leave if Bella doesn't change her attitude.'

Paula's mouth had dropped open at hearing Cherry's tirade.

'I can hardy believe it. Sweet little, butter-wouldn't-melt-in-her-mouth Bella? It don't sound like her at all, Cherry.'

'Who knows what ideas they get in their heads once they start to outgrow their childish ways? I'm the first to admit that Bella's been spoilt, and Lance has always given in to her over everything. At least she hasn't been given the pony she talks about from time to time,' she added.

'So what are you going to do about it?'

Cherry sighed heavily. 'Well, because of Nanny Green practically having hysterics one day at Bella's rudeness, Lance has now decided that the children should have a proper tutor, and a male one at that. He says that because Georgie still has babyish tantrums, he needs a masculine influence in the school-room, and Nanny Green's just not qualified enough, and Bella would benefit from a sterner hand in things too. So I have no say in things.'

She couldn't hide the bitterness in her voice. She loved Lance dearly, but she had to admit that since coming home, partly because of the atmosphere with the children and Miss Green, things had been somewhat prickly between them. Lance had been adamant that things couldn't go on as they were, and that Bella had to learn to behave like a lady and not like a Hottentot.

Cherry couldn't help feeling he was partly blaming her, although it was totally unjustified. There were times when she was made to feel not only like the proverbial little woman, meekly doing everything her husband said, but also as if she had no concept of how the children of a lord should behave.

Well, why the hell should she know? She hadn't been born a lady, and, to her shame, she knew she had avoided telling Lance that she was inviting Paula here today. He never actively objected, but she knew he would prefer her to be on a more social footing with Cynthia Hetherington and her dubious friends than with Paula. Guiltily, she had also made sure that he would be out for several more hours yet. Perhaps, whatever the outer trappings, a person never completely escaped their roots, and hers were very firmly below stairs.

'Cheer up, girl. It won't be so bad,' Paula was saying, with no idea of the way she was churning inside. 'He might be some handsome bloke straight out of Hollywood who takes a shine to you, and then old Captain Lancey will have to look to his laurels, won't he?'

Cherry forced a laugh. 'You may be right. Anyway, it might never happen. Bella could turn into a little angel overnight, and then there'd be no need to hire a perishing tutor at all.'

And pigs might fly, thought Paula.

'So what interesting people did you meet on this wonderful voyage, then?' she went on, trying to lift Cherry's spirits. Though, considering Cherry was living the life of Riley, she couldn't see why on earth they should need lifting.

Cherry's eyes suddenly sparkled with remembering. 'Well, we met one couple who were very odd. She was obviously a lady and a good twenty years older than him, and she thought she recognized me from somewhere, which made my blood run cold for a bit.'

'Blimey, I bet it did. Did she twig anything? She wasn't one of Lady Muck's cronies, was she?'

Cherry shook her head. 'She thought she'd seen me with another girl at a hairdressing salon years ago after having our hair bobbed. Can you imagine?'

Paula was hooting with laughter now. 'Well, we did go a bit crazy that day, didn't we? What about her old man? Did he think he knew you too?'

'No, not me. That was another funny thing. He was brash and loud and horrible, and it turned out he was once Lance's batman when they were in the army. He made a point of contacting us, but Lance didn't care for him either, and we did our best to avoid them both. It gave us a turn, though – especially me, after what the woman had said. Somehow I never expected to meet anyone we knew among two thousand passengers. Perhaps I should have done.'

'Well, you couldn't be prepared for everything, and it turned out all right in the end, didn't it, and you didn't have to see other people all the time. I mean, this was supposed to be a second honeymoon,' she added archly.

'Yes, and it was,' Cherry said softly, her face relaxing again. 'And that's all you're going to hear about it!'

* * *

Sara O'Neill lay on her narrow bed in the mean little house, trying to catch her rattling breath. She was exhausted after the simple effort of writing a letter. But she knew it had to be done, and time was getting short. She knew it without any bastard doctor giving her the once-over and telling her the grim reaper was on his way. Not that they ever told you something so stark, anyway. They just gave you a bottle of gruesome-smelling medicine, providing you could pay for it, then went away and left you to rot.

She hated doctors. They hadn't cared when her husband was in dire need of one. They'd taken one look at him and more or less said he deserved all he got. As if being a bareknuckle fighter wasn't a worthy enough occupation to warrant proper medical care. As if his once-handsome bashed-in face and the hideous purple bruises spreading all over his body didn't mean he desperately needed help. As if the gang of blokes who had done this to him weren't in need of locking up, the key thrown away, until they rotted. He'd won his fight, fair and square, and got good money for it. It wasn't Brian's fault that the poor bastard had since died, but it had resulted in his mates deciding to get their own back on Brian one dark night behind the shearing sheds. He'd stood no chance among six of them, and they'd left him cut and bleeding and near death himself.

Their kid had found him. Poor little bugger. Six years old at the time, he was, and finding his father gasping and moaning had sent him screaming and terrified into the big house to tell the boss and to find his mother. The boss had been sympathetic enough, but he didn't want any trouble, and there would be sure to be an investigation if he called in the rozzers, so he merely gave Sara some painkilling sedatives and strong-smelling salve that smelled like horse liniment for her to put on Brian's bruises, and left them to it. The one good thing the boss's wife did was allow young Ethan to sleep in the big house that night, away from his parents' mean little shack, so that he wouldn't hear his father's agonizing groans.

Sometime during that long and terrible night, Brian died in her arms, and the last insistent words he was able to croak was that she should take the boy to England to his sister. She would take care of them both. Sara had no option but to agree to everything he said, knowing he wouldn't be around to know if she carried out his wishes or not. Though how a woman on her own, with no money to speak of and a small son to support, would ever afford the boat fare to England, to dump them both on a woman they didn't know, she had no idea.

But worse was to come. She had heard the bitter tale many times of how the woman's husband had sent Brian packing to Australia, and that his own sister had disowned him. She didn't know all the details, and she was well aware that Brian was clever at papering over the cracks when he chose, but she knew enough to resent the very sound of the Melchoir name. But she had agreed to his laboured words, and when it was all over, she was horrified to find she was expected to pay off his many debts, and how very little he had left her, and she had wept furious tears for ever getting entangled with such a rogue.

But she was no angel herself. She had been working the waterfront at Sydney harbour when the boat came in carrying Brian O'Neill, and, with it, her destiny. She had picked quite a few pockets by the time the rozzers caught sight of her and began shouting, and she had bumped right into Brian as she was scarpering. It took no more than a second for him to twig what was going on, to grab her hand and start running and laughing with her, until they found themselves in a maze of little back alleys beyond the waterfront.

Two of a kind, that's what they were . . . him with his handsome, gypsy good looks that could devastate any woman, and her with her dancing black eyes and tousled hair . . . and within minutes the sex-starved man and the easy woman were frantically coupling and enjoying each other. Next minute, they heard the rozzers shouting again, and she had pulled him with her, back to her lodgings, where they hardly moved for the next few weeks. By then, Sara was pregnant, and they decided to throw in their lot together.

She thought she must be hallucinating now as she lay on the narrow bed in the house on one of the poorest streets of Bristol, because those times were clearer in her mind than anything that had happened recently. They had had some good old times, she and her brawny devil-man, and some bad ones too; near misses with the law, and nights spent under the stars when they'd been thrown out of lodgings, with nothing but each other and the growing babe beneath her heart, and all around them the sweet smell of the eucalyptus trees and the furtive scuttles and mournful night cries of wild animals. But they had feared nothing then. They had been young and strong . . . but when the babe was born, they had decided they had better settle down to some degree. So Brian had combined his bouts of bare-knuckle fighting with working on the sheep stations where he could, until that fatal night when his opponents came gunning for him, and it was all over.

She moaned in her throat as the memories washed over her. Some legacy they had left for Ethan. But that would all come right now, when he took the letter she had written, together with their marriage certificate and Brian's death notice, to his sister. She would do the right thing by the boy, before she got properly sick and had to take to her bed for most of the time. Especially now that they had had a glimpse of her and her kids on the Downs. The woman was a mother herself, so Ethan would be all right. Everything he needed to take to his aunt was in the small tin box that Sara had carried with her all the way from Australia as though her life depended on it. Hers, and Ethan's.

The boy had had his instructions drummed into him. He knew that if anything should happen to her, he was to take the tin box straight to the big house up on the hill and give it to the woman. First, he would alert one of their neighbours who had been kind to them, and she would see to the things a young boy should never have to do for his mother. As the acid, sawing tightness in her chest overcame her to the point of delirium again, she knew it must be soon.

The boys by the evil-smelling stream, full of rubbish and unmentionable bits of flotsam, cared nothing for any risk to their health. They were more intent on catching minnows and tiddlers that afternoon, cheerfully jeering at the one with the strange accent, throwing pebbles and sticks at him and getting them hurled back. But it was all good-natured sport, and Ethan O'Neill revelled in it. His pa had always said that sticks and stones were the least troublesome of a good bloke's armour. His fists could do far more lethal damage, he'd said with justifiable pride. His pa had had plenty of such sayings, but because he had died when Ethan was only six, the boy hardly ever remembered them properly, except when his mother reminded him.

As the sun began to go down, he suddenly remembered that she was extra sickly that day, and had told him not to stay out too long in case he needed her. Reluctantly, he yelled g'day to his fellow roughnecks, who responded with more jibes and guffaws, and he ran all the way home, his jar of tiddlers bumping along beside him and spilling half of the muddy water as he went. He flung open the front door and yelled out that he was home. There was no reply.

'Mum! I'm back, Mum!' he hollered out. 'What's for grub?'

When he still didn't get an answer, he peered into his mother's bedroom, and his throat seemed to close up. His heart stopped beating for a horrified minute, and then raced on so painfully fast he thought he was going to die. He dropped his jar of tiddlers unseeingly, turned and tore out of the house, his eyes bursting with unmanly tears that his pa would have clipped him for, bawling and yelling frantically for Mrs Laidlaw down the road to come and see what was wrong with his mum.

But he already knew. Of course he bloody well knew. The minute he had seen her, half-fallen out of the bed, her eyes wide open and vacant, her scrawny arm wrapped around the tin box she set such store by, he knew. Just as he knew by Mrs Laidlaw's scratchy voice that he should come away now, and go and sit with her kids while she got the doctor and did what had to be done. He knew.

And in a week or two, when he had come to terms with his grief, and the knowledge that the one person he loved in all the world was gone, he knew what he had to do too.

Seven

It was more than two weeks before the boy felt able to put his few belongings into a bag, together with the precious tin box, and say goodbye to the house that was empty now. He had wept all his bitter tears and dried his eyes, and his mother had been buried in a corner of the churchyard. The landlord had allowed him stay because Mrs Laidlaw vouched for him, but nobody was going to let a young boy have possession of a house that could bring in good rent.

He trudged all the way up through the busy Bristol streets, avoided by people who looked down their noses at him and sniffed at his unkempt and unsavoury appearance, and he registered none of it. He was intent on his purpose. His intermittent sleep ever since his mother's death had been beset by ghoulish nightmares, and he moved as if in a dream.

But at last he arrived at the big house, and for the first time he baulked at what he had to do. His pa would scoff at him for being a chicken, but his mum would be urging him on with that weird look in her eyes, saying he had every right to be here, and that these people were his kin.

He'd seen the woman with the fiery red hair, and his mum said, according to his pa, that she had a temper to match. He'd seen the girl with the matching hair who'd been tickled at his accent when they'd met and gossiped at the funfair, and the small bloke with her who'd looked a bit scared of him until he'd shown him a few tricks. Well, he was the one who was scared now, and he had to swallow down the bile that kept coming up to choke him before he could move an inch forward.

He edged nearer, but there was no way he could go boldly up to that imposing front door and bang on it. He scuttled around towards the stables and the garage, where a snooty-looking young bloke in his shirtsleeves was polishing a large black car. He tried to dodge back out of sight, but he was big for his age and there was nowhere to hide, and Dawkins stopped his polishing and yanked out an arm to catch hold of him.

'Here, what do you think you're doing? If you're thieving, I'll have the cops on you and you'll be down the Bridewell quicker than blinking.'

'I ain't thieving!' Ethan yelled, suddenly finding his voice. 'I've got to see somebody here.'

Dawkins let him go and began grinning. 'Oh yes, and who do you think wants to see you?'

Before he could answer, the boy's stomach gave an almighty rumble, startling them both. He clutched it in embarrassment, feeling the gnaw of hunger as he did so.

'You look as if you could do with a square meal,' Dawkins said sharply, suddenly taking in the dishevelled appearance of the kid and his wild eyes. Like Cook, he was a sucker for any kid in trouble.

'Hungry, are you?'

Ethan nodded wordlessly, the smallest hint of kindness making his eyes well up. He dashed the tears away furiously, and Dawkins pretended not to notice. He spoke cheerfully.

'Tell you what. You come into the kitchen and we'll ask Cook to give you a bite to eat and a drink of tea before you go on your way. Come on. She's always been partial to the odd waif and stray.'

And there was none odder than this one. He hadn't fathomed out the boy's accent yet, but he caught hold of his arm and marched him determinedly towards the kitchen door, where the warm, mingled smells of baking and cleaning fluids wafted out towards them. Once inside, he called out to the cook.

'Here's somebody in need of a bit of pie and a hot drink, Cookie.'

He pushed Ethan ahead of him and left him to it.

Cook was in the middle of haranguing the kitchen-maids as usual, and ignoring their insolent giggles. Gerard was just coming down to the kitchen from upstairs, wondering what the devil the trouble was now, when Cook turned around and saw the boy.

Her hand went immediately to her mouth, her eyes widening.

'Oh, my good God!' she mouthed, as if she could hardly breathe the words.

For a minute, she thought she was seeing a ghost. Her old ticker was pounding fit to burst, and she had to clutch at the edge of the scrubbed table for support.

'Who are you, boy, and what do you want?' she heard Gerard say, his voice not quite normal, and Cook knew he had seen it too.

Ethan saw the kitchen-maids still giggling behind their hands at the unlikely sight of their betters so unnerved, and then the hot and steamy room seemed to swirl in front of him, and he crashed to the floor in a dead faint.

Cherry was glad of a quiet afternoon with her embroidery in the drawing room on her own. Lance had gone out on business, and the children were in the nursery with Nanny Green, doing their lessons. At least, she hoped they were. Lately, Bella seemed to be doing her best to drive Nanny Green wild, and, as ever, Georgie was ready to follow where she led. Lance had informed the girl on more than one occasion that she looked like an angry young colt tossing its mane when she flung her red hair about in that disdainful manner, and Cherry had to agree with him.

In fact, she was reluctantly coming around to the idea that a male tutor was probably the only way to curb their impossible rudeness and instil some discipline into them, since Nanny Green was still repeating her threat of leaving. Cherry stuck her needle savagely into her tapestry, wondering why things ever had to change.

With no idea of how her life was about to be thrown into complete chaos, she heard a tap on the door, and, with a sigh of resignation at having her afternoon interrupted, she called out to whoever it was to enter.

'Yes, what is it, Gerard?' she said, forcing a smile.

He was paler than usual, she registered, and he looked unusually agitated and unlike his usual suave self. Perhaps it was time he retired too, although she would hate to see him go.

'Madam, we've been looking after a young person in the

kitchen for a while. He seemed to have fainted from lack of food. Cook has given him something to eat and drink, and wanted to send him on his way, but he insists that he's here to see you, and he refuses to leave.'

'Oh, does he?' Cherry said wearily, assuming it was someone from one of the charitable organizations that she and Lance supported. 'I suppose I'd better have a few words with him, then.'

Gerard hesitated, but it wasn't his place to say too much. 'Madam, I beg you to be careful. He may be a young rogue, and I feel I should warn you.'

'I assure you I'm quite capable of judging for myself, Gerard,' she said sharply. 'Please send him in and let's get it over with. But wait outside until the interview is over.'

He shrugged in a way that surprised her. The look in his eyes was almost insolent, as if he knew something that she didn't. She thought they had assumed an easy relationship over the years, but that look threw her back to the first time he had come to meet her and Lance from the ferry, when they returned from their exile in Ireland on the death of Lance's father. It had been the first time the then haughty chauffeur had been obliged to address the former kitchen-maid as the new Lady Melchoir.

It had stung him then, and something had stung him now. But he went outside the drawing room, preparing to take up his post until he was required, which he suspected wouldn't be long, and ushered the boy inside.

By now, Cherry had learned the toff's ropes of dealing with unwanted visitors. You didn't look at them straight away. You let them stand awkwardly while you fiddled with paperwork on a desk, or finished a line of stitching before you looked up. Only then did you deign to give them your attention, when they were perfectly sure who was in charge of the situation.

Except that, on this occasion, she was never going to be in charge. She looked up from her embroidery, preparing to put it aside, and looked straight into the eyes of her brother as she stabbed her finger with her needle. Her cry of pain alerted Gerard at once, and he opened the door without ceremony.

'It's quite all right, Gerard,' Cherry gasped. 'I've just pricked myself, nothing more.'

Of course, he knew very well that it wasn't all right, and she knew very well that he knew why. Her reaction to the boy would be reported downstairs to Cook, who, together with Gerard, would have seen what she had seen. Thank God none of the newer servants would have done, she thought fleetingly.

'Who are you?' she whispered, when she could get her voice back.

'Ethan O'Neill, missus.'

Ethan O'Neill. Her thoughts whirled like lightning. There could only be one reason in the world why this boy had such a name. Or maybe two. Either it was a cruel act in his twisted mind that Brian had seen a boy who resembled him and sent him here to taunt her . . . or he was Brian's son.

She gathered her senses. She was the mistress here, not this boy with the fearsomely similar resemblance to her brother. Why had he been sent? To extort money out of them, the way his father had tried to do all those years ago when he had mistakenly thought she was pregnant and sent the blackmail demand to Lance's father? Why otherwise?

'What do you want?' she said, her voice a husk of sound.

'Me mum said I was to come and give you this,' he said, in an accent she didn't know, his voice turning up at the end as if he was asking a question.

He rummaged in his bag and held out a small tin box to Cherry. She looked at it with her heart thumping, wondering just what horrors she was going to find inside it.

'Put in on the little table beside me and open it,' she said at last.

He did as he was told, and now that the first shock of seeing him was over, Cherry was overcome with all kinds of emotion. He was so like Brian as he had been as a child, when they were orphaned and Brian had promised to always look after her. She had loved him so much then, her strong and handsome brother, but that was long before he had turned into the grasping, evil monster he became.

The tin box was open now, and she could see papers and

a few mementos inside it. On the top was an envelope with her name on it. It simply said 'Lady Cherry Melchoir'. She couldn't remember Brian ever writing to her, so she had no idea if it was his hand or if he was mocking her. In any case, it was such a bad scrawl that it could have been written by anybody. She took it out, ignoring it for the moment as she looked at the folded papers beneath.

The boy stood silently by, watching her warily and saying nothing. The first object was a foreign-looking marriage certificate, and her brother's name leapt out at her. She forced herself to read the details.

Brian O'Neill, bachelor, occupation bare-knuckle fighter and itinerant worker, had married Sara Jane Cooper, spinster and casual worker, not long after Brian would have arrived in Australia. So that meant that if this boy was their offspring, he was at least legitimate.

Cherry swallowed hard. It also meant that he was her legal nephew, but right now she wasn't going to think about that.

'Is your father here in Bristol?' she managed to say.

'No, of course he ain't.' The boy's lips clamped together then, and Cherry picked up the next folded document.

Her eyes blurred as she realized what the black-edged paper meant. It was a death notice. She scanned it quickly.

'Your father has been dead for four years?' she said painfully, the shock of it all washing over her in waves of nausea.

He nodded. 'Me mum said I was to come and find you,' he snarled.

Cherry found it difficult to look at his accusing eyes. She had no idea what stories he had been told of how and why his father had come to be in Australia, or how devious his mother was in sending him here. That it could only be for some kind of extortion she had no doubt, and Lance would immediately think the same. Oh dear God, *Lance*. He had thought them rid of her wretched brother for good, and now Brian had come back to haunt them in the shape of his son.

Her finger throbbed with pain as she muttered to the boy to sit down. He perched himself on the very edge of a chair as if he was about to take flight, and she gingerly opened the envelope with her name on it, wondering what demands she was about to read. What she saw gave her a fresh shock. It had been dated more than two weeks ago. There was no preamble, no pretence at niceties, just a page of explanation for the presence of the boy.

'My name is Sara O'Neill, the widow of your brother Brian, who died in a brawl four years ago. By the time you read this, I will also be dead. It was your brother's insistence that, if anything happens to us, you do your Christian duty by our son, Ethan, your rightful nephew. I leave him in your care.'

Cherry couldn't speak for a few moments. The sheer gall of the woman, even though the letter must have been written on her deathbed, left her speechless. Any compassion she might have was felt was tempered by rage at the arrogance of her brother as well, as if he was speaking to her from beyond the grave. She had almost forgotten the boy for a moment, and then she heard him give a huge sniff as he brushed his grubby sleeve across his eyes, and she tried to control her emotions and remind herself that none of this was his fault. He was a victim as much as she. And he had so recently become an orphan. She knew how that felt.

'So your mother is dead too,' she said, with as much control as she could muster. It clearly wasn't enough, because he suddenly railed at her.

'I didn't want to come here. I hate it here,' he bawled. 'I want to go home. I want my mum. I don't want you buggers, I don't want none of you!'

The door opened quickly, and Gerard came inside the drawing room, clearly having heard much of what was going on. He was shocked at the language, and not about to risk his mistress being injured by a young thug.

'It's all right, Gerard,' Cherry began, and then another door burst open, and Bella and Georgie rushed in, followed by a flustered Nanny Green.

'I'm not doing any more lessons today,' Bella yelled.

'Be quiet, Bella. Both of you, you'd better meet this – this – your – well, your cousin – who's come to visit,' Cherry said, completely floundering, and not knowing what else to say to diffuse the sudden tension in the room.

'I don't have a cousin,' her daughter said rudely, and then

she took a good look at the unexpected visitor. '*Ethan*, what are you doing in our house, and looking so horrible and *dirty*?'

The imperiousness and disdain in her young voice was too much for him. He simply stood and screeched out all kinds of abuse and words that even Cherry didn't know. This time it was Nanny Green who unexpectedly took control.

'From the look of him, the boy is sure to have fleas, Madam. If he's here to stay, and perhaps if I could enlist Mr Gerard's help, you would permit me to take him for a bath and a change of clothes, if he has any.'

'I think that would be a very good idea,' Cherry said with relief, as both her children stood dumbly now, uncertain of what was happening.

'Come along, young man,' Gerard said, gripping him firmly by one arm while Nanny Green took the other. The boy had no option but to be dragged along with them, kicking and screaming all the way. Nanny Green would probably be black and blue by the time they reached the bathroom.

Then Cherry was left with her bewildered children, and Bella's face was filled with fury as she faced her mother.

'He's horrible, Mummy. He was quite funny at first when we talked to him at the funfair, but he was really rude to people as well. We don't want him here. He's not staying, is he? And he's not really our cousin. He can't be!'

'He showed me how to pinch stuff when people weren't looking. He said it was a game,' Georgie piped up, and Bella shushed him furiously.

Oh God. It was a nightmare coming true. Brian didn't need to come back from his banishment all those years ago to bring chaos into their lives all over again. His disreputable offspring was perfectly capable of doing it for him. Cherry swallowed hard, knowing she would have to tell the children a little of why he was here. As little as possible.

'I want you both to listen to me, and not interrupt,' she said. 'A very long time ago, I had a brother and he went to live in Australia. Eventually, he had a wife and a son, and that's your cousin, Ethan. His father died some years ago, and now his mother has died, and so he has no one else in the world except us. It's very sad, my darlings, and that's why we must be kind to him, and why he'll be staying with us for a little while.'

She felt like a hypocrite saying these things, and she prayed to God that it wouldn't be for long, although what they were supposed to do with him, Cherry couldn't think. The future yawned ahead of her like a never-ending black pit. Yesterday she had still been happy in the afterglow of the sea voyage, even though she had had the temerity to tell Paula she was bored with her life. How shallow it all seemed, now that everything had changed. She was desperate to talk to Paula again and hear her no-nonsense opinion on what could be done. But there were others who would need to know too. There were their many social acquaintances, such as the Hetheringtons, who would be more than curious as to why the Melchoirs were taking in a young ruffian.

There would inevitably be more gossip. There might even be those who knew something of the story of how Lance had fallen for a kitchen-maid and married her against his family's wishes. Might there not be some who would question this boy's parentage as well, and lay it at Lance's own door?

Oh God, oh God, the possibilities got worse and worse. But most of all there was Lance himself, and she dreaded telling him more than anything. He loved her dearly, but she couldn't deny that everything that had gone wrong in his life was because of her.

After her brief explanation, Bella and Georgie had been momentarily too shocked to speak, but now she was aware of Georgie's snivelling at the sad tale, and of Bella curtly telling him not be so stupid and to behave like a little man. If only Lady Elspeth had been here to witness her granddaughter's cold-heartedness, she would have been proud, Cherry thought bitterly.

'I won't speak to him, anyway,' Bella declared now. 'He's not our sort, is he, Mummy? I know Daddy won't want me to have anything to do with him.'

The pompous little miss had said something similar about Paula's son, Thomas. But this boy was so much worse. So very much his father's son. But Cherry could be just as hard-hearted when it was necessary.

'You *will* be civil to Ethan, Bella, and you will make him welcome in our home for the time he remains here. You will show him as much courtesy as you would to any of our friends. And Ethan is more than just a friend. He's part of our family and nothing can change that. Please remember it.'

Bella sullenly refused to answer, and she finally asked if she and Georgie could be excused. Cherry thankfully let them go, and then she wilted. She desperately wanted Lance here to lean on, and just as quickly she prayed that he would stay away a while longer, to put off the moment when she would have to reveal what had happened. It could be another hour or more before he returned, and presumably the bathroom ordeal was still going on, but there was still one person she could turn to, the one she could always rely on. Paula. She had to speak to Paula . . .

And then, to her horror, the door opened, and Lance walked inside. For a few seconds, she simply froze. She sat so still she could have been a statue. For one idiotic moment, she wished that she was, so that she need never say the things that had to be said, things that were going to turn his complacent world upside down.

'Well, that's all arranged,' Lance said with satisfaction. Before even saying hello, he went straight to the sideboard to pour himself a glass of whisky, even though it was only late afternoon. 'Mr David Trelawney will be coming to the house for a brief interview with us both on Monday. He has excellent credentials, and I've no doubt you'll find him pleasant and capable.'

Cherry flinched, not understanding what on earth he was talking about, and caring even less about who this David Trelawney was, or why she had to meet him. Another of Lance's upper-crust friends, she supposed, although why she should be interested in what credentials he had, she couldn't imagine. Her mind was in a complete state of cotton wool. And when she continued to say nothing, he finally turned to her and spoke sharply.

'Cherry, I know you don't approve of my suggestion, but can't you show at least a little interest in your children's education and the tutor I've hired to turn them into some semblance of a little lady and gentleman?'

Without warning, her temper flared so fast she thought she was going to explode. What she might have said to him then, she didn't know, because there was an almighty noise coming from outside the drawing-room door, and the next minute the door burst open and Lance was greeted by the extraordinary sight of a street child being hauled into the room by a beetroot-faced Nanny Green and a furious Gerard, and they were all dripping wet.

'What the devil's this? Lance roared. 'Is this some wretched sneak thief who's infiltrated my house?'

Oh God, Lance, forget the long words for once . . .

'I'm sorry, Sir,' Gerard gasped, while the boy continued yelling and kicking where he could. 'Lady Melchoir suggested we take the boy for a bath, but I fear he behaves more like a wild animal that any normal child.'

Lance was incandescent with rage now. He turned on Cherry. 'You mean you've allowed this little thug to desecrate my children's bathroom?'

Cherry could finally stand it no longer. She leapt to her feet now, her hands clenched so tightly her nails were digging into her flesh, and she found herself shrieking like a fishwife.

'This little thug, as you call him, is your nephew, Lance. *My* nephew, anyway, and in the eyes of the law, that makes him yours too.'

The boy found his voice as well, even though he was unable to suppress the frightened tears in his eyes. 'I ain't his nephew!' he bellowed. 'I ain't nothing to him, and I ain't staying here no longer. Give me my tin, missus.'

Cherry hardly knew how the small tin box came to be in her hands, but now she clutched it to her. It contained everything she had left of her brother, and the only proof that Ethan O'Neill was who he said he was. Without it, Lance would never allow him to stay. And he had to stay. She knew that. For all that they had once been to one another as children, she owed Brian this much.

She took a deep breath, and since Lance seemed too stunned to speak for the moment, she spoke to the boy with as much authority as she could muster.

'The tin stays with me for now,' she snapped. 'And you will

stop shouting and behave yourself. You will go with Miss Green and Mr Gerard and get yourself properly tidied up, and then you may have tea with your cousins in the nursery. Now go, go, *go!*'

To her relief, they did as instructed, and she bit her trembling lips, wondering how she had had the nerve to defy Lance and do what she had just done. She dared to glance at him, and the coldness in his eyes made her blanch.

'Will you please tell me what the devil has been going on here?' he demanded. 'And why that pathetic apology for a civilized child claims to be your nephew?'

'And yours,' Cherry said, before she could stop herself.

After a moment, he spoke with an ominous softness. She couldn't miss the way the once-livid scar on his cheek, inflicted by her own brother all that time ago, seemed to be standing out like an accusation.

'I'm waiting, Madam.'

Cherry had heard that tone before, though never to her. It always preceded some cruel act of dismissal to a servant who had offended him. Like the servant she had once been.

She lifted her head. Even to her own ears, her voice sounded strangled and strange. 'I think you had better look in this tin box. Read the letter first and then look at the rest. It explains everything better than I could, since I can hardly bear to speak to you now.'

She knew she was doing him an injustice. If she had been in any state of mind to look at it from his point of view, how else could he have reacted when he came home to this holocaust, and a strange boy, whom his wife claimed to be her kin, and which the boy himself was seemingly denying?

She handed him the tin and sat down again with her arms firmly folded. If she hadn't done so, she would probably have fallen down. And her arms needed to be kept folded to hold her body in check, to prevent it from shaking uncontrollably at the enormity of what was happening.

Her brother had been dead for four years. At the bottom of the tin, there had been a small poster, proclaiming the bare-knuckle fighting skills of Brian 'Knuckles' O'Neill, and his wickedly good-looking gypsy face had smiled up at her, making her heart turn over. She should have taken the poster out and destroyed it before Lance saw it, but it was too late for that now, and, besides, it didn't belong to her. It belonged to the boy. They thought they had been rid of her brother for good, and that he could never hurt them again. But he was still here, in the shape of his son, and when Lance realized the truth, she had no idea how he was going to deal with it.

Eight

How long Lance stared at the letter and documents she could never have said. His silence seemed to go on interminably, as if he too was struck dumb by what was happening. But with cold deliberation, he finally put everything back inside the tin box, closed it up, and strode out of the room.

'Where are you going? Lance, we have to discuss this,' Cherry called distractedly, but he didn't answer, and the door banged behind him.

She simply didn't know what to do, or what to think. Was this the end for them? Had they come through all the trauma of the past, all the desperation to be married and to share their lives, against so much opposition, and then to be finally rid of her brother, only to have it end like this? She wanted to weep, but, with an inner steel she hardly knew she had possessed, she told herself that this was not the time for weeping. Now was the time for seeing that the three children now in her care were not going to be at one another's throats for the foreseeable future.

She smoothed down her skirts, walked out of the drawing room with her head held high, and went directly to the nursery. As she did so, she encountered one of the housemaids in the process of carrying a large tray of sandwiches and cakes for the children's afternoon tea.

'Thank you, Josie, I'll take that,' she said, ignoring the girl's startled eyes.

Cherry didn't care what she thought, or what anyone else thought. If her own husband thought so little of her that he wasn't even prepared to talk about the shock that they had both had that day, then what did anything else matter?

She took the tray out of the girl's hands and sent her on her way back to the kitchen, no doubt to gossip to all and sundry that her ladyship had looked far less than her usual happy self.

*And her with all that money and privilege and sea voyages too.
She should try doing what them below stairs have to do for their
pittances, and then see how happy she'd look.*

Cherry could anticipate every word of it, for hadn't she
once said the very same thing a thousand times about Lady
Elspeth and Lord Francis Melchoir, and Captain Lance as well?
She smothered the lump in her throat and pushed open the
door of the nursery with a free hand.

She was surprised to see that Gerard was still there, for
dealing with unruly children was surely beyond the call of
duty. But Nanny Green still looked flustered, and she flashed
him a grateful look, and put the tray down on the small dining
table. In any case, since everything on this day was so topsy-
turvy, she shouldn't be surprised at anything any more. And
even though she seemed to have lived through a lifetime of
emotion since Ethan O'Neill had first arrived in her drawing
room, in reality it had been little time at all.

'So what are we all doing?' she asked with false brightness.
Daft too, since she could see very well.

Bella was sitting in the window seat, her arms clasped tightly
around her body in much the same way as Cherry's had been.
She could hardly tell her daughter it wasn't ladylike to sit
hunched up in that way, when Cherry had been doing the
very same thing a short while ago.

Nanny Green was trying to coax Georgie to come and learn
his letters, while Gerard was standing near the other boy in
case of trouble. Cherry could hardly think of him by name,
and yet she knew she must. He was Ethan O'Neill, and he
was her nephew, and right now he was sprawled out on the
floor, staring vacantly into space. No doubt he was missing his
mother, she thought with swift compassion, and wondering
what kind of a world he had suddenly been thrust into. He
probably didn't want it any more than the rest of them did.

When nobody answered her question, she forced a smile.

'Well, if nobody's going to eat these sandwiches and cakes,
then Mr Gerard, Nanny Green and I will have to have a feast
all to ourselves. It's a shame, since there'll be nothing more
for you all until bedtime.'

Georgie was the first one to run to the table and sit down.

'I'll help you eat it, Mummy,' he said.

Bella slid off the window seat and came sullenly across to join him, as a tight-lipped Nanny Green distributed the plates.

Cherry looked at Ethan.

'I think you had better have some food as well, young man, or you'll be hungry by bedtime.'

'He's not sleeping here, is he?' Bella said aggressively.

Cherry's heart lurched uneasily. Of course he was sleeping here. But everything had happened so quickly since the boy's arrival that her thoughts hadn't gone any farther than that. But where else would he go? And where would they put him? Not in the servants' quarters, since he wasn't a servant. Nor in one of the guest bedrooms, since he wasn't exactly a guest either, and certainly not a welcome one.

She saw Gerard encourage him curtly to get up from the floor, and he eventually slouched over to the table. Clearly, the lure of food was going to be the way forward, as with most children, Cherry thought with a sliver of relief.

'Mr Gerard, would you ask one of the maids to prepare the bedroom at the end of the children's landing for my nephew, please?'

She stared him out as she said it, willing herself not to flinch at her use of the word 'nephew'. But she could no longer deny it. Not while Ethan O'Neill was looking at her now with his father's eyes and his father's calculating expression.

Oh yes, he might be a bereaved child, but he was already starting to realize which side his bread was buttered, she thought.

The nursery where they were now was the largest room on the children's landing. The empty bedroom at the far end of it was well away from Bella's and Georgie's rooms, with their bathroom and the nursery in between. To Cherry, it seemed like a small point to score, but one that was best for all concerned. He would be included in the life of the children here, but still kept well apart.

'I'll see to it now, Madam, if I may take my leave,' Gerard said, clearly wanting to be sure it was safe to leave them with the boy.

'Please do, Gerard,' Cherry said evenly.

He left them to it, and God only knew what tales he might be telling below stairs, thought Cherry, nor how much gossip would be going on among the kitchen staff. But only he and Cook would be aware of the real identity of the boy and his background, and she knew she could count on their loyalty.

When the nursery door opened a while later during the uneasy meal, Lance stood contemplating the cosy little scene, which Cherry knew very well he would detest. He spoke abruptly before he left them.

'I'll see the boy in my study when he's finished his tea.'

'I expect he'll send you packing,' Bella muttered to her new cousin, bolder now that she had heard her father's words.

Bella knew that being asked to go to his study was not just an invitation. It always meant a reprimand for something or other, and she relished the fact that this interloper was going to get the rough end of her father's tongue. She had thought him quite exciting when she'd first met him at the funfair, intrigued by his looks and his funny way of talking, in the way that gypsies were exciting at a distance. Then, to her horror, she had become aware that he was showing Georgie how to pick pockets. She had dragged her little brother away from the boy then, and still remembered the way he had been laughing at them as they went. She definitely hadn't liked him after that, and she wasn't going to like him now.

Lance sat at the desk in the study that had been his father's, where he had suffered so many tongue-lashings himself when he was a boy and learning how to be a young gentleman. It hadn't been that much of a hardship to him, since he had known no other life, but the prospect in front of him now was more distasteful than he cared to admit. He had thought that Cherry's bastard brother was long out of their life. And so he was. Unknown to them, he had been dead for four years, and that should have been an end to it. But who could have predicted that the thug would have married and produced a son, and that that son would come here to bring the past back to them?

The sins of the fathers . . . and perhaps there were some who would say that it was *his* sin that had begun this chain of events in the first place. If he hadn't lusted over a kitchen-maid, taken her to the stables that dark night and ravished her . . . and if she hadn't been oh-so-willing, and, later, played her own little game with him, pretending that she pregnant. And if her evil brother hadn't overheard her discussing it with her bosom friend and seen a way to extort money out of Lord Francis Melchoir, his father, so that by the time his lust for Cherry O'Neill had reached fever pitch, he knew he had to have her at all costs . . . If none of that had happened, they would never have faced the wrath of his parents with their desire to be married, reminding them that the supposed child would be their grandchild, and never been grudgingly given permission to marry, providing they were exiled to a Melchoir property in Ireland.

In due course, he had learned that there had never been a child. Cherry had been as devious as her brother in what she and Paula had still considered a bit of sport to tease him, but by then he had been too besotted to care. And he *had* loved her, so much . . .

He caught his rambling thoughts up short. He still loved her, God damn it, with a wild and raging passion that could still take him by surprise. But because of her, and because of the lust in his loins that would never go away, he was about to face this young upstart who thought he was going to muscle in on the Melchoir fortune. Well, never in a million years, Lance thought savagely. His lawyer, and a new clause in his Will, was going to set that straight at the first opportunity.

There was a tap on the door and he barked an instruction. The boy stepped inside uncertainly, seeing the large man behind the desk, and his small tin box in front of him. Not knowing what to expect, and having had the strap put about him many times in the past, the boy prayed that he wasn't going to piss himself with fright. All the guts had gone out of him, and he wanted his mother.

'You'd better come and sit down,' Lance snapped. 'I can't speak to you while you cower by the door.'

He took a proper look at the boy for the first time. *Christ*, he was the image of his father. There could hardly be any doubt as to his parentage. The dark, unruly hair, the black eyes, the belligerent mouth, the build of the lad, all shrieked Brian O'Neill to him. He could also see the rough charm in such looks that could appeal to the female sex, and it bothered him that he had such a young and beautiful daughter. She wasn't yet of an age to care about boys, but it would come, and he prayed to God that the unwanted but undeniable relationship between them would squash any future thoughts of that nature.

If anything was destined to make him want to send him packing, it was that. But he cleared his throat, forcibly reminding himself that this boy wasn't Brian O'Neill, and that he looked scared to death right now.

'So, this tin box,' he said, tapping it.

'It's mine,' the boy said at once. 'You ain't keeping it!'

'Why would I want to keep it?' Lance said disdainfully. 'What I will want to do, though, is show the contents to someone and verify everything that's inside it. You know what a lawyer is, do you?'

''Course I do. I ain't daft.'

'No, I don't believe you are.'

He was playing for time, of course. There was little need to verify the contents of the box, probably no need at all, since all the documents looked perfectly legal. But he wasn't taking any chances, and he still wanted his lawyer to check them over and to revise his Will. He still couldn't rid himself of the suspicion that, since the boy was so much like Brian O'Neill, it could still have been a lucky chance that the O'Neill couple had seized upon in a warped attempt to make Lance pay for transporting Brian to Australia all those years ago. However far-fetched it might seem, Lance would have put nothing past him.

'Am I staying here, then? The lady told the stuffed shirt to get a bedroom ready for me,' Ethan said, slightly bolder when the man seemed to be doing a lot of thinking and not saying much.

Lance tried not to smile at hearing Gerard referred to as a stuffed shirt. God knows he hadn't done much smiling since he had come home that afternoon, so it didn't do his facial muscles much harm to let them relax a mite.

'Are those the only clothes you have?' he asked, changing tactics.

'They're my seconds. The stuffed shirt and the old woman took me others off me when they shoved me in the bath, and these are my seconds.'

Lance leaned forward, his voice hardening again. 'Now, you just listen to me, boy. You will not refer to my butler as the stuffed shirt. His name is Mr Gerard, and the governess is Nanny Green. You will please use their proper names at all times. In a week's time, you will attend lessons in the nursery with my children under the tutelage of Mr David Trelawney.'

'I ain't come here to do no lessons,' the boy howled. 'And I'm too old to spend my time in a perishing nursery like a babby.'

'You have no option,' Lance said coldly. 'You are too young to live on your own, and you will do as you are told. You will be taken to a suitable establishment to be fitted out with some decent clothing to replace those rags, and you will respect everyone in my household at all times, do you hear?'

Ethan felt his lower lip tremble, and he bit it furiously.

'I like the fat woman and the girls in the kitchen the best,' he muttered.

Of course he bloody well did, thought Lance savagely. It was his natural habitat, below stairs where his father had also grubbed his way into Cook's affections, by all accounts, and where his Aunt Cherry belonged.

He was truly aghast at the sudden thought that had come into his head, putting his wife on a par with these louts.

'You may go back to the nursery now, and remember all that you've been told,' he said sharply.

'So what do I call you?' he said insolently.

'*Sir* will do,' Lance said.

The boy left him, banging the door behind him, and for the first time in Lance's sheltered life since he had been faced with the fury of his parents at ever having associated with a common kitchen-maid, he felt out of his depth. But not for long. He reached for the telephone and put a call through to his lawyer.

★　　★　　★

By the time the house settled down for the night, Ethan O'Neill had been given a new bedroom, and although it was a modest child's room by Melchoir standards, to him it was more palatial than he had ever seen in his life. After inspecting every bit of the room to see if there were any knick-knacks he could take to the pawn shop, since it was second nature to do so, he finally buried his head beneath the bedclothes and wept the bitter tears for his mother that he had kept in check for so long, and wished himself back in Australia where he belonged.

In the master bedroom on the floor above, Cherry and Lance might have been oceans apart in the large bed where they had spent such passionate and loving hours. They lay without touching, each enveloped in the turbulent images that swirled round and round in their heads like a bottomless vortex.

Until now, their lives had been so serene, bereft of anything troublesome. They were wealthy landowners, wanting for nothing, their children healthy and happy, their social scene a vibrant and busy one. And now this . . . He had told her nothing of his meeting with Ethan, only that the boy was staying.

Cherry's heart jolted, suddenly remembering the invitation for herself and Lance, delivered by hand, to the Hetheringtons' tomorrow evening, to hear Cynthia's tales of her trip to Germany and the Olympic Games. They couldn't go now! *They simply couldn't go!* How could they sit there and pretend nothing had happened when their whole world had been shattered? She found herself suddenly so short of breath that she was gasping.

'Do you need some water?' Lance said, with so little concern in his voice that she could have wept.

'No, I don't want water. I want all this to go away,' she burst out.

'Well, it won't, and there's nothing we can do about it.'

She turned her head to look at him. But she couldn't see him properly in the darkness, only the harsh outline of his uncompromising profile.

'You're blaming me, aren't you?'

'Well, he was your brother.'

How dare he be so cruel? But she wouldn't rise to the bait. She just wouldn't.

'We can't go to the Hetheringtons' tomorrow evening, not until things have been sorted out. They're your friends, so you'll have to make some excuse.'

She was ashamed of herself for making this a tit-for-tat affair. But she was as stunned by the sudden chaos in their lives as she assumed Lance to be. She soon learned that it wasn't the case at all, and that he had very definite ideas of what was to occur.

'We *will* go to the Hetheringtons' tomorrow evening as planned, and you will behave in a proper way as befits my wife. This relative of yours is not going to disrupt our social life, nor any other part of it. If he is to stay, he will learn to conform or he will be sent away to some establishment that will care for boys of his type.'

Cherry couldn't believe what she was hearing. She hadn't wanted to have Brian's son foisted on them, but he was a living, breathing, recently orphaned young boy who was her flesh and blood, whether she wanted it or not, and she couldn't turn her back on him.

'I never thought you could be like this,' she burst out. 'I'm beginning to think I don't know you at all.'

'It's taken you a long time to find that out, then,' he snapped back. 'Did you expect me to forget everything in my own background to accommodate you and your brat of a nephew?'

'I expected you to be my husband, and to support me.'

'I shall do what's necessary for the boy, and no more. After what his father did to my family, can you really expect anything else?'

It was true, then. He *did* blame her, for being who she was, for her brother's evil ways, for everything. Cherry felt as if her whole life was collapsing around her, and she didn't know how to deal with it any more.

She turned her back on him and curled up into a ball, hating him for the first time in her life. The Cinderella story ended here, she thought bitterly. For her, at least. But maybe not for Ethan. He had probably had a rotten life with his father and whoever his mother was, and at least now he had the chance to make something of himself, with her help. If Lance wouldn't do it, then she would.

Lance had gone out early the next day, and Cherry guessed he had an early appointment with his lawyer. She was glad he wasn't in the house. She couldn't bear to look at him any more. She checked with Nanny Green that the children had had their breakfast, and saw the three of them in the nursery, preparing to do some lessons that morning. Nanny Green could always take a firm hand when necessary. But since Ethan's arrival, Cherry could see that she was more than relieved now that a male tutor would be taking over very soon, even though she had been affronted by the idea at first.

'The young boy was more docile than he was last night,' she reported to Cherry in an aside. 'I think he was overcome with nerves yesterday, if I may say so, Madam, but Georgie really seems to have taken to him, and it has settled him down a little.'

'And what about Bella?'

The woman sighed. 'She's behaving a little strangely, and simply ignores the boy completely. It's obvious that she resents his presence deeply.'

'I'm afraid she must get used to it, Miss Green. Please remind her that he is her cousin, and we'll have no nonsense. I will see them again at teatime.'

She should really stay with them now, she thought guiltily. But she knew very well she had to remove herself as much as possible from any further confrontation for the moment. If it was the coward's way out, she didn't care. They had all had a tremendous shock yesterday, and it would take time for them to adjust. And she still had to accept the news that her brother was dead. She should probably not be too sorry, but what kind of person was ever glad that somebody who had once been so close to them was dead? It wasn't right, and it wasn't decent, and she could still be sad that Brian had turned out the way he had, so different from the loving brother she had known as a child.

She took a deep breath and told herself there were things to do, and she couldn't spend the time wallowing over something that couldn't be changed. For a start, as Lance had said, the boy needed a complete new set of clothes, but she absolutely baulked at the thought of taking him to one of the better establishments that the Melchoirs patronized. She could just imagine the raised eyebrows when she walked in with the rough and ready Ethan O'Neill.

Paula. Paula would know what to do and where to go. She had to buy clothes for Thomas, and they certainly didn't come from the upper-class emporiums that the Melchoirs visited. She hated Lance all over again for putting her in this impossible position, and making her demean her old friend's taste, but she didn't know what else to do. In any case, she badly needed to speak to Paula, who, as yet, knew nothing of what had happened yesterday.

That it was only yesterday gave her a shock. So much had happened since then. So much to tear her and Lance apart . . . She smothered a sob and went through to the drawing room and picked up the telephone.

Paula went through her usual frantic fluff of answering, until Cherry managed to stop her by croaking out, 'Paula, stop it. It's me.'

There was a momentary silence before she heard a reply.

'Blimey, kid, what's wrong? It don't sound a bit like you. I thought it was some poncey heavy breather on the line for a blooming scary minute.'

She could hardly speak at all now. How could she spill out everything that had happened and ask Paula for this enormous favour, knowing her friend would know immediately why she had to be the one to help her buy the boy's clothes?

'Paula, I've got to see you,' she said, her voice desperate.

There was another pause, and Cherry guessed that Paula was anticipating all sorts of problems. But she could never have guessed in a million years what had actually happened.

'Do you want me to come up there? Thomas is at school, and I can cheerfully skip the ironing for a couple of hours.'

The so-ordinary words made Cherry close her eyes for moment. Sweet darling Paula, doing her domestic chores and loving them. Why couldn't she too have been satisfied with the life that should have been mapped out for both of them?

'I'll come to you,' she managed to say huskily. 'I've got to get out of here, Paula, and I've so much to tell you. I'll be there soon.'

She put down the telephone quickly, forcing herself not to burst into tears at Paula's homely, concerned voice. She hadn't needed to tell her that something was seriously wrong. Paula could always tell. This time, though, it was something that neither Paula nor anybody else would be able to put right.

Nine

It was a long walk across the Downs and down the steep hills of the city, through the busy, bustling streets and along the waterfront, to the street not far from Temple Meads railway station, where Paula and Harold lived. But Cherry hardly noticed the distance. She had walked the streets of this city too many times in the past to be daunted by it. But she kept her head down, not wanting to meet anybody she knew, and almost fell through Paula's front door when her friend answered it. She was immediately enclosed in the cosy, steamy warmth of the house, and the noisy kettle whistling on the hob was the most welcome sound she had ever heard.

'Come and tell me what's happened,' Paula said at once, and at that so-familiar sound of her voice, which always gave her the feeling that between them they could solve everything as they had done in the past, Cherry burst into noisy tears again.

'My God, Cherry, what the hell is it? Nothing's happened to one of the kids, has it? Or his lordship?' she said in a fright. 'You're really scaring me now. Come and sit down while I turn off this ruddy kettle, and when you've spat it out, I'll make us some tea.'

Every part of her shaking, now that she was actually here, Cherry sank down on one of the armchairs that had definitely seen better days. But what did any of that matter when there was love to spare in this little house? She heard Paula turn off the kettle, and then her friend pulled up a chair right next to her and caught hold of her cold hands.

'Now tell me before I bust a gut with curiosity and worry,' she ordered.

Cherry couldn't even raise a smile at that. But where could she start? Where else but at the source of it all?

'You remember my brother, don't you?'

Paula drew in her breath. 'Oh my God, you ain't telling me that that kid I saw had anything to do with him, are you, Cherry?'

Cherry stared at her, her heart doing somersaults.

'What kid?'

Paula spoke uneasily now. 'Harold said I was seeing things that weren't there, and that I wasn't to tell you in case it upset you. He said it was all a figment of my imagination, whatever the hell that meant.'

'I don't think it was, so you'd better tell me what you saw, hadn't you?'

Paula was agitated now, not least because of Cherry's accusing eyes.

'Here, don't go blaming me, Cherry! It was a just a kid who looked a hell of a lot like your brother, that's all. But it couldn't have had anything to do with him, could it? I mean, he's thousands of miles away, ain't he?'

Cherry's defensiveness drooped. 'He's dead, Paula. He's been dead for four years and I never knew it.'

'Well, then,' Paula said after a second or two, 'don't expect me to be sorry about that, after everything he did to you. And unless the kid I saw is his ghost come back to haunt you, I'd say forget it.'

'The kid is his son.'

'What? Bloody hell, Cherry, he can't be!'

'Of course he can,' Cherry said angrily. 'And he bloody well is.'

Paula stood up. 'I'm making that tea, and then you'd better tell me everything that's happened, because I can't think straight now.'

She went out to the kitchen and turned the gas on again, while Cherry slumped in the armchair. Even saying it made her feel sick. Ethan O'Neill was her brother's son, and there wasn't a damn thing she could do about it. She guessed that Lance would be verifying the documents in the boy's tin box, but there was no doubt in her mind — nor in his — that they were legal.

She closed her eyes for a moment, feeling, now that she was away from the house, that she could relax a little for the first time since the whole horrific business began. But she had to go back, of course. She couldn't just run away and forget that it had ever happened. She had responsibilities. She was a wife and mother – and an aunt, she thought, with a catch in her throat.

'Here, drink this,' she heard Paula say. 'I've laced it with plenty of sugar for shock, as Cook used to say.'

Hearing the words, Cherry found it hard to swallow a mouthful for the lump in her throat, but she did as she was told, hoping the scalding liquid would revive her.

'So come on, then. I'm not sorry I didn't tell you about the kid, Cherry. Like Harold said, it might all have been a coincidence, and one of them figment things, but now that I know it wasn't, what happened? Did he just walk in and say he was Brian's son? And does he have a mother in all this? I bet they're after money. You'd better be ruddy careful, girl. You don't owe them nothing.'

As she gabbled on, Cherry felt mildly hysterical. 'I'll tell you if you let me get a word in edgeways. For a start, his mother's just died as well, so he's completely on his own.'

'Oh, blimey,' Paula said, silenced for the moment.

Cherry had thought it would be difficult and painful to tell the whole story, even to her best friend, but, once started, it all came spilling out, until in the end she was gasping and sobbing, because the most painful and hurtful thing of all was telling another person how betrayed and humiliated she felt by her own husband's attitude.

'What a bastard,' Paula muttered.

'Yes, but I can't really blame him, can I?' she said unhappily.

'Of course you can! Don't start defending him now, Cherry. He should stand by you, no matter what! God Almighty, he got you into this whole mess in the first place, didn't he?'

'So now you're calling my marriage a mess, are you? My children too?'

'Oh, don't be so daft. You know I didn't mean it like that. But if he hadn't bedded you in the first place—'

'And if I hadn't been so willing to be bedded, as you put it, as you very well know—'

Unwillingly, and almost unbelievably, there was a small smile tugging at each of their mouths now as Paula went on more calmly.

'And you can't say you haven't had a bloody wonderful life with his lordship all these years, can you? You've had more than your fair share of luck in this world, girl. So a little setback's happened now, but you'll get over it.'

Cherry's smile faded. 'You think Ethan O'Neill is a little setback, do you? I'd call him a monster of a setback!'

'Oh, come on, Cherry, if *you* can't get round your man, I don't know who can. He'd do anything for you, including taking in this kid. He's hardly going to put him to work in the stables, is he?' she said with a grin.

'No. He's hiring some chap called David Trelawney to come and tutor the children, since he doesn't trust Nanny Green to do it any longer, and that means all three of them. That's something else I wanted to see you about, Paula,' Cherry said, going off at a tangent. 'The boy needs some decent clothes and I don't know where to get them. Nanny's always taken Bella and Georgie to kit them out, or we've had samples sent to the house, but you'll know the kind of places where you get Thomas's clothes, and I wondered if you'd help me out. I'd have to bring him along for measuring, of course.'

Even to her own ears, it sounded so ruddy patronizing. But Paula, being Paula, merely shrugged and told her to set the date, and she'd come with her and the boy to do the necessary.

'Tomorrow afternoon?' Cherry said gratefully. 'It needs to be soon, before the tutor meets him and thinks we've got some street urchin in the house. You know what these people are. He'd probably turn up his nose at the sight of him.'

'No, I don't know what these people are, but I'll take your word for it,' Paula said shortly, a touch ruffled now.

'I'm sorry, Paula. I know I'm doing this all wrong.'

'I said I'd help, and you're only doing what you think best for your family. So let's meet about two o'clock tomorrow afternoon outside Smithy's Tea Rooms. You won't want to take him inside any more than I want to set foot in it with all the swanks, but it's near enough to the big stores.'

She couldn't have made it plainer that she thought Cherry had turned into a prize snob, and Cherry thanked her humbly. She had wanted to see her old friend so much, but now she couldn't wait to get out of there. The cosy atmosphere that had welcomed her so much was suddenly stifling her.

Once away from the street where Paula lived, she took in great gulps of air. The long walk ahead now seemed an endless distance to cover, but she was near enough to Temple Meads railway station, so she walked up to the taxi rank, sank into the back of a taxi thankfully, and allowed it to jolt her all the way home.

When it arrived at Melchoir House, she sat in the back without moving for a minute, until the driver spoke to her sharply.

'Are you all right, missus? This is the place you wanted, is it?'

He thought it must be, since she wore the kind of clothes suited to such a mansion, and didn't look short of a bob or two. But she didn't seem to be carrying a handbag, and he still had to earn his living. And as Cherry realized why he was sitting there without opening the door for her as she would have expected, she realized she had no money with her, and she spoke quickly.

'Please wait here a minute while I send someone out with your fare,' she said, and rushed into the kitchen to ask a startled Gerard if he would please see to the taxi driver for her. Then Cook and the rest of the staff had the extraordinary sight of Lady Melchoir rushing through them towards the stairs and banging the door behind her.

'You'll never guess!' Paula greeted Harold, the minute he stepped inside the door at midday.

'You'd better tell me, then,' he said good-humouredly, 'providing you don't make me wait for my dinner. Is that fried bacon I can smell?'

Her news was far too important to wait. 'Cherry's been here, and, by all accounts, all hell's been let loose up at Melchoir House.'

'Oh yes? What now? Has my lady broken a fingernail or something equally disastrous?'

'Don't be daft, Harold. This is serious! You know that boy I told you about? The one who looked the image of Cherry's brother, and you told me it was all a figment of something or other? Well, it wasn't, see? It turns out that he's Brian O'Neill's son, and he's an orphan now, and he's turned up out of nowhere to live with them, and his ruddy lordship is throwing a purple fit because of it!'

'Good God!'

Paula could see that he was gratifyingly shocked, and she knew that she'd been right all the time in her suspicions about the kid who looked frighteningly like Brian O'Neill.

'So what did Cherry have to say about it, then? I suppose his lordship's sent him packing like he did her brother.'

Paula frowned, slapping his meal on the table, unable to stop a growing sense that she was somehow being given a servile role in having to help Cherry buy the kid's new clothes, in stores that Cherry wouldn't normally set foot inside. When she got as far as mentioning that fact, Harold obviously thought the same.

'Well, that's rich, that is! She's got very high and mighty now, hasn't she? You'll be having to call her "my lady" soon – if she deigns to speak to you at all.'

'You can't blame her, Harold. And nothing's going to change our friendship.'

'No? I'd say this has gone a long way towards it.'

'Well, you're wrong. I was the first person she came to talk to, wasn't I? Same as always,' Paula said, but feeling more and more distressed.

'But nothing's the same as always, is it, girl? Look at you now, red-faced and flustered, and piping your eyes over summat that don't concern you.'

'No, I'm not,' Paula snapped. 'You never did understand, did you? We've been friends too long for me not to know when Cherry needs me, and I'll do as she asked tomorrow. If it was the other way around, I know she'd help me out.'

'That's never likely, and we don't need her handouts,' Harold said predictably. 'Now, get me some more sauce, woman, before this bacon goes completely cold. My dinner's ruined with all this damn Cherry talk.'

Cherry reached the sanctuary of the drawing room and leaned against the door thankfully, knowing there'd be plenty of gossip downstairs at her unexpected appearance in the kitchen. It was the least of her worries, though. She'd done what she had to do, and Paula would be there for her tomorrow. All she had to do now was be sure Ethan was informed, and that Lance would give her the money to pay for the clothes. There was no way he would want them put on an account at these shops, and nor could she sign a cheque in his name that would raise even more comment. She ran a shaky hand across her eyes, wondering why everything had to be so blessed complicated. It was all a damn sight simpler when she was a kitchen-maid, she thought ironically.

By now she had a throbbing headache, but after a few moments she went to the nursery to see how things were getting on there. The children should be having a meal shortly, and morning lessons would be at an end. She was greeted by Nanny Green's raised voice as she entered the room, and Bella was arguing volubly with her. Ethan and Georgie had their heads together, which wasn't necessarily a good sign, but Cherry held up her hand for quiet, refusing to get into whatever was going on between them.

'I just want to tell you that Ethan will be excused lessons tomorrow afternoon.' She looked at him as he gave a small cheer. 'It's not for your pleasure, Ethan, it's so that you will come with me to be fitted for some new clothes to replace those you are wearing.'

'I ain't going to be dressed up like some dog's dinner,' he retorted.

'I've no idea what that is, but you will do as you're told,' Cherry said icily. 'And I'll see you all again at teatime.'

There was an immediate outcry from her own children as Nanny Green tried to control them, but if Cherry was taking the easy way out by leaving them all to the governess, she was past caring. It was all getting too much, and she went to her bedroom and lay down for ten minutes, hoping the throbbing headache would calm down.

Lance found her an hour or so later. 'What's all this? Are you ill?'

His voice probably wasn't as cold as she imagined it to be, but, right now, all she could see and hear was the accusation oozing out of him for the way his ordered life had changed. What about *her* life too, she wanted to shriek . . . but she was just too drained.

'I have a bad headache,' she mumbled.

In other times, he would have come to her and pressed a soothing cool hand on her forehead. Or taken her in his arms until the tension went away. But these weren't other times.

'Then I hope you've taken something for it,' he said. 'You'll need to be feeling well and alert by this evening.'

Oh God, she had forgotten all about this evening at the Hetheringtons'.

'Must we go?' she said weakly, knowing how futile the question was.

'Of course we must. Cynthia will be agog to show us her photographs and to tell us all about the Games. And you will put on your best acting performance, my dear, which I know you can do so well.'

She flinched at that. 'Why are you so intent on hurting me, Lance? None of this is my fault,' she said, struggling to sit up, since to remain lying down gave her a disadvantage when he was glowering at her.

'I think we can safely say that all of it is your fault, however indirectly. But none of us can help our relatives, and I just thank God I had no siblings to bring shame on me. But, regardless of all that, I have seen our solicitor, and you can be assured that your nephew will inherit nothing from this estate, whatever his devious little plan in coming here.'

'For pity's sake, Lance, he's ten years old,' she said angrily. 'What kind of devious plan can a child of that age have?'

'With his parentage, I would say he had plenty of opportunity to learn. Now, I have other business to attend to, so please calm yourself before this evening. Wear something bright and glittery tonight, and be at your most charming and beautiful.'

He was so mocking she could have wept.

'And do we tell the Hetheringtons about Ethan?' she demanded. 'Or is he to be kept my guilty secret?'

'We can hardly spirit him away, much as I would like to, so

if the time is ripe, I will mention him, and you will take your lead from me. Is that clear?'

'Perfectly,' Cherry said.

She turned her head away. For a moment he said nothing, and then she felt his hand on her shoulder.

'We'll get through this, Cherry. It's not the end of the world.'

And then he was gone, leaving her fighting back the stinging tears at the slightest crumb of comfort he had given her.

She went through the rest of the day like an automaton. Having tea with the squabbling children and a tight-lipped Nanny Green made her all the more aware that the tutor was probably going to be their salvation, after all. She had been so opposed to him, but a bit of male discipline was clearly what was badly needed now. So much for female emancipation, she thought bitterly. There were still times when only the firm hand of a man would do.

Any invitation to the Hetheringtons' was more in the nature of a command occasion, and Cherry knew they would all be in evening wear. She chose a soft cream silk gown that hugged her shape discreetly, a long rope of pearls at her throat and matching earrings. The contrast between the delicate purity of it all and her dramatic coppery hair was stunning. When she went to say goodnight to her children before she and Lance left, Bella told her she looked beautiful.

'You look like an angel, Mummy,' Georgie said.

'Do I, darling?' she said, hugging him tightly for a moment. He was like a little angel himself, she thought, so small and vulnerable, and, not for the first time, she prayed that Ethan O'Neill wasn't going to be a bad influence on him.

She hesitated outside the boy's bedroom door. It was her ritual to say goodnight to the children before she and Lance ate supper together. Tonight, supper would be at the Hetheringtons', of course, but she supposed she should say goodnight to Ethan as well. Without giving it another thought, she opened his door. He was huddled up beneath the bedclothes, and she felt a pang of sadness for him. Through no fault of his own, he had been thrust into this unfeeling household, having just lost his mother.

'I've just come to say goodnight, Ethan,' she said quietly.

His head jerked up, and she could see that he had been crying. But his eyes widened at the sight of her and she knew it would be wisest not to comment.

'You look different. I didn't know who you were for a minute. 'Night, then,' he mumbled.

'I'll see you tomorrow,' she said, unable to say anything more, and realizing he was truly startled at her changed appearance. It probably set her even more apart from him and the life he had recently led, so perhaps this brief visit hadn't been such a good idea, and she decided not to mention it to Lance.

Dawkins drove them in the limousine to the Hetheringtons', a large establishment as grand as Melchoir House. He would spend the evening yarning with the Hetheringtons' staff until they were ready to leave, probably spreading whatever gossip he knew. Which probably wasn't much, thought Cherry, though she knew of old that it was often the kitchen staff who got to know things before their betters.

'You look lovely, Cherry,' Lance said at last before they entered the house. It was the first time in a long time he had said anything remotely complimentary to her. She had tried to dress to please him, even though it had been hard to shake off the memories of the past few days. He looked as handsome as ever, and, to outward appearances, as if he didn't have a care in the world, though she could tell by the tightness of his jaw that it wasn't the case.

Impulsively, she slipped her hand in his. 'As you said, we'll get through this, Lance, providing we tackle it together, the way we've always done.'

He gave her hand the smallest squeeze before he let it go, and she didn't know whether to be rebuffed or reassured. In any case, there was no time to ponder as they were let inside by the Hetherington butler.

Then Cynthia was upon them, sparkling in green and gold, her close friend Monica not far behind. 'At last, darlings,' she said gaily. 'We thought you were never coming. And how marvellous you look tonight, Cherry darling. You're an absolute vision of loveliness.'

As the ghastly Monica agreed, Cherry could just imagine Paula's comments at hearing such gushing platitudes.

Watch out, girl, I think that means they both fancy you. You ever heard of a threesome?

Hearing her friend's voice in her head, with such ridiculous words, relaxed her more than anything else, and she smiled back at the other two and thanked them naturally. As Lance had reminded her, if ever she needed to put her acting skills to the test, tonight was the night. And she wouldn't let him down, she vowed. Even if she felt that he had let her down in the worst possible way over the whole Ethan affair, she wouldn't do the same to him.

Cyn linked an arm through hers and Lance's as they joined her parents and several other guests in the spacious drawing room.

'We've got so much to tell you, and so many souvenirs to show you, haven't we, Mon? The *Schloss* was simply divine, of course, and our hosts so hospitable, and at the Olympic Games we nearly forgot who we were, we were shouting ourselves so hoarse along with everyone else. And I'm sure you heard about the awful moment when Herr Hitler refused to shake the hand of the black athlete, whatever his name was. So embarrassing for everyone, but those people seem able to rise above it all, and it didn't spoil things for the rest of us.'

As she prattled on and on, Cherry found herself cringing at the sheer crassness of such remarks. But that was Cynthia, and nothing was going to change her. All through supper there was a lengthy discourse on the merits of the German countryside and its architecture, and the splendour of the Games, and afterwards they were subjected to all the photographs that had been taken, until Cherry felt drunk with so much information.

'We want to hear all about your sea voyage too,' Cyn said at last, turning to her and Lance. 'I'm so sorry to have gone on and on, but now it's your turn!' she added with a laugh.

The remark startled Cherry. So much had happened since they had been aboard the *Queen Mary* that she had almost forgotten their wonderful trip, but, to her complete shock, Lance picked up on it at once.

'It was a wonderful trip, and since we considered it to be

our second honeymoon, it could hardly have been otherwise, could it, Cherry-ripe?'

If she had been stunned before, she was even more so at his use of her pet name in this company. But before she could say anything at all, he had moved smoothly on.

'With two thousand people on board, I suppose it was inevitable that we would see someone we knew, and one couple in particular homed in on us. The man was my old batman when I was in the army, and his wife, a surprisingly aristocratic lady, remembered seeing Cherry and her friend Paula years ago on the day they had their hair bobbed. What a memory was that!'

'Goodness me,' Cyn said, looking nonplussed.

'It was very odd,' Cherry continued. 'I didn't recognize her at all, but I daresay Paula and I were a bit conspicuous coming out of the hair salon laughing like a pair of loons, and wondering what we had done!'

'How very amusing, my dear,' Cyn's father said indulgently.

'And, since then, we've had another shock,' Lance said deliberately. 'Not altogether a welcome one, but we shall cope with it. I'm sure you'll all get to know about it soon enough, so do you want to tell it, darling, or shall I?'

His eyes challenged her, and Cherry could hardly believe he was humiliating her like this. Did he really want her to blurt out the truth about her brother's son landing on them? Was this a kind of revenge for bringing more disgrace on his name? She felt her blood seethe, but she spoke with deliberate coolness, a fixed smile on her face.

'Oh, I think you could tell it so much better than I, Lance.'

Ten

By the time Lance finished speaking, Cherry conceded that if he thought she was a good actress when the need arose, he was just as good a performer, if not better. He carried off the arrival of Ethan O'Neill so smoothly and with such aplomb that half the company would surely think the boy was almost a child prodigy and an asset to the family. Only Cyn was fully aware of the disgrace that Cherry's brother had threatened the Melchoirs with all those years ago, and how it had been dealt with. She was the only one who knew why Brian O'Neill had been banished to Australia, but to hear Lance speaking of him now, he was being elevated to the status of some brave adventurer going forth to a new land.

'So that's the story,' he said in conclusion. 'Our family has now expanded by one, and since it's unfair for Miss Green to try to teach three children instead of two, especially a young boy of Ethan's age, we are hiring a splendid new tutor for them all. He's originally from Cornwall, but has been educated and trained at Cambridge. He recently tutored the young sons of a friend of mine in government, and he comes with excellent qualifications and will be joining the household in just over a week's time.'

Cherry kept the smile fixed on her face, even though she had been told nothing of David Trelawney's apparently excellent qualifications, nor that he was Cambridge-educated, and certainly not that he would be joining the household. If that meant that he would be living in Melchoir House, she had known nothing of it. It showed how far apart she and Lance had come in terms of communication.

'Well,' Mrs Hetherington said at last, 'this is certainly a surprise for us all, Lance. It takes my breath away to know that Cherry had relatives as far away as Australia, but how good it is of you both to take the poor orphaned boy in.'

'It's no more than I would have expected of Lance and

Cherry, Mother,' Cyn put in, 'and it's almost a more exciting tale than mine and Monica's.'

Lance gave a tight smile. 'Hardly. And we certainly didn't mean to steal your thunder, dear girl.'

She laughed and squeezed his hand. 'You haven't. But I'm sure Cherry and I will get our heads together sometime soon to learn more about this intriguing situation.'

Cherry was quite sure that they wouldn't if she had anything do about it. But she muttered something appropriate and let the conversation drift on all around her, still completely bemused that Lance had chosen to say anything at all. But she supposed it was better to get it out in the open in one fell swoop, while other people were here, than to let them discover it all gradually. And, by now, she was sure Dawkins would have alerted their servants about the strange kid who had arrived in their midst out of nowhere.

A short while later she realized that Cyn was by her side in one of those rare moments in the middle of a crowd when two people could manage a few private moments.

'Well, this is a turn up, isn't it?' the other girl said softly. 'And hardly one as welcome as Lance made out, I'm sure. He explained it all very smoothly, but when you've known someone as long as I have, you know when all is not as it seems. If you need a friend, Cherry darling, you know I'm always here.'

She moved away as Monica claimed her, leaving Cherry with prickling eyes, knowing how she had misjudged her earlier words as she so often did. Cynthia Hetherington might be a prize snob in many ways, but, underneath it all, she had a sympathetic heart. And she shouldn't forget that Cyn had always championed their cause in the past. But how far that generosity went once she came into contact with Brian O'Neill's son, they had yet to discover.

At last, the interminable evening came to an end, and Cherry sat stiffly and silently beside Lance as the limousine took them back to Melchoir House. If she said anything at all, she knew she would burst into a torrent of rage at him, and it was better left until they were inside the house and out of range of the curious eyes and ears of the chauffeur.

But, once in their bedroom, it didn't take a moment for Cherry to tear off her pearls, fling them on the bed and to round on Lance.

'How could you go on and on about the tutor like that, without letting me know the first thing about him other than his name?'

'All you need to know is that he will instil some discipline in the children, which seems sadly lacking from Miss Green, and as for the other one—'

'You mean my nephew?' she said sarcastically. 'The one you practically implied was a boy genius this evening.'

'I could hardly do much less. Or did you want me to tell them all that he seemed an illiterate lout like his father?'

'He's hardly illiterate. He was perfectly able to read all the documents his mother had trusted him with.'

'And no doubt he gloried in all the various posters regarding his father's dubious bare-knuckle fighting,' Lance retorted. 'I wonder he isn't planning to follow in his footsteps. Or perhaps he is.'

'You know very well that it's illegal in this country now.'

'And always disreputable!'

'Perhaps you'd like to ship him to Ireland when he's old enough, then, where I believe it's still considered a sport. After all, your parents were quick enough to send us both there to avoid damaging the precious Melchoir reputation,' Cherry blazed at him.

She was too incensed to be upset at the furious row they were having, or to care what she was saying. This evening had never been destined to be an easy one, and it was simply going from bad to worse.

'I begin to think my parents were right in the first place, and that chalk and cheese are never likely to be anything but bad bedfellows,' Lance said coldly.

Cherry gasped at the inference. 'If that's what you think, then I'm sorry I ever bloody well married you!'

'And so am I. And, by the way, your accent's slipping.'

He turned on his heel and slammed out of the bedroom, leaving her stunned in the middle of the room.

Her head whirled sickeningly and she couldn't think

straight for some minutes. They had once vowed never to end an evening on a row, and they had never done so before. However bad the problem, there was always the making-up to follow, and it was often all the sweeter because of what had gone before, and the mutual apologies and forgiveness . . . but tonight it would take a great deal more than usual before Cherry could feel able to forgive his harsh words.

She undressed with trembling hands, wondering how it had come to such a pitch. She finally slid under the bedcovers and waited for Lance to return. She guessed he would have gone to the drawing room for a stiff drink of whisky, or perhaps to his study, and then he would come back to their bedroom, if not contrite, then at least ready to forget the dreadful accusations they had both made to one another.

She was so tired after so much stress that she must have drifted off to sleep, because she awoke with a start. She was still alone, the bed was cold, and when she realized how long it was since Lance had stormed out, she lay rigidly, wondering if she should look for him. He had surely calmed down by now. Unable to rest properly, she finally looked in the dressing room adjoining the bedroom, but the bed there hadn't been slept in either. She was torn between looking for him and trying to put things right, and leaving him to stew in his own juices.

But it was only when she went back to their bedroom, still undecided, that she heard the sound of the motor start up. She rushed to the window and saw the limousine leaving the house, and she could just see two shapes in the car. She swallowed hard, wondering where Lance could be going at this time of night, especially without telling her. Before she could stop to think, she had pressed the bell at the side of her bed, and one of the maids appeared shortly afterwards, clearly having dressed hastily.

'I'm sorry to disturb you, Josie, but I have the most terrible headache. Would you please bring me a sedative for it? And would you happen to know where Dawkins has driven Lord Melchoir at this hour? I fear he has forgotten something.'

The girl answered without expression, even though Cherry knew to her cost that the question would be the talk of the kitchen in the morning. It sounded feeble, even to her, and she hated having to ask such a question. And how stupid she was not to have thought of a more plausible one.

'He asked Dawkins to take him to his club, Madam. Should I ask him to report to you when he returns?'

'There's no need. I'm sure it was nothing important. Now, if you'll just bring me that sedative, please, Josie, and then I won't disturb you any longer.'

She sank back against the pillows, shaking badly now. If Lance had gone to spend the night at his club, it didn't bode well for his state of mind. He was obviously furious with her, when she hadn't done anything wrong. Nothing, except to be saddled with a wicked brother, and now his offspring. But he had said the unforgivable to her. He had said he wished he had never married her. She felt the sobs rising in her throat and fought them down until the maid had come and gone again. After that, she couldn't fight them any more.

'I tell you, she looked near to weeping, and ever so wild-eyed,' Josie said excitedly early next morning as soon as the kitchen staff had all assembled for duty. 'And she didn't know where his lordship had gone, neither, even though she tried to pretend that she did. I reckon they'd had an almighty bust-up, and I bet it was over that new kid too.'

'He's gone to his club, and I reckon he was stayin',' Dawkins, the chauffeur confirmed. 'And I can tell you, he looked fit to blow a gasket as well, but I'm to collect him at eleven o'clock this morning.'

'So he did stay away all night, then,' Josie muttered with a snigger to the other maids. 'It must have been serious if he was prepared to go without his bedroom comforts, if you know what I mean.'

'That's enough of that,' Cook told her sharply. 'I won't have you talking about your betters in that coarse way.'

Then she hesitated. So far, she and Gerard had been tight-lipped over the true identity of the boy who had arrived at the house, but if he was staying, and these upsets were due to his presence, then it was all going to come out in the open before long. And better from somebody who was sympathetic than from gossipy outsiders. She looked at Gerard who gave her the nod.

'Now, you just listen to me, you girls, and Dawkins too. I'm going to tell you something, and I want you to swear that it won't go any farther than these four walls. I also want to be sure of your loyalty too, since Lord and Lady Melchoir are good employers and you won't get nobody better.'

They looked mystified for a moment, but agreed eagerly, sensing a bit of spicy gossip and maybe a family mystery too. What they heard had them practically reeling.

'You mean her bleedin' fancy ladyship was once one of us?' Josie spluttered. 'She worked in the kitchens like the rest of us, bowin' and scrapin' to them buggers upstairs?'

'I don't see you doing much bowing and scraping,' Gerard said sharply, 'and you mind your language, girl. They're still your employers, no matter where they came from.'

'So who's this boy that's caused all the ructions, then?' Dawkins put in, his eyes narrowed. 'I knew there was summat funny about him the minute I laid eyes on him. Where does he come into it?'

The tale had gone too far now for them not to hear the rest of it. And this time they were silenced at learning of the evil ways of Brian O'Neill, her ladyship's brother, how Cherry and Lance had overcome all the odds to be married, and how the brother had been banished to Australia all those years ago.

Agnes, the youngest kitchen-maid, and watery-eyed at the best of times, was sobbing quietly now.

'For God's sake, Agnes, pipe down. You'll be watering your porridge,' Josie told her irritably.

'I can't help it. It's such a romantic story,' she girl wailed. 'It's like one of them sad films you see at the pictures.'

Josie snorted. 'You're a daft little bugger, aren't you? Anyway, after all that, I'm never going to look at her bloomin' ladyship in the same away again.'

Gerard took control.

'You will and you must,' he thundered. 'Otherwise I shall

recommend that you seek employment elsewhere. And before you think that will give you free rein to spread gossip about your betters, let me assure you that if you leave here under a cloud, I shall make it my personal business to see that no other God-fearing establishment employs you, not in this town or any other.'

'And that goes for me too,' Cook said loudly. 'The Melchoirs have always been good and generous employers, and no scumbag skivvies are going to put the boot in when they're in trouble, do you all understand? We're here to serve them, not to condemn them. Remember that.'

She was greeted with various mutterings, but it wasn't good enough for Gerard. Startling them all, he declared that he was going to his room to prepare a document for them all to sign, swearing total loyalty to their employers. But while the others grumbled and muttered at the very idea, the young Agnes obviously saw this as an important sense of belonging.

'It's just like they was royalty, ain't it?' she squeaked.

Gerard turned on his heel before he exploded with a mixture of fury over what was happening and a wild desire to laugh at the girl's gullibility. He was halfway up the stairs to the servant's quarters when he became aware of a shadowy shape ahead of him. He looked up, and his heart jumped.

'I heard,' Cherry said, choking. 'I was coming to look for Dawkins, to find out what was happening, and I heard everything. You're a loyal friend, Gerard . . .'

Her voice cracked and her hand almost slipped on the banister. He involuntarily gripped her arm to steady her, and he saw her eyes, large with tears and pain, her mouth trembling with anxiety and hurt. And in that moment she was no longer the lady of the house, but the bewildered, vulnerable little Cherry O'Neill, part of his kitchen family, and in need of his help and guidance. And her unfinished words told him she was badly in need of a friend.

'May I take you to my room for a few moments until you recover, Madam?' he said gently, and with a small nod she allowed herself to be taken the last few steps until she was safe inside his room, where she had been reprimanded so many times in the distant past.

Hardly knowing what she did, she sank down on his hard, narrow bed, and felt his arm go around her shoulders. It should have been quite unseemly, given their situations, but he had always been a stern father figure to the skivvies in the old days, and right then it seemed the most natural thing in the world to be here with him and to be comforted.

'Oh Gerard, what am I to do?' she wept. 'How could we ever have expected this to happen? How could I ever have thought that my brother would come back to haunt me in this way?'

'That's the trouble with life, Madam. The unexpected can always catch us out when we least want it to,' he said awkwardly.

With a semblance of her usual self, she made a small gesture of annoyance. 'Please, Gerard, stop calling me Madam while I'm in your room. I'm not here as your employer now, and you know my name as well as I do. Can't we just be normal for once?'

He gave a small smile. 'If we were to be normal, Cherry, I would be telling you to pull yourself together and not let the buggers get you down, but I'm not sure that's what you want to hear, nor that I should be saying it.'

She straightened up slightly. 'Yes, you should be saying it, and I should be taking heed of your wise words as always. I didn't always appreciate them, but Paula and I always respected you, even when you were so shocked and disapproving when I married into the family. I'm sure you hated me then for risking the pride of the Melchoir name.'

'I never hated you, my dear.'

She sniffed back tears. 'Well, you were certainly outraged, weren't you?'

He actually laughed then, removing his arm from her shoulders as if knowing that this brief interlude of nostalgia was coming to an end, as it must.

'I think we always knew that you were destined for being more than a kitchen-maid. The performances you put on for us, especially imitating Lady Elspeth's voice so well, made us all think you were destined for the stage. You may have missed your vocation, but you have certainly graced this house over the years, my lady.'

Cherry swallowed the lump her throat as she stood up, humbled by such an unexpected compliment. 'Thank you, Gerard. I feel all the better for having talked with you, and ready to face whatever I have to. And I believe you have a certain document to prepare, for which I thank you from the bottom of my heart.'

Without thinking, she pressed a small kiss on his cheek. Then she walked out of the room quickly and continued back upstairs to her own domain, to steady herself and to splash some cold water on her heated face.

By the time Lance returned to the house, she was clear-eyed and much calmer, on the surface at least. Yes, she could have gone on the stage. She could have been an actress. And she was very much acting a part now, as she spoke to him as if nothing of last night had happened at all. She forestalled whatever he had to say by relating a little of what had transpired with Gerard, without letting him know her humiliation at overhearing everything from the kitchen stairs.

'Gerard is the most loyal friend, as well as a servant,' she went on finally. 'I'm sure the staff will be under no doubt that the document he makes them sign is as good as being legal and binding.'

'Well, you've certainly been busy this morning,' Lance said guardedly, not sure how to take this new show of confidence. 'Just how did you accomplish all this, may I ask?'

'Oh, I have my methods,' Cherry said coolly. 'I also understand the way that those below stairs think and react, which is something of an asset, wouldn't you say, my dear?'

She was mocking him now, throwing back in his face the way he seemed intent on demeaning her, and not for a moment letting him guess how her heart was breaking at the tangible animosity between them.

'I shall be away for the rest of the weekend,' he said without further comment. 'Our meeting with David Trelawney is arranged for two o'clock here on Monday afternoon. Please be sure to be available.'

She just managed not to click her heels and salute. Instead, she shrugged as if it wasn't of the least interest to her.

'*Cherry?*'

'Of course I'll be here,' she snapped. 'Would I do otherwise than obey what my lord and master commands?'

'Now you're being ridiculous,' he said coldly.

There was nothing she could sensibly reply to that if she didn't want to scream with rage and frustration, so she merely walked out of the drawing room with her head held high. She simply didn't know what to do next. It was Saturday tomorrow, and as long as the days remained fine, she and Paula always met with their children on the Downs. Maybe being with them all would calm her frayed nerves, she thought, avoiding the fact that Ethan O'Neill was unlikely to be anyone's favourite. There was also something she had to do today . . .

For now, that gave her scattered thoughts a purpose, and she went to the nursery to see how they were all getting along. Once on the nursery landing, however, she was met with a small tornado rushing through.

'Now then, where's the fire?' she said involuntarily, grabbing hold of the boy's arm.

He tried to snatch it away, but she held firm. He looked mad-eyed, and her heart sank, remembering her so-recent hope of a pleasant afternoon on the Downs with her friend tomorrow.

'I ain't here for those kids to make fun of me!' he shouted.

Cherry sighed. It was too much to hope that they would all get on together. Far too much. 'What have they done, Ethan?' she asked quietly.

'All I said was that I had to go to the dunny, and they started laughing and telling me I was the *dummy*. That ain't what I said at all, and they're the dummies, not me. And then the old witch started shouting at me for being rude.'

He was talking double Dutch as far as Cherry was concerned, but this had better be sorted out, and quickly. She couldn't have Nanny Green referred to as an old witch, either, even though she had a brief sympathy with the boy.

'Look, love,' she said, trying to be a calming influence, 'this is a new situation for all of us, and we all have to learn to get to know one another, don't we? They obviously didn't under-stand what you were saying, so why don't we go to your bedroom for a few minutes while you explain it to me?'

'If I wait many more minutes, I shall piss meself!' he shouted again.

Cherry saw him cross his legs tightly, and even if she didn't know the words, she knew the meaning of that gesture all right.

'Go to the bathroom quickly then, and I'll wait for you outside.'

She let him go and he tore along the landing to the bathroom at the end. Poor little devil, she thought with real compassion. It must be hell on earth for him to be thrust into this household, and she guessed that Bella wasn't doing very much to help. A few minutes later, the boy returned, looking sullen.

'Sorry, missus,' he muttered.

Cherry forced a smile. 'Let's get one thing straight, Ethan. Nobody's disputing that I'm your aunt, so you should call me Auntie Cherry, all right?'

He nodded uncertainly.

'So now we'll go back to the nursery, and it would be sensible if you would explain what you meant earlier. I'm coming with you and nobody's going to laugh at you, I promise.'

She hardly knew why she was championing him like this. He looked at her with her brother's eyes and scowling expression, and she should hate him. But it was dawning on her that if she didn't stand by him, nobody else would. Certainly not Lance, who detested the very name O'Neill, she thought with a shudder.

But she caught hold of his hand and they went into the nursery together. Bella hid stifling laughter behind her hand, Georgie giggled nervously, and Nanny Green told them to be quiet while their mother was here to speak to them.

'Now then, let's get this sorted out, shall we?' she said pleasantly, but with steel in her gaze. 'We have a guest in our house, but he is far more than a usual guest, since he is also a relative. The fact that he comes from a different country means that he speaks differently, and probably uses different words from ours. That doesn't mean he is inferior to us. Or that he should think of us as snobs,' she reminded Ethan when he gave a little snort.

'So why don't you tell us what you meant just now that caused such merriment, Ethan?'

He glared at her, unsure if she was helping him or not. Then he shrugged.

'I needed the dunny.'

Bella started to snigger again, and Cherry held up her hand.

'You will be quiet, Bella, or you will go to your room for the rest of the day. And you, Ethan, will please explain what a dunny is.'

She had already worked it out, but she needed to hear him say it for the benefit of these idiot children. Aghast that she could think of them in those terms, she kept her face straight while the boy spoke.

'It's the lav, the privy. Whatever you call it, it's where you go for a—'

'Thank you,' Cherry broke in quickly. 'Now then, if we've got that clear, I should just explain to you, Ethan, that in future you should just say that you need the bathroom. That should satisfy everybody, shouldn't it, Miss Green?'

The woman agreed stiffly, clearly affronted by the boy, by the term he'd used, by the need for Lady Melchoir to come and do her job for her.

'Good,' Cherry said. 'And this afternoon, you will be excused lessons, Ethan, since you and I will be going shopping for your new clothes before you meet your new tutor.'

She ignored the outcry from Bella and Georgie and continued doggedly.

'Then, tomorrow afternoon, children, we shall be going out on the Downs as usual, to meet Paula and Thomas. I'm sure you'll get along with Thomas, Ethan, as he's about your age.'

She left them all before she had to listen to any comments one way or another, with an uneasy feeling in her heart that Ethan wasn't going to like Thomas Farmer one bit, any more than Thomas Farmer was going to like him.

Sometimes, she thought wearily, everything could get so complicated, especially having to juggle other people's lives and trying to keep them all sweet. It had been so much simpler when she and Paula had worked in the kitchens, with no more responsibility than scurrying around to Cook's demands, and the prospect of a Saturday night off to go dancing with the local lads. And that was not the kind of nostalgic memory she ever thought she would find herself thinking.

Eleven

There were never any definite plans to meet on the Downs on Saturday afternoons, it was simply a long-standing date. In fact, Cherry wondered if Paula would even turn up this week, or if she had taken the huff after their last meeting. She couldn't even remember what had been said, but she knew Paula thought she was being a proper swank over the buying of clothes for Ethan O'Neill. But she was sure she wouldn't let her down over the arrangement to meet outside Smithy's Tea Rooms on Friday afternoon, and Cherry was mightily relieved to see her old friend waiting there when she and Ethan arrived.

'So this is Brian's son, is it?' Paula said at once, looking him up and down with a critical gaze. 'I thought so, as soon as I laid eyes on him. He's got the same daredevil look, and pretty much the same everything else, I daresay.'

'His name's Ethan, Paula,' Cherry said quickly, wishing she wouldn't talk about him scathingly as if he wasn't there. It wasn't the boy's fault that he was his father's son. 'And Ethan, this is Mrs Farmer, who I told you about.'

He muttered something unintelligible until Cherry prodded his arm and then he spoke more clearly.

'I said, nice to meet you, missus.'

'Mrs *Farmer*,' Cherry hissed.

'Mrs Farmer, then.'

'Charming, ain't he?' Paula said, but with a hint of a smile on her lips now. She had met boys like him before, more than Cherry had, she guessed, living in her organized little world of governesses and servants. With a suddenness that surprised her, Paula felt sorry for Cherry, and that was a turn-up for sure!

'Come on, then, if we've got to get you kitted out,' she said more generously to Ethan. 'Want to be a proper little Lord Fauntleroy, do you?'

As Ethan looked totally blank, Paula grinned. 'Never mind,

we'll just do the best we can with the material we've got, eh, kid?'

To Cherry's astonishment, she tucked Ethan's arm in hers, and even more amazingly he let it remain there as they walked off down the hill at a brisk pace, with Cherry following behind on the narrow pavement. She felt suddenly redundant, as if these two had somehow discovered they had far more in common than she did with her own nephew. Which was hardly surprising, since Paula spoke in the same kind of loose, slangy way that Ethan did . . . the way that she too had spoken once, she reminded herself with swift shame.

By the end of that exhausting afternoon, amid much laughter and coaxing from Paula as she persuaded Ethan into trying on shirts and shoes and everything in between, there were more than a dozen bags and boxes ready to be taken back to Melchoir House.

'You two ain't thinking of carrying this lot back on your own, are you, Cherry? I'd help you, but I need to get back for when Thomas comes home from school. It looks like rain and I don't fancy getting soaked,' Paula said at last.

'Don't worry about that, I'll have it all put aside and send Dawkins down to collect it later,' Cherry said quickly.

Paula looked at her silently for a moment. The words were innocent enough, but they seemed to say that now Paula had done her job, Cherry could get back to the real world of having everything done for her with no more than a click of her fingers. It was an irrational thing to think, but think it she did.

'Oh well, if you don't need me any more, I'll be getting back home.'

Cherry saw at once the way her friend's thoughts were going. 'We can go and have some tea first if you like. There's no hurry.'

'There is for me,' Paula said. She looked at Ethan, busily fingering some oddments on the shop counter now, and hid a slight smile. For two pins, he'd pick something up and be off with it, she guessed. He caught her glance and grinned at her.

'So it's goodbye for now, young feller-me-lad,' she told him cheerily. 'Or should that be g'day? I'll see you tomorrow unless it's too wet to come out to play,' she added with a wink.

He hooted, and, to Cherry's surprise, Paula put her arm around him and gave him a smacker of a kiss on his cheek, which was more than she had been able to unbend enough to do herself!

They parted outside on the street after Cherry had given her instructions to the shop assistants that the parcels would be collected later that afternoon. She merely gave the name as Dawkins, collecting parcels for O'Neill, and let them make of it what they would when the smartly dressed chauffeur arrived.

She and Ethan walked home together, saying little. Once at the house, they quickly parted company. She really didn't know what to make of him, she thought crossly. She always thought she could get on with anyone, but it horrified her slightly now to realize she was more at home with the likes of Cynthia Hetherington and other toffs than with her own kind. She had come up in the world in more ways than one, which just went to show how far she had come in the last few years, but the thought wasn't exactly a comfortable one. She sought out Dawkins and gave him her instructions, and an hour or so later all the bags and boxes had been collected and brought to the house.

By then the rain had set in steadily. Cherry hated this kind of oppressive weather. Lance was out, God knew where, probably at his club as he so often was these days, and she didn't want to disturb Miss Green with the children, so there was nothing more for her to do until she joined them at teatime. An old saying of Cook's flashed into her mind.

The devil makes work for idle hands . . .

She and Paula had scoffed and giggled every time she said it, likening Cook to a follower of old Nick himself for giving them endless tasks to do. There had been no time for idling for kitchen-maids then, with their fingers pricked by endless mending tasks, their hands red raw from scrubbing and cleaning . . .

Well, she didn't choose to be idle these days, Cherry thought in annoyance, and nor did she want to be. It was simply that everything was done for her now, and she sometimes felt that she had no real purpose. Ever since the heady days of the ocean voyage with Lance, she had seemed to be just marking time. The thought shocked her, because what better purpose was there in life than being a loving wife and mother?

A tap on the drawing-room door made her jump, and she composed herself quickly as the butler came inside.

'Miss Hetherington is here to see you, my lady.'

'Oh, please show her up, Gerard,' Cherry said with relief.

A few minutes later, Cynthia Hetherington entered the room, full of apologies at an impromptu visit and not having telephoned first.

'It doesn't matter a bit, and I can't tell you how glad I am to see you, Cyn. We'll have some tea sent up in a minute, please, Gerard,' she said as he waited for her instructions.

'Well, you seem to be in low spirits, or am I imagining things?' Cyn said shrewdly. 'Don't tell me the little interloper's not playing the game. It's turning into a beastly afternoon, by the way, enough to make everyone miserable, so I wouldn't blame you if that's the case.'

Cherry gave a shaky laugh. 'He's all right, Cyn, and we've been out earlier buying him some decent clothes. Not that I did much about it, but Paula managed to take him under her wing and do the necessary.'

'Do I detect a small sign of the green eye?' Cyn said archly.

'Don't be daft! Why would I be jealous of Paula?'

Why indeed? Then she wilted. 'Oh well, perhaps I am, a little, since Paula seemed able to make more headway with my own nephew in an hour or so than I have all the time he's been here.'

'I didn't think you were so enamoured of having him here, darling.'

'Maybe I wasn't, but I've no choice, have I? You can't turn your back on blood, however disagreeable it may be.'

The arrival of a maid with a tray of tea and biscuits interrupted their talk for a few moments. Still disgruntled at the way the afternoon seemed to have disintegrated, Cherry became unduly indiscreet.

'I'm not exactly having much support from Lance, either. He's hardly ever here and I know he dislikes Ethan intensely, and of course I'm the source of his displeasure. He's forever getting his head together with his lawyer for some intelligent conversation, no doubt —oh Lord, I'm sorry, Cyn. I shouldn't be saying these things to you. Please forget them.'

She was so distressed that at first she hardly noticed the uneasy look that her friend was giving her, or registered her silence until it became obvious.

'There's something else, isn't there?' she blurted out. 'Is there something I should know? It's not Lance, is it? He doesn't have – he hasn't been straying, has he? You were always his confidante, Cyn, and if anybody would know such a thing, it would be you!'

Cynthia put her cup down on the saucer with a clatter and spoke soothingly.

'You goose, of course Lance hasn't been straying. Why on earth would he want to, when he's always been besotted by his lovely wife?'

'But you do know something, don't you?'

Cynthia shrugged her elegant shoulders.

'Well, I know he's been consulting James Fitzherbert on some legal matters, but that's all I do know.'

'For what reason? What legal matters?'

'I've already said I don't know, Cherry, and if you really want to know, you should ask him yourself, darling. I always think that ladies should stay out of such affairs and leave it to the gentlemen. It's usually best to leave things be and let them sort themselves out as they always do.'

That's because you were born a lady, thought Cherry, *serenely moving through life with everything taken care of for you.*

'So tell me more about this tutor that Lance has hired. I understand you'll be meeting him on Monday,' Cyn went on, adroitly changing the subject.

'Lance told you about him the other night,' Cherry said sullenly, 'and since he comes with excellent references from Lance's well-heeled friends, he's probably no end of a toff, and I'm sure I won't like him.'

Cynthia burst out laughing, her eyes bright with amusement as she pressed a manicured hand over Cherry's.

'Oh, you're such a sweetheart, Cherry, and so transparent!

I'm sure he'll be perfectly respectable and agreeable, and if he takes the responsibility for tutoring the children off poor old Nanny Green's hands, so much the better. I imagine she's having a rather strenuous time of it with the new arrival.'

'That's putting it mildly,' Cherry said, allowing herself to smile at last.

By the time her friend had left, zipping away in the sporty little car that was her new toy, she was determined to tackle Lance after dinner that evening, to find out just what was so important that he had to see James Fitzherbert constantly on legal matters.

She was thankful to see that he was in a more relaxed mood than of late. He had visited the children in the nursery, and Cherry was glad that Nanny Green had persuaded Ethan to wear some of his new clothes, which were more suited to the household. Even so, for a moment Cherry had seen Lance's eyes narrow, as if he still couldn't resist seeing the boy as a little upstart, and showing far too much resemblance to his father for him to accept his presence. No amount of finery and new clothes was ever going to change that.

But the time passed amicably enough, and when they met for dinner, Cherry had chosen a soft creamy gown that she knew he particularly liked, coupled with the pearls he had given her on her last birthday. The muted colours complemented her glowing hair, fastened with an elaborate tortoiseshell pin, and she could see that he appreciated her effort. So after a splendid dinner, when they had retired to the drawing room for drinks, now was the time . . . and she was unaccountably nervous.

'Have you had an interesting afternoon, Lance?' she began.

'Good enough. Fitzherbert's got a clever head on his shoulders.'

He gave her the lead she wanted. 'Was this an important meeting, then?'

He poured himself a large whisky before he replied. 'Nothing that you need to worry your pretty head about.'

'So it wasn't anything to do with Ethan, then?' she persisted, ignoring the slight for the moment.

'I've better things to do with my time than discuss your brother's brat,' he said shortly, making her gasp. She felt her face flame with anger.

'That's an unnecessary remark, isn't it? Besides, it's only since Ethan arrived that you seem to be spending so much time with your lawyer, so, as I have reasonable intelligence, even for a woman, it's obvious that his presence here is causing you concern.'

'What else would you expect when I assumed that we were rid of your bastard brother for ever? The arrival of his offspring was hardly welcome. How many more of them are there, one wonders? Will we be greeted by an entire army of them in due course?'

Cherry jumped up from the sofa, infuriated by his sarcasm, and realizing he had already had more than enough to drink that evening. But by now she was beyond caring what she said.

'You're being perfectly hateful, Lance, and no matter what you say, I've no doubt you and that poncey lawyer of yours have been discussing how best to get rid of the boy, and I have every right to know what has been said.'

He glowered at her, his eyes dark with fury now. 'You have no such rights, my dear, and never did have, any more than your common nephew does. I've made damn sure of that.'

She felt a shiver run through her. He looked so condemning, as if she had done something terrible. As if all of this was her fault. As if she had brought him to this . . . and as if she had been the one to encourage him all those years ago, when it had been *him* seducing her, not the other way around . . . The shivers wouldn't leave her, but she had to go on now.

'Please explain yourself, my lord, unless you want me to go to the lawyer myself, and demand to know what provisions you have made for me and my brother's child. Or have you forgotten that we have children of our own? Are they to be thrown out of the house too, simply because my inferior blood runs through their veins?'

'God Almighty, Cherry, stop being so melodramatic,' he snapped, brushing an unsteady hand across his eyes. 'I don't expect you to understand the finer points of the law.'

'Why not? Do you think me so stupid? I don't remember you thinking any such thing when you took advantage of me in the stables.'

She flung the words at him and was immediately furious with herself for doing so, knowing very well what would come next.

'And I don't remember you putting up much resistance to my advances, my sweet! In fact, between you and that simpering friend of yours, it was a toss-up which one of you would give in first.'

Cherry gasped again at his arrogance. But this had gone too far to bother about what she was saying now.

'Well, don't you think you're the ruddy high and mighty one? For your information, Paula never thought much of you, and she never understood why I ever took a fancy to you at all. And now I wish I hadn't.'

'And so do I,' Lance snapped. 'I should have listened to my father before I let myself get tangled up with the likes of you.'

Angry and humiliated, Cherry's eyes were blurred with tears now, and she dashed them away. She wanted to rush out of there, out of the house to anywhere, and never come back. But she knew she could never do that. Not while the children needed her – all three of them.

The memory of why this tirade had started stopped her in her tracks, and how she managed it, she never knew, but her voice became icily calm as she sat down and folded her arms tightly across her chest.

'So are you going to do me the courtesy of telling me what's so important that it has to be discussed with your lawyer, and not with me? Or would you prefer that I do as I've already said and go to him and ask for myself? Because one way or another, Lance, I will get at the truth.'

He poured himself another whisky, and she became alarmed at the quantity he was drinking, but she didn't dare to start discussing the merits of sobriety.

'Very well, then. Do you know what the term "entail" means?'

Damn and blast it, no, she bloody well didn't! So that little bit of ignorance would be another feather in his cap for him to crow over . . .

'Don't bother, I can see that you don't,' he went on coldly. 'Briefly, it's something that all great houses have enjoyed for generations, and although Melchoir House hardly comes into the category of a king's palace, it has been in my family for generations, and my great-great-grandfather took the precaution of ensuring the entail clause in his Will.'

Cherry looked at him unblinkingly, knowing that his sense of family pride would compel him to explain further now, and not giving him the satisfaction of asking any more questions until he did.

When he spoke, it was curt and to the point.

'What an entailed estate means, my dear, is that it can only be inherited by a son, and not a daughter.'

'I see,' Cherry said. 'So Georgie would inherit Melchoir House after your death, and Bella would presumably marry a rich man well up to your standards and have no need of it anyway. Is that right?'

'Correct,' Lance said coldly. 'Since my great-great-grandfather's time, there has always been a son, so there was no problem.'

'There's a son now,' Cherry pointed out, tiring of a conversation that seemed to be going nowhere.

He went on as though she hadn't spoken. 'According to the legal requirements of an entailed estate, if there is no son, or should anything befall him, the next male relative will then inherit.'

For the next few moments, all Cherry could hear was the ticking of the grandfather clock in the corner of the drawing room, and the sick drumming of her heart at the implications of what he was saying.

'Oh my God,' she whispered.

'Exactly. I can see that light has dawned,' he said sarcastically. 'The next male relative would be your brother's brat, who, if he has inherited all of his father's delightful traits, would be perfectly capable of dragging the estate down and abusing its good name by whatever means.'

The horror of it washed over Cherry in waves for a moment.

'You're totally mad,' she said flatly. 'You can't think that Ethan would do any harm to Georgie so that he could take control of this place? He's only a child and he has no idea about inheritances and entails or any other blasted legal term.'

Lance gave a harsh laugh, 'It's no matter, anyway. Fortunately, Fitzherbert is a top man, and he has been delving into the archives and found something that solves the whole problem.'

'Which is?'

'It appears that my great-great-grandfather was a wily old fox. His first child was a stillborn son, and fearing that his wife might be unable to conceive another, and that the estate should fall into less noble hands, he added a precautionary codicil to his will that was uncontested. Entails are normally watertight, so my guess is that he also had his lawyer in the palm of his hand. I care nothing for the details, but, thankfully, there was another son, so the codicil was not needed, but it remains legal and survives to this day, and I have stressed its existence in my Will.'

'And what is this wonderful codicil?' Cherry said without expression.

He ignored the sarcasm. 'Briefly, it states that in the event of the incumbent's death, the estate naturally goes to the eldest son, and then to subsequent sons. A wife or daughters may remain here as long as they wish, barring a wife's remarriage. After that, a daughter may inherit, but no other male relative has any entitlement to the estate. When all legatees are exhausted, the estate will go to the Crown.'

'Well, you certainly seem to have swallowed enough of Fitzherbert's legal jargon to fill a book,' Cherry said heatedly. 'And, in the process, you've neatly avoided the trap of letting my brother's son have any entitlement to the estate whatsoever. Not that I would ever have wanted him to have it, any more than you would, and it shames me to think that you could ever have imagined otherwise. But that was the purpose of this whole spiteful exercise, wasn't it?'

'Absolutely right, my dear,' Lance said, 'and I for one will sleep easier in my bed tonight for having settled the matter.'

'Then I'll leave you to gloat on your successful day,' Cherry choked.

She stood up, her eyes murderous. Such matters had never bothered the likes of her and Paula when they had worked below stairs, and there had surely been no need for all of this. They weren't royalty, for God's sake, but Georgie was Lance's legal heir, and she could hardly imagine that Ethan would have any interest in the whole business, other than having a roof over his head. She remembered hearing him tell Paula that he'd rather spend time in the kitchens, entertaining Cook and the maids with his tales of life in the Outback, wherever that was. But that was something she hadn't told Lance, knowing it would only incense him more and cause him to sneer that the kitchen was clearly the right place for minions.

When had he changed so much?

She had been in bed for a while before she heard him open and close their bedroom door. She kept her eyes determinedly shut, not giving him the satisfaction of letting him know that she was still feeling bruised and distraught. She wanted to weep at the way they seemed to be tearing one another apart, but tears wouldn't come.

She had half-expected him to sleep in his dressing room, or to fall into a stupor in the drawing room after the copious amounts of whisky he seemed to have consumed. She could smell the fumes of it as he blundered about the bedroom until he finally slid into bed beside her as she lay rigidly.

'So what should we do to ensure that the inheritance remains even more firmly where it belongs, my sweet?' he slurred.

She pretended to be asleep, but he was having none of it. She felt his hands begin to roam over her flesh, and no matter how upset or how furious she was with him, her skin tingled at his touch as always, and she was aware of her body's treacherous response and the involuntary little murmurs of pleasure that escaped her lips. It was a wife's duty to give in to a husband's needs, she thought weakly, even as she despised herself for being so spineless.

Then he was upon her, pushing up her nightgown with rough hands, and forcing himself into her, and if she had ever thought this was to be an act of love, she was cruelly mistaken. There were no tender words of love from his lips, only obscenities that shocked her. She had never known him like this before. She wasn't ready, and he hurt her, thrusting himself into her again and again until he was spent, ignoring her cries of discomfort as if she was less than nothing. As if she was no more than a servant with whom he could take his pleasure any time he chose. At last, he rolled away from her, gasping at her side, while she wondered desperately if she was bleeding and damaged.

'With the devil's luck, that will give us the obligatory heir and a spare,' he snarled, and then he got out of the bed and strode unsteadily across the room, slamming the door behind him.

Cherry felt the hot trickle of tears running down her face now. So that was what this had all been about. He was still punishing her for her brother's wickedness all those years ago, but tonight he had humiliated her beyond words. It couldn't be called rape, for the law said that a husband couldn't rape his wife, but it was exactly how she felt. She felt raped and abused, and she prayed with all her might that this night wouldn't produce another child for his satisfaction.

When she had got her senses together, she finally staggered out of bed and went to the adjoining bathroom, where she washed and scrubbed herself until her skin felt raw. But there had been no sign of bleeding, and she hoped savagely that she had washed every bit of him out of her.

Twelve

When Cherry awoke after a fitful few hours of tossing and turning, one look in the mirror showed her pale face and swollen eyes. Her head throbbed appallingly, and the day seemed as dark as night. Outside, the rain was coming down in torrents, and there was no chance of anyone going out of doors today, so she wouldn't be able to see Paula as usual. How far she would have confided in her friend, she wasn't sure, but not being able to see her at all was one more thing to add to her despair.

She realized she was also very sore, but the familiar dragging pains in her stomach told her that Lance was not going to get his way, and that her monthly visitor had arrived. She was faintly triumphant, but it was a poor triumph, since she knew they had lost something very precious between them.

She didn't intend to linger in bed all day, though. In the past, she and Paula had just had to get on with it, no matter what their ailments, she thought, gritting her teeth. But she certainly needed something to ease her headache and her stomach cramps, and she rang the bell for Josie to fetch something for her.

She sat on her dressing stool with her eyes closed for a few minutes, then, hearing the door open, turned around with her thanks, only to see Lance enter the room with a small tray containing the tablets and a glass of water.

Without thinking, she flinched, and had the satisfaction of seeing him look wary and somewhat shamefaced as he put the tray down on her dressing table.

'I waylaid the maid,' he said in an oddly stifled voice by way of explanation. 'I want to offer my apologies for my behaviour last night, and to assure you that it won't happen again.'

She inclined her head, hardly knowing how to answer, and nor did she entirely trust this newly contrite Lord Melchoir. It didn't suit him, and it wouldn't last. She merely murmured

something unintelligible and left it at that. Let him hope for
a while that his actions last night had done what he wanted.
He would learn otherwise soon enough.

She had a sudden weird sense of déjà vu. After she and
Lance had first shared those moments of passion in the stables,
she had thought for a while that she was pregnant, only to
discover later that she wasn't. It was then that her devious
brother had heard her and Paula discussing the possibility, and
he had seized his chance to send the incriminating anonymous
note to Lance's father, demanding money or he would tell the
world how his precious son was going to father a brat by their
kitchen-maid.

Cherry felt the same sense of betrayal and shock as she had
felt then, that her own brother could do such a thing. And
her own sense of shame that she and Paula had perpetuated
the lie for as long as it suited them, not knowing how badly
it would all go wrong, and that she would be hauled to account
by the so very autocratic Lord Francis and Lady Elspeth
Melchoir. She remembered, too, that even though she had
finally confessed to Lance, risking his anger – and relief – that
no child was expected, he had stood up for her and kept the
truth from his parents, adamant that he intended to marry the
kitchen-maid.

So many things were spinning around in her head right
then, adding to the headache that still throbbed incessantly and
the griping stomach cramps. Finally, she knew she should give
in to it all and lie down for a while, leaving it until later to
face the day ahead. She rang the bell again, and this time it
was Josie who entered the bedroom.

'Please bring me some weak tea, Josie, and inform Nanny
Green that I shall be staying in my room this morning. I'm
still feeling unwell and I will see the children this afternoon.'

'Very well, Madam,' the girl said sympathetically. She hesitated, and then decided to speak up, eyeing Cherry keenly as
she did so. 'Lord Melchoir has already gone out and has given
instructions to Cook that he will be dining at his club this
evening.'

Cherry waved her hand feebly as if she already knew. She
wasn't in the least surprised. The farther apart they were right

now, the better for both of them. They both needed time to cool down and examine what had occurred between them if there was to be any hope that their life could be restored to the way it was before.

'I tell you there's summat going on between 'em again,' Josie said excitedly to the other maids as she prepared the tray of weak tea. 'She looks like death, and Dawkins said his lordship didn't look much better when he drove him down to that snooty club of his.'

Doris snorted. 'Probably had one of them tiffs over what to wear at somebody's coming-out ball or whatever they call it.'

'Nah, I reckon it was more than that from the look of 'er, all red-eyed and sniffly. It's more'n just the guts-ache too. P'raps we'll get summat out of his young nibs if he comes down here for a chinwag today, braggin' about livin' Down Under or whatever it's called.'

'Or p'raps her ladyship's been getting a bit too much of the other kind of *down under* from his lusty lordship,' Doris chortled, which sent them both off into gales of laughter, until Cook told them to stop their chattering and get on with some work before she cuffed them both about their ears.

'Silly old trout,' Josie muttered 'It's time she was put out to grass if you ask me. She must have been here since the year dot.'

But they were denied any sneaking visit from Ethan O'Neill and the reminiscences of his life in Australia. Since there was little else to do on such a wet and windy Saturday, and Nanny Green couldn't abide the miserable faces of three children around her all day, she had reluctantly decided to ask him about it too. At least it would prevent the constant sniping between him and Bella with her superior sneering. And once started, Ethan was only too glad to oblige, with the upshot that all three children spent much of the day drawing pictures at Ethan's instruction of strange animals like kangaroos and wallabies and koalas, trees with names too long to pronounce, and colourful birds that neither of the Melchoir children nor Nanny Green had seen before.

By the middle of the afternoon, Cherry's headache had

lifted, and the cramps had merged into a manageable ache, and she finally felt able to venture out of the bedroom and go down to the nursery, guilty that she had neglected the children all day so far. To her amazement, she found them all absorbed in their tasks, until Bella and Georgie rushed up to her to show her their drawings. Nanny Green spoke quietly if grudgingly.

'I reckon that boy could turn out to be a teacher, if nothing else.'

'Let's hope Mr Trelawney will think so too,' Cherry murmured, knowing it would take more than a talent with art to curb the boy's impatience with anything too educational.

'Where's Daddy today? He never comes to see us now,' Georgie asked her with a pout, making her heart jump.

'He's had to go out on business, darling, but I'm sure he'll be back soon,' she said, with more hope than certainty.

'He hasn't gone riding, has he? He always smells so horsey when he comes in if he's been riding Prince in the rain,' Bella said, wrinkling up her nose.

'That's nothing. My pa used to ride in camel races, and you ain't smelled nothing until you've smelled camel stink!' Ethan bragged before Cherry could reply.

Nanny Green tut-tutted at once. 'Now then, young man, we've heard all about some of the strange animals that live in Australia, but don't start filling the children's heads with fairy tales. Camel racing, indeed!'

Cherry saw the boy's face darken, and the other two sniggered as he flung down his crayons and began shouting.

'It ain't no fairy tale, and I bet my pa was stronger than any soppy horse rider. I seen him ride in the camel races when I was a nipper, and he won prizes for it as well. My mum would tell you if she was here.'

His voice died away and he brushed the sleeve of his new shirt across his eyes and nose. As Cherry could see that Nanny Green was about to explode with anger at being spoken to in such a way, she intervened quickly.

'Well, I'm sure none of us knew that camels lived in Australia, Ethan, so that's something else we've all learned today, isn't it?

Now then, shall we all have some tea and talk about other things?'

Thankfully, the maids had arrived with the afternoon tea and the moments passed. But Cherry intended going straight to the library afterwards to try to discover if what Ethan said was correct. She had had no idea that camels existed in Australia either, but if they did, she could well imagine her devil-may-care brother entering the races, especially if there were money prizes to be won. He would win, too, she thought, with a sliver of sisterly pride that annoyed her even as she thought it

As soon as she could, she left the nursery and went to the library. It took a while before she could find any book with a reference to camel habitat, but when she did, it took her completely by surprise. There were apparently many thousands of camels, mostly in the arid parts of the continent, some used for working and many more free-ranging, and she could no longer dispute what Ethan had said. She was so immersed in her reading that she looked up, startled, when she heard the door open.

'What's all this? Are you attempting to educate yourself?' she heard Lance say, in what was probably meant to be a gently teasing tone.

Unfortunately, Cherry didn't see it that way. In view of what had happened last night, she merely saw his words as taunting, reminding her of her previous status in this house. She slammed the covers of the book together.

'I was merely confirming something I needed to know,' she said quickly, 'and I was told you wouldn't be dining here this evening.'

'That's correct. I'll also be spending a couple of nights at my club, to give us both breathing space, and I'm just collecting a change of clothes and the necessary. I shall be here in good time for our meeting with Mr Trelawney on Monday, so I'll leave you to your studies.'

He gave what Cherry considered a mocking small bow and then he was gone, leaving her with her eyes smarting, and wondering how things had ever come to such a pitch. But after a few moments she dashed the tears away and went back to the nursery, to inform them all that Ethan had been quite right about the camels, and it should be a lesson to them all not to be so sceptical about things that happened in foreign lands.

'Australia's not foreign!' Ethan burst out indignantly. '*England's* foreign. Me mum always said so when she said we had to come here, even though we never wanted to in the first place.'

'Just be happy that we don't think you're telling fairy tales, Ethan,' Cherry said evenly, wondering if there was ever such a contrary child, and ignoring the rest. '*Do* we, Nanny Green?'

'I'm sure I'm glad to agree with you, my lady,' the woman said stiffly.

God Almighty, why she did ever have to take on the job of acting as go-between? So there were bloody camels in Australia! Who cared? Hopefully, when David Trelawney arrived, he'd be better informed than Miss Green, and know how to handle boys like the aggressive offspring of Brian O'Neill.

But once she had left them again, she had to face the realization that she was going to spend the rest of this miserable weekend without Lance's company. In his present mood, she shouldn't care, but of course she did. She wanted him back the way he was before Ethan had turned up. She wanted the old carefree days back when she had nothing more to worry about than settling the petty squabbles between her children, without dealing with the monumental ones that seemed to erupt whenever Ethan was around – and even when he wasn't. His very existence had triggered a total change in the tempo of their lives. It wasn't his fault, and she kept trying to believe that . . . but she couldn't escape the fact that nothing was ever going to be the same again, because of him.

The rain looked as though it was set in for the entire weekend. Even the elements were against her, Cherry thought miserably. They couldn't go for walks, and she couldn't see Paula to let off steam. She could telephone Cynthia Hetherington, she supposed, if she wasn't out with her ghastly friend Monica, but then she would be tempted to confide in Cyn over how things were going so very wrong between her and Lance, and that was the last thing she needed to do.

She resorted to trying to do some of the despised knitting

she hated, but it only irritated her more, remembering how it had been old Lady Melchoir who had shown unexpected patience in teaching her how, when she wanted to make a shawl for Paula's baby and was making such a pig's ear of it. Resentfully, she wanted nothing to remind her of those times, when she had been considered the lowest of the low in ensnaring Lady Elspeth's precious son into marriage.

As the lady's image entered her mind, without warning, she was suddenly seeing things through the older couple's eyes. Their army captain son, of whom they were so proud, and who would naturally be expected to marry well and produce male children to carry on the Melchoir line, had instead chosen a kitchen-maid to be his wife. She had nearly put the word *humble* in front of it in her mind, but there had never been anything humble about Cherry O'Neill . . .

Be that as it may, she put the knitting down and clasped her hands together tightly, her heart beating faster. Now that she had heard the full story of the entail and of Lance's frequent discussions with the lawyer to try to thrash things out, she realized instantly how he must also have felt. If anything happened to their darling Georgie, then Brian O'Neill's son would be entitled to Melchoir House, the estate and everything that went with it.

But that was never going to happen, and if Lance was mightily relieved because of it, then so was she. How could he ever think otherwise? It was many years since she had been Cherry O'Neill, kitchen-maid. In some ways, it was like another life, dimly remembered. On their marriage, they had been banished to one of the Melchoir properties in Ireland by his irate parents, who had finally given in to the union, assuming that Cherry was pregnant . . . Or had there been something at the back of Lord Francis Melchoir's mind, even then, that sometime in the future the bastard child of an unmarried kitchen-maid would claim his title, so it would be better to take the lesser of two evils and allow the marriage to take place so that at least any child would be legitimate?

Cherry brushed the unsavoury thought from her mind. In any case, it was pointless to brood over something that had never happened that way. Lance had stood by her, declaring

his love and his intention to marry her, and his parents had
given way. And she and Lance had been happy . . . so
happy . . . The weak tears started to her eyes again and she
longed for the comfort of his arms and for him to tell her that
everything was going to be all right, and that he loved his
Cherry-ripe as much as ever.

Saturday came and went, and Sunday was much the same, with
the rain falling incessantly. The children were fractious and
squabbling, and Cherry didn't feel inclined to suggest church,
with this little band of irritants sitting beside her, and no Lance.
Halfway through the afternoon, she finally sent for Dawkins
and instructed him to take her and the children for a drive to
blow the cobwebs away.

'In this weather, my lady?' he said dubiously.

'In this weather, Dawkins,' she snapped. 'Unless you have
something else you would rather be doing?'

She looked at him coolly, her manner and her gaze reminding
him of who she was, and that he was here to do her bidding.
In her heart, she prayed that he would say he had to fetch
Lance from his club that afternoon, but instead he gave the
smallest of shrugs.

'Very well, my lady. I'll have the car at the front of the
house in fifteen minutes if that will suit you.'

She nodded and went to tell the children that they were
going for a drive.

'It's raining,' Bella complained predictably.

'A little rain won't kill you, Bella,' Cherry said.

'I like rain,' Ethan put in. 'When I was little, me pa used
to say the rain washed all your sins away, not that he ever had
any.'

'How could anybody like rain? You're so stupid, Ethan, and
was your father a saint or something?' Bella said rudely.

Cherry kept her expression firmly neutral, but *oh, my Aussie
lad, I could tell you things about your father that would prove he was
sorely in need of redemption!*

'I like rain because most of the time we never saw any!'
Ethan was shouting again now. 'It was as dry as the desert in
the Outback where we lived, and when we got dust storms,

it got into your throat and nose so you could hardly breathe, and it killed animals and people too.'

Georgie was starting to snivel at the spectre of animals and people being killed by dust, and Cherry took control before they were all at one another's throats again.

'Right. So we're going out in the rain for a drive. Get your coats and hats, and we'll all meet in the front hall in five minutes exactly, and we'll have no more arguments or discussion.'

She was exhausted already, and they hadn't started on this expedition yet. But the more she heard about Ethan O'Neill, and his life in the Outback of Australia with his parents, the more she realized how little she knew of him, and of the later life that her brother had led. And since Ethan had been only six years old when Brian died, it was natural that he had an idealized memory of him.

'Where do you wish to go, Madam?' Dawkins said, once they were all bundled inside the limousine. His annoyance at having to turn out on such a day was tangible, and it made Cherry even more determined to exercise her wishes over him. Damn it, who was the mistress here!

'We'll go to the seaside, Dawkins. It's hardly bucket-and-sand weather, but the children always enjoy the ride, and it will be a novelty for my nephew.'

To them, she said, 'I have your pencils and drawing pads in my bag, and tomorrow you'll be able to show Nanny Green what you've seen today, as well as your father and uncle.'

She distributed them quickly, and saw the spark of interest in Ethan's and Georgie's eyes, even if Bella was still sullen. It was no matter, and, as if by magic, the rain began to ease off at last, and by the time they reached the seaside, a watery sun was overhead. Dawkins stopped the limousine alongside a group of other cars, their owners walking the promenade and enjoying this breath of fresh air after a stuffy couple of days.

Cherry and the children stepped outside. Ethan's eyes were gawping now as he took in the shingle beach, and the pier stretching out into the sea, its Victorian edifice at the far end.

'There are people walking on it,' he said, mystified. 'Is it safe?'

'Of course it is,' Cherry said, thankful to have caught his interest at last. 'We can do the same, if it's what you all want.'

The clamour this time was unanimous, and Cherry breathed a sigh of relief, thankful that she had found something to interest them at last. She wished she had thought to contact Paula and ask if she and Thomas wanted to come too. It would have been a squash, even in the limousine, but it would have been more fun. For a moment, she remembered years ago when she and Paula had taken a charabanc ride to this same seaside, and had gone scampering along the pier, laughing and screaming at the waves far below that lashed the wrought iron sides of the old construction. How very long ago it seemed now. Another lifetime . . . If she didn't stop being so maudlin, she would be the one to ruin this day yet.

Georgie was holding tightly to her hand as they took their first steps along the boards that stretched towards the pavilion at the end, while the other two leaned over the railings to watch the ebb and flow of the tide below. Ethan was clearly fascinated, and Cherry realized anew how little he would have seen of anything like this – apart from the sea voyage from Australia. She didn't think he and his mother could have travelled in any comfort, and it must have been horrendous, she thought for the first time.

'I don't like it. The waves frighten me,' Georgie whispered, and she decided it was best not to make this a very long excursion away from shore.

'We'll just walk halfway and then go back to the car,' she said. 'I don't think it's going to stay fine for much longer, anyway.'

Almost to her relief, she felt a few spots of rain, and the sun had disappeared again. The waters of the Bristol Channel had become pewter grey, as people came hurrying back from the far end of the pier to regain shelter in the safety of their cars before the torrent began.

'The wind's getting up, which will whip up the waves a lot more, and we'd have a fine view from the car,' Cherry suggested. 'You could do your drawings there before we turn for home. Does that sound like a good idea?'

She made it sound as if it was their choice, and to her relief they all agreed. She could see how glad Georgie was to get back inside the limousine, where Dawkins had been waiting for them.

'What's that place over there?' Ethan said, pointing to a distant shoreline through the mist. 'Is it another country?'

Bella whooped with laughter, ready to throw scorn on his assumption, but Cherry corrected her at once.

'Yes, it is, Ethan. It's called Wales, but it's a part of the British Isles. You can look it up on a map when we get home if you like, and see where it joins on to us. Scotland, too.'

She told him naturally, realizing she had referred to Melchoir House as home just as naturally, but at least the boy was showing some interest in the geography of the country, which was more than Bella ever seemed to do. It was still foreign to him, she remembered, all still new.

By the time they reached home, despite the rain coming down heavily again, there was more harmony inside the car, with the older two ready to go indoors and demonstrate which of them had done the best drawings in a healthy state of competition. Georgie had become increasingly pale-faced, and, once inside the house, was immediately sick, which had the maids rushing around him and cleaning him up. Cherry put him to bed for an hour with a cool cloth on his forehead until he felt better, promising to read to him until he fell asleep. When she finally tiptoed out of his bedroom, Ethan was outside the door.

'Will you show me the map like you promised, Auntie Cherry?' he asked. 'I want to see where we've been today, and me and Bella want to show you our drawings so you can say which is best.'

'Come into the library, then, and we'll take the atlas to the nursery together,' Cherry said.

Since he had arrived at Melchoir House, it was one of the very few times he had called her Auntie Cherry, and she choked slightly. She also knew that she had better be very careful choosing which of today's drawings was going to be called the best. Ruffled feathers on her prickly little daughter's part was not something she wanted to provoke, but nor did she want to dampen Ethan's enthusiasm in his new surroundings. So tact had to be the order of the day, and she hoped fervently that, for all her frazzled nerves over these past few days, she would have enough of it.

Thirteen

Dawkins was to fetch Lance from his gentlemen's club at eleven o'clock on Monday morning. The meeting with David Trelawney at Melchoir House had been arranged for three in the afternoon, by which time the children were to be polished and spruced to meet their new tutor once the meeting with his parents was over. There was no doubt that he would be hired, and Cherry knew it was merely a formality. If Lance approved of the man, then she must do so too.

She couldn't decide which was making her more nervous: the reunion with her husband after the heated exchanges that had gone before, which was ridiculous in itself; hoping that the children were going to be on their best behaviour, especially the unpredictable Ethan; or meeting this unknown, well-educated man who was going to play such a part in their lives from now on.

By the time Lance arrived home, she was very sure which was making her more apprehensive: wondering what his mood was going to be. To her relief, he greeted her with a brief smile and said he would join her in half an hour. No kiss, she noted, but perhaps that would come later. So now she had nothing to do but wait in the drawing room, wishing he was here to reassure her that this meeting was nothing to be nervous about.

All the same, she couldn't help feeling that meeting this Trelawney was putting her on parade as much as the children. Although Lance had a much higher social status than the tutor, Trelawney was still streets above Cherry Melchoir *née* O'Neill . . . and if she didn't stop thinking of herself in that way, she told herself severely, she'd be a nervous wreck by the time they all met.

So it was an even greater relief when Lance joined her again, appearing far more natural than before. Of course, he already knew very well that he was going to get his way over the tutor, and in doing so presumably he expected the O'Neill boy to be brought into line in manners and education, so that at least he wouldn't show up the proud name of Melchoir. She could see it all so clearly now, but she couldn't blame Lance for it, either. Why wouldn't he want all the children in his household to conform to the comfortable life they experienced?

'I presume Mr Trelawney will be living in, once he begins his work here, Lance,' she said a little awkwardly, knowing she should have clarified this before now. 'Should I instruct the maids to prepare a room for him?'

'It won't be necessary. I understand he has some relatives living just outside the town, and he intends to lodge with them and drive himself to Melchoir House daily.'

'I see.' She felt like childishly clapping her hands with relief. The last thing she wanted was a stranger in the house at all hours, sharing their meals, having to make polite conversation with him constantly . . .

'I can see that you're pleased,' Lance said, allowing himself a real smile now. 'It doesn't altogether displease me, either. Far better to have the house to ourselves, eh, Cherry-ripe?'

She caught her breath at the sudden use of his pet name for her. She gave a shaky laugh.

'Well, apart from the children, and Nanny Green, Mr Gerard and Dawkins, and the stable-boys, and Cook and the maids—'

Lance laughed back. 'Old Uncle Tom Cobley and all, you mean! But they have their quarters and we have ours. So they don't bother us, do they?'

'Not at all,' Cherry said, thankful that this was the first natural conversation they had had in what seemed like weeks. And if she had once been one of those others, confined to lesser quarters, that was a very long time ago.

She just hoped this Trelawney was going to have a good influence on Ethan, knowing, to her chagrin, that it was because of him that they had to go down this road at all.

Despite all, though, by the time the meeting drew near, she was a bundle of nerves again, and some of her apprehension was starting to affect Lance.

'For goodness' sake, Cherry, don't look so worried. The man's a servant like the rest of them, that's all. He's coming to do a job, for which he'll be well paid, providing he does it properly. Just remember that you're the lady of the house, so stop looking so servile. It doesn't become you.'

Oh God, couldn't he see the irony of his words? But apparently not, and she should be pleased. She *was* the lady of the house . . .

Promptly, at the appointed time, Gerard came to the drawing room and announced that Mr Trelawney had arrived, and then moved away from the door as Lance and Cherry stood up to greet him. And Cherry had her first shock.

She didn't know what she had expected. The whole prospect of some learned male tutor invading the house had been on her mind ever since Lance had suggested it. In her mind, she had had the vague image of some stern, elderly professor who was going to scare her to death with his superior knowledge, and undoubtedly scare Georgie as well.

Instead . . . here was this absolute vision of manhood . . . she tried not to let the superfluous words enter her mind, but she could think of him as nothing less. He was almost beautiful, if you could call a man beautiful. He was slim and young – not much older than Lance himself, she guessed – his hair a shock of gold, his eyes as blue as the sea, his smile attractively wide. She was struck dumb, thankful that at least Lance had met him before and knew what to expect, even if he hadn't thought fit to inform *her*! So she could stand as still as a statue as Lance stepped forward to shake his hand and introduce him to his wife.

'I'm delighted to make your acquaintance, Lady Melchoir,' the tutor said, the underlying traces of a Cornish accent delightful and warm to her ears.

'Thank you, Mr Trelawney,' Cherry murmured, extricating her hand from his, while hardly knowing how it had got there.

She felt as if she was in a grip of some madness. Her head swirled and her stomach felt tight. It absolutely *couldn't* be, of course, but for one crazy moment she felt totally smitten.

The feeling passed, and she shook herself as Lance bade them all to sit down while they discussed their business before the tutor was introduced to the children. Not that there was anything for her to say. This was men's business, dealing with hours and tuition, the names and ages of the children, and so on.

'You'll find my wife's nephew a difficult boy at first, Trelawney, not being native to this country, but I have no doubt you'll find a way to overcome his resentment at being here far easier than Miss Green,' Lance was saying now.

Cherry noted that Ethan was now definitely *her* nephew, but she hardly cared. The fact that this beautiful young man was going to care for him would surely bring out the best in him. Georgie would love him, and as for Bella . . . During all the hours they would spend together, Bella would probably adore him too, Cherry thought generously, not for a second letting a thread of jealousy for her own daughter enter her head.

After what was obviously a satisfactory meeting between the two men, at which Cherry merely had to sit and listen and put in the occasional comment, Lance suggested that it was time for Trelawney to meet his new pupils. He turned to Cherry.

'Would you ring down for tea to be sent up to the nursery in half an hour, my dear? For the children, Mr Trelawney and Miss Green, and ourselves, and please join us shortly.'

'Of course,' Cherry said, and waited until the two men had left the room, practically as thick as thieves, while she sat and wilted for a few moments.

This was how things were done in the best households, of course. Even if she had wanted to have a say in her own children's future education, it was not the done thing. The important decisions in any marriage were still the man's role . . . and no matter how triumphant the day when women had finally got the vote, things were unlikely to change for a good while yet, if ever. While men held the purse strings, how could they?

But she knew very well that all this idle surmising was only to put off the instant when she faced the fact that, for a few blinding moments, she had been wildly attracted at first sight to the handsome young tutor who had come into their lives.

Madness it certainly was . . . and it wouldn't last, of course. It couldn't, and *mustn't* last . . . not while she still loved her husband to distraction, the way she always had.

Pushing all other idiotic thoughts aside, she hastily rang the bell and gave Josie her instructions as soon as the maid arrived – turning up so promptly that she must have been hovering fairly near, Cherry guessed. The next minute she was proved right.

'Was that the new young gentleman who's going to teach the children, my lady?' Josie said excitedly. 'Me and Doris were in the kitchen garden pulling carrots when we saw the car arrive. Ever so handsome, ain't he? Like one of them Greek gods!'

Cherry managed an amused laugh. 'Greek gods indeed! Where did you ever hear of such things?'

'It was in a book that Mr Gerard showed us once. They all had this golden hair and lovely smiles, just like the new young gentleman.'

'Well, never mind about all that, Josie. Just get the tea and cakes sent up to the nursery in half an hour, and don't waste time daydreaming about such things as Greek gods!'

Not that she could have described him better herself . . .

Minutes later, she joined the company in the nursery, and found the three children listening dutifully to what Mr David Trelawney was telling them. It seemed that he was a fairly progressive teacher, keen on things other than learning the three Rs. Healthy in mind and body was to be the order of the day, he told them, and Cherry kept her thoughts steadfastly on the words and not the images he evoked. There would be plenty of nature walks, no matter what the weather, and they would learn about birds and flowers and trees and the native habitat of where they lived, as well as faraway places.

'I approve, Trelawney,' Lance told him later, after one and another of the children had clamoured to ask more. 'You've clearly captured their interest, and for that I applaud you.'

And it seemed to be the type of outdoor lesson that the stout Miss Green had certainly never have considered. Ethan was certainly emboldened to ask the tutor about camels, and was rewarded by hearing that Trelawney did indeed know that camels lived in Australia; he knew when they had first arrived there, and the work that they did. All of which made Ethan throw a triumphant glance at both Cherry and Nanny Green.

She was glad when the afternoon tea arrived, and she didn't miss the admiring looks that Josie gave the tutor, nor the way in which he smiled back at her so freely. So he was a ladies' man, Cherry thought, and it shouldn't surprise her. Though whether a university-educated man would be attracted by Josie's flashing eyes and pert figure was something else. At the thought, she almost dropped her cup, for nothing of the sort had prevented Captain Lance Melchoir, as he had been then, from pursuing *her*. For centuries it had been almost an accepted sport for the higher classes to take their pleasure with the lower ones, if both sides were agreeable. And even if they were not . . .

'Do I take it I have your approval on my methods too, Lady Melchoir?' she heard Trelawney say a little while later in that seductively attractive accent.

'I approve of any method that my husband does, and which will benefit the children,' she said sweetly, not betraying for a moment that she suddenly recognized the challenging look in those blue eyes.

My God, he knows exactly what power he has over women, she found herself thinking, whatever their role in life. What was more, she intended to warn Josie delicately to be careful. It was her duty to look after the kitchen-maids, and she knew only too well how easy it was to be carried away by lust disguised as love. Except that in her case it had always been love.

She was very glad when the afternoon came to an end, and the arrangements for David Trelawney to begin work with the children on the following Monday morning had been put in place. She was even more thankful that it was not a living-in post, and she decided there and then that she would be the one to inform the kitchen staff. There was no hurry, and first of all she wanted to telephone Paula. But not today. Tomorrow would be soon enough, when Lance was out riding Prince in the morning, exercising man and beast, as he called it, and she could speak to Paula at leisure and in private.

At least she and Lance were being sociable towards one another, she reflected. Almost too polite . . . as though they were tiptoeing around one another for fear of saying the wrong thing or letting tempers flare. He shouldn't worry, she thought bitterly. He had got his way in everything, as usual. Nearly everything . . .

That night she lay in bed beside him rigidly, knowing he wouldn't bother her since she had left a clear message that her monthly visitor had arrived, still feeling a small triumph that his savage treatment of her wasn't going to give him another child. Even as she thought it, she felt a small tear trickle down her cheek, sad that the love and passion between them had turned to this. She must have made a small moan in her throat, because he turned to her at once, his hand on her shoulder.

'Don't ever be afraid of me, Cherry,' he said in a low voice. 'I know what I did was wrong, and I bitterly regret it. I hope you know that.'

And, as always, her generous heart forgave him at once.

She was impatient for him to leave the next morning to go riding across the Downs, joined by one or other of his friends – part of 'the horsey set', as Paula called them. And once everyone was settled, the children in the nursery with Nanny Green, and breakfast long over, she went into the drawing room to telephone Paula, knowing she wouldn't be disturbed. The minute she heard her friend's diffident voice on the phone, her face relaxed into a smile.

'Good morning, Mrs Farmer,' she said in an imperious voice. 'I trust I'm speaking to the lady of the house?'

There was silence for a moment, and then Paula shrieked into the phone, forcing Cherry to hold the receiver away from her ear.

'God Almighty, Cherry, you nearly gave me a heart attack. I thought it was the bailiffs or something – not that I know any lady bailiffs, nor that me and Harold are in any kind of trouble, but hell's bells, it nearly gave me the squits!'

Cherry was laughing by the end of the tirade, glad to know that at least something in her world was exactly the same as it had always been. She could always rely on Paula!

'I'm sorry about that, Paula,' she said contritely, 'but I couldn't resist it.'

'Well, try and resist it next time. Anyway, what's up?'

'Why should anything be up?'

Paula snorted. 'I know you, and I can guess this ain't just a social call. So what's he like?'

'Who?'

'Oh come on, Cherry, aren't you about to give me the low-down on this new tutor fellow for your kids? I bet he's proper toffee-nosed, old and balding, and so professor-like that he scared you half to death. Am I right?' she finished on a giggle.

'You couldn't be more wrong,' Cherry said, her breath catching for a moment as the image of David Trelawney filled her mind, blue eyes and wide smile, and that soft hint of a Cornish accent . . .

'Blimey, don't tell me he's like one of them film stars, and that you've fallen for him. Old Lance will have to look to his laurels, won't he?' Paula chuckled, clearly not believing it for a minute.

Cherry blinked the unwelcome image of a young, virile David Trelawney out of her head. 'Don't be so daft, and stop calling Lance old. Anyway, that's not the main reason I'm calling you.'

'What is it, then?'

Cherry hesitated again. They had always told one another everything in the past, but the past was a long time ago, and time and circumstances changed people. There had just been the two of them then, sharing secrets in the dark of their servants' bedroom, confident of one another's loyalty. She was just as sure of Paula's loyalty as she had ever been, but it was no longer just the two of them to consider. Now there were other people deserving of their loyalties, and she couldn't betray what had happened between her and Lance the other night, nor her own shame and humiliation because of it.

'I'm wondering when we're going to see each other again,' she said hurriedly. 'This weekend was so miserable with the rain, and I missed you, Paula. I'm sure the children missed seeing Thomas too.'

'Ah,' Paula said.

'*Ah*? What does that mean? Didn't you miss seeing me?'

'Of course I did, but Thomas had a few of his pals round playing with his train set in his bedroom, so it was a pretty noisy Saturday afternoon in our house, with me baking cakes and pouring glasses of lemonade all afternoon to keep up with their appetites.'

In other words, Thomas was perfectly happy not to continue their usual Saturdays on the Downs, and his rowdy Saturday afternoon with his pals clearly couldn't compare with having to make small talk with the prissy daughter and small son of a Lord, not to mention the other one . . . She caught herself up short.

'Well, let's hope this Saturday will be sunnier, then,' she said at last.

'As a matter of fact, Cherry – and don't take this the wrong way – I don't think it's such a good idea any more.'

For a few seconds, Cherry felt as if her whole world was falling apart. First, the arrival of Ethan had thrown her life into chaos, then Lance's attack on her the other night, and now her best and dearest friend was telling her she didn't want to know her any more. It was too much . . . too much . . .

'Paula, don't do this,' she said in a choked voice. 'Why don't you want to see me any more?'

'Of course I want to see you . . . it's just what Harold said, that's all.'

'What did Harold say?'

Dear God, it was like drawing teeth . . .

'You're not going to like this, Cherry, but I knew I'd have to tell you sooner or later. Harold don't want our Thomas having anything to do with your brother's kid. There, now I've said it, and I'm sorry if it offends you, but I've got to do what Harold says in this, Cherry. I did promise to love, honour and obey him. You do see that, don't you?' But despite what she was saying, her voice was becoming increasingly agitated and upset.

Oh yes, Cherry saw it all right, and how could she blame anybody for not wanting to get tangled up with Brian O'Neill's son? It was the last thing she herself had ever wanted to do.

But she had had no choice, and she wanted to shriek down the phone that, irritating though Ethan was, he wasn't Brian. She tried desperately to hold herself in check. If it was ironic that the plain-speaking railwayman, former house painter and decorator, should have the gall to look down his nose at the nephew of a Lord, she managed not to say it.

'Of course I do, Paula, and I'm not blaming you for Harold's views. I don't always agree with everything Lance says, but we both made our vows, didn't we?'

It was the most she was ever going to say about what had happened between her and Lance, and how their idyllic marriage was no longer quite as idyllic any more.

'But there's nothing to stop you and me from meeting, is there?' Paula said hopefully. 'I couldn't bear it if this spoiled our friendship, Cherry.'

'And we won't let it,' Cherry said emphatically. 'Let's decide to meet one afternoon every week at Smithy's for afternoon tea, starting tomorrow. Truth to tell, it will be good to be able to talk without the children around, won't it?'

'That sounds smashing,' Paula said, and Cherry could hear the break in her voice, knowing very well that when she hung up the phone, Paula would go off and have a good howl, the way she always did when they had had words.

'I'll see you there tomorrow, then, about two o'clock,' she said efficiently, just as though it was a business meeting.

She put down the phone carefully and sat staring at it for a few minutes. How odd it was, how very odd, that the very ordinary, working-class Harold Farmer should be so damn snobbish over having his son mix with Ethan O'Neill! If Lance got to hear of it, he would be furious. So that was why he was never going to know, she thought doggedly.

She felt more restless than she had expected after talking to Paula, who could normally bring her down to earth with a tease and a laugh. But today was different. They had both been keeping things from one another, and even though Paula's concerns were now out in the open and the air had been cleared, Cherry felt that somehow something very dear had been lost between them.

She was hot and upset. The children were at their lessons

with Nanny Green, Lance was out, and she suddenly felt very alone. The house was stifling her, and she needed to get outside. For October, the weather was still very mild, and after the weekend's rain the air was fresh, and all the leaves that were starting to turn into glorious autumn colours glowed like fire. She slipped on a coat and wandered out into the garden, breathing in the stillness and the remaining fragrance of late-blooming flowers.

The sound of giggling alerted her. It came from the kitchen garden nearby, and she could see two of the maids there now. They saw her at the same time, and one of them darted back indoors as if being caught slacking, while the other bent down to continue pulling up carrots for the evening's meal and putting them into a trug. On an impulse, Cherry walked purposefully towards her.

'Good morning, Josie,' she said.

'Good morning, my lady,' the girl said in some confusion. 'I'm sorry if me and Doris disturbed you. We were just having a bit of a gossip.'

'It's no matter. But I'm glad to have this moment with you.'

The girl looked at her warily, saying nothing as she waited for Cherry to continue.

'Josie, I hope you'll take what I'm about to say very seriously and understand that, as your employer, I'm duty-bound to say it.'

'Have I done something wrong, my lady?'

'No, and nor will you, I hope. But it's very easy for a servant-girl to get carried away by what she imagines to be a young man's attention. I'm trying to be as delicate as possible, but I couldn't help noticing the way you were looking at the children's new tutor yesterday.'

'I never did, Madam!' Josie said hotly, her face scarlet.

'I'm not saying you did anything wrong, Josie, and I'm sure there's nothing to worry about at all. But I want you to be aware that an educated person of his class may be just as flattered by the glances of a pretty girl as someone in your position would be in return. Just be careful, my dear, that's all I'm saying.'

Oh God, she was making such a clumsy mess of this. A real

pig's ear of it, as Paula would say . . . and the redness in Josie's face had now turned into something far uglier.

'Well, I'm sure you'd know all about that, Madam – far more than a poor servant-girl like me would do,' she said insolently.

Dear God, she knows! She knows all about Lance and me . . . but how could she know? Cherry would have counted on Gerard and Cook's loyalty to the death, and no one else here had any idea . . . but if there was any time to put her acting skills to use, it was surely now.

Her voice was calm and concerned. 'What I know, Josie, is that if any servant in a good household was caught in salacious circumstances with someone above their station, they would face instant dismissal with no references. Her reputation would be ruined, and her good name would be sullied for ever.'

And, for all her control, she knew she spoke with very good authority. But for the grace of God and the love of a good man, it could so very easily have happened to her. She looked at the girl unblinkingly, half-expecting some further sly remark as to what she knew – or surmised. But whatever was going around inside her head, after a few seconds Josie wilted.

'I understand completely, my lady,' she said humbly. 'I know there are always rogues who would take advantage of girls like us – like me and Doris, I mean – and I'll be very careful in future.'

Or, as both Cherry and Paula might once have said, 'be sure to keep your 'and on your ha'penny' . . .

'Well done,' Cherry said aloud, in some relief. 'And I only felt obliged to say this to you because it's always the pretty ones that such men see as fair game.'

Josie gave a little bob. 'Then I thank you for the compliment, my lady, and if you'll excuse me now, I must get these carrots indoors for Cook.'

Cherry let her go, feeling completely wrung-out. She wasn't even sure if she had done the right thing, or if Lance would have approved, and not for a single moment would she admit that the last thing she would have wanted to see was the new tutor and the maid making eyes at one another.

In any case, since talking to Paula, and now to Josie, the

brief sense of madness she had felt at his presence was fast starting to wane, and she wondered if he was indeed something of a womanizer, with his warm eyes and ready smiles, and, if so, just how much she wanted him in her house. However, there was nothing she could do about it now. Lance approved of the man, the children seemed to like him, and so she must learn to tolerate him too.

Fourteen

The following afternoon, Cherry arrived at Smithy's Tea Shop before Paula did, knowing that her friend would dither if she got there on her own. Cherry was already seated at an alcove table when she waved to Paula through the window. The other woman came inside, looking a little uncomfortable at the smart interior, but Cherry said brightly that she had already ordered tea, so that once the waitress brought it, they could have a good gossip. Her chatter was intended to put Paula at her ease, but it did the same for Cherry too, breaking the first awkward moments after yesterday's conversation.

She couldn't resist saying something, all the same.

'We're all right, aren't we, Paula? You and me, I mean.'

Or should that be 'You and I'?

''Course we are. 'Twould take more'n a few bad words to break us up, wouldn't it?' Paula said.

That was the best thing about long-standing friendship. You could easily take a running jump over any fancy, long-winded apologies and get right back to where you were with the minimum of fuss. And as the waitress was approaching their table now, all they had to do was wait for two cups of tea to be poured out, choose one of the delicious cream cakes, and enjoy each other's company.

'So are you going to tell me some more about this teacher chappie, then?' Paula said.

'He's called a tutor, *actually,* darling,' Cherry said, poker-faced. But her lips twitched, and then they were both laughing.

'Whatever you say! So is he really gorgeous-looking?'

'Well, I can't deny that.' A small frown crept between her eyebrows and Paula noted it at once.

'You ain't really expecting trouble in paradise, are you? I was only kidding when I said Lance would have to look to his laurels, Cherry. I know you've only got eyes for him.'

Cherry shook her head. 'It's not that. It's one of the maids – Josie. I had a few words with her yesterday after I'd telephoned you, and warned her delicately not to get carried away by a handsome young man above her station.'

'Blimey, that was rich, coming from you, kid, if you'll pardon me for saying so,' Paula said with a chuckle.

'Don't worry, I didn't miss the irony of what I was saying, but it was what she said in return, and the way she said it, that shook me.'

'Well, what did she say?' Paula asked, when Cherry fell silent.

She hadn't been going to tell her anything. She had intended keeping it to herself, but it would only have festered there, and if she couldn't confide in Paula, knowing she could trust her discretion, she couldn't confide in anyone.

She spoke slowly, feeling as if the words were being dragged unwillingly out of her. 'She said, "Well, I'm sure you'd know all about that, Madam – far more than a poor servant-girl like me would do."'

'*Bloody hell*,' Paula said, loud enough for several ladies at other tables to glance their way and tut-tut disapprovingly.

'I think she knew very well what she was implying, Paula, and it shook me rigid, I can tell you. I mean, how could she possibly know the truth about Lance and me? There are so few people who do. Only Gerard and Cook downstairs, since the other skivvies are new, but I do know they felt obliged to tell them something, and Gerard made them sign a document of loyalty to us.'

'Blimey, did he? But they're not the only ones, Cherry,' Paula said.

'Well, my brother's dead, and even if he told his wife everything, I'm quite sure they wouldn't have told their son about such things.'

'I didn't mean Brian.'

'Who, then?' Her heart was beginning to pound now. She had only considered Gerard and Cook when she thought about who could have let slip anything to Josie, but Paula was scaring her now.

'There's Cynthia Hetherington and her parents, and anybody

else of their acquaintance, although, knowing their sort, I don't suppose they'd care to brag about Lord Melchoir marrying beneath him, since it would rub off on them, wouldn't it? So we can forget them. And then there's Harold and me.'

'Harold and you?' Cherry echoed.

Her face suddenly flooded with colour as she saw the guarded look in Paula's eyes. 'My God, Paula, you don't think I would ever dream of thinking you or Harold would go gossiping about me and Lance? Such a thing never entered my head, not for a single minute!'

'Good. It might have done, though,' Paula muttered.

'It never would. I would trust you with my life, and if I trust you, then I trust Harold too.'

'Well, just to clear the air between us once and for all, let me assure you that me and Harold have never discussed what happened from that day to this. And if we had — which we haven't — we would certainly never do it in our Thomas's hearing either! I know what trouble kids' tittle-tattle can cause, so you can feel easy about that as well.'

'I'd never even thought about any of it, Paula,' Cherry said, feeling more distressed now as all the possibilities Paula was putting in her head began to take shape. But she was sure Josie hadn't been talking idly, so there must be more to it, and she had to find out . . . and she was still torn over whether or not to tell Lance.

'I can see I've upset you even more now, haven't I?' Paula was saying. 'Perhaps us meeting like this wasn't such a good idea, after all.'

'Don't say that. It was the *best* idea,' Cherry said fervently. 'You've always been my best friend, and nothing's going to change that. You're the only one I can tell what's in my heart, so don't desert me now, Paula.'

'I ain't deserting you, you ninny. Pour us out another cuppa, if it ain't beneath you, your ladyship. I'm parched with all this talking, and then tell me how long this teacher-tutor chap is staying.'

Cherry did as she was bid while she collected her thoughts together.

'Initially, it's for six months, but probably longer if Lance is satisfied with him. I must say, he has some rather progressive ideas.'

'Does he? What does that mean?' Paula said, with raised eyebrows.

Cherry shrugged. 'He seems very keen on outdoor pursuits and exercise, and, as you know, Nanny Green is definitely not an outdoor person. The children will be getting plenty of nature walks and studying plant life, as well as art and geography and the usual lessons. Mr Trelawney believes in widening the mind in all directions.'

'Blimey. He sounds a bit of a nutter if you ask me.'

Cherry laughed. 'Lance approves of him, anyway, and as he's not living in, I doubt that I'll need to see much of him.'

Her look dared Paula to make any further comment. Instead, she asked about Thomas's progress at school, and listened to chapter and verse about his general lack of interest in schoolwork.

'Never mind. With his dad behind him, there'll always be a job for him on the railways, I'm sure,' Paula finished cheerfully. 'So what happens to young Ethan when his six months or so with golden boy is up?'

'I don't know. That's up to Lance.'

'And Bella? Or doesn't she need anything other than to grow into a beautiful young lady and marry the right kind of beau, don't-yer-know?'

Cherry grinned, refusing to take offence, because it was all so bloody well true! 'Something like that,' she said airily.

They parted on good terms, promising to make their Wednesday afternoon a regular occurrence now, and Cherry admitted it was a relief not to have had the children around. It was also a refreshingly rare occasion, and she wondered why they hadn't done it before. Always having to keep their eyes on their offspring, especially any problems between Ethan and Thomas Farmer, was only going to stretch their friendship. It was far better this way, just two old friends chatting socially over afternoon tea in a congenial location.

Cherry walked home thoughtfully, glad of the pale October sunshine that had dried out the dampness of the grassy Downs by now. And as she neared the estate, she thought how beautiful Melchoir House looked, its mellow stones washed clean by the rain, its solid foundations reeking of old money. She could understand so well how the classes that had owned and cared for these old houses for generations would want to preserve them for the future. How they would resent upstarts from the lower classes or, God forbid, from people in *trade* muscling in on their proud domains . . . She could finally understand old Lord and Lady Melchoir's horror when Lance had professed his determination to marry a kitchen-maid.

She could understand it, because, imperceptibly over the years, she had become just as fierce in her longing to keep everything the way it had always been kept. As for Paula's casual remark that the Hetheringtons, too, had known all about the circumstances of her and Lance's marriage . . . well, they were of the old school too, and for once she was heartily glad of it, knowing they would simply close ranks if their own were threatened in any way.

She gave a rueful smile. Had she at last become one of them? Her children clearly thought so, knowing nothing else of her but the genteel tones in which she spoke, betraying nothing of her background in word or deed. Yes, the actress in her had carried it off well, and Lance should be glad that she had never once let him down. Remembering that, she held her head high as she went indoors to resume her role as the lady of the house.

There was a note for her on the silver tray in the drawing room, requesting her to have a word with Cook about some problem in the kitchen when she could spare a moment. She felt a small upheaval in her heart. Was this fortuitous? Should she seize the moment to sound out Cook about whether anything had ever been said about the circumstances that had brought her and Lance together?

She wouldn't plan or anticipate anything. How could she? She would simply let events dictate what happened. She ran lightly down the stairs to the kitchen to see what problem demanded her attention.

'Oh, my lady,' Cook said, all of a fluster, as soon as she arrived.

'I'm sorry to have bothered you. It was all a misunderstanding and it's been resolved now. That silly maid should have removed the note before you saw it.'

'Never mind, Cook, as long as all's well with you. So where is everybody?' she asked, realizing that the kitchen was unusually quiet.

'I've sent two of 'em to buy provisions. T'others are doing jobs, and Mr Gerard's taking his half-day as usual. I trust that's all right?' she said. Having known Cherry for so long, she was suddenly aware that she looked less than easy. 'Is there summat else you wanted to say to me? If it's not overstepping the mark, there's a pot of tea brewing.'

There was always a pot of tea brewing . . . and although Cherry thought she might well be wallowing in liquid if she wasn't careful, she sat down at the scrubbed table and allowed Cook to pour her a cup.

'Now then, my dear,' Cook said with long-used familiarity. 'I know when summat's troubling you, so let's have it. Is it summat to do with the young boy?'

'Not that I'm aware of, Cook,' Cherry said with the ghost of a smile. 'It's something Josie said – and I may have been imagining it, but it's been worrying me ever since, and although I hate doing this, I have to ask.'

She stopped abruptly. What was she doing, about to accuse her most loyal of supporters all these years of betraying her and Lance's deepest secret?

'Then I think you'd better ask it before you explode,' Cook said dryly.

She repeated the incident quickly, and she saw the woman's face blanch. Oh God, had she right after all? Had talk about the scandal of Captain Lance Melchoir falling for a kitchen-maid been bandied about downstairs, when it had all been forgotten years ago?

'Cherry, my dear, I can only offer my apologies and try to explain what happened. It came about because of your brother's son appearing out of the blue and giving me the fright of my life, and then me trying to explain in my clumsy way how he came to be related to you. The maids wouldn't let it go, and we didn't know how much of it the boy himself knew, so in the end, after a lot of discussion, me and Gerard took it upon ourselves to give them the very briefest details, and nothing more. And we made them all swear on the Bible never to divulge any of it to a living soul.' She was clearly agitated and distressed now. 'I'm deeply sorry for it, my lady, but it seemed best to stop them speculating any more, and if you want me to leave, I'll go at once.'

'Don't be so daft, Cook. Of course I don't want you to go! What would I do without your pies and pastries?' Cherry said in a choked voice.

All the same, she couldn't deny that her head was whirling. So those maids did know, and Josie had been doing her insolent best to let her know it. But remembering the outcome of that little spat, Cherry knew she had put her firmly in her place. If she began any gossip and was dismissed without a reference, she would get no more work in any respectable household.

'What are you going to do?' Cook went on uneasily.

Cherry took a deep breath. 'Absolutely nothing except finish my tea. And as far as you and I are concerned, this conversation never took place. I think that's best, don't you?'

'Then I thank you humbly, my lady.'

Cherry gave a short laugh, 'Oh come off it, Cook. You've never been humble in your life, and it's a bit late to start now, isn't it? Just carry on ruling the kitchen with a rod of iron the way you always have.'

She stood up and pressed the older woman's shoulder for a moment before going back upstairs, into her bedroom, and sagging on to her bed. These last few days had been some of the worst in her life – almost – but somehow she had come through them the way she always did. Brian 'Knuckles' O'Neill wasn't the only family member with steel in his heart when it was needed . . . and the unbidden thought opened the floodgates of tears and memory. It lasted longer than expected, but she finally emerged, dry-eyed and pale, but once more the lady of the house, ready to join her children in the nursery, now to be called the schoolroom, to hear how they had spent their day.

For Lance, the week had resumed its usual pattern. He exercised Prince in the mornings, and he spent the afternoons in his study attending to estate work, or driving around the various properties that were part of the estate, or ensconced with his lawyer at his club. Cherry suspected there was always a certain amount of libation at the latter, as she could always detect it on his breath. Not that he ever overstepped the mark, and it was presumably just enough to relax him. Ever since Ethan O'Neill had arrived in their lives, he was more tense than he had ever been, she thought miserably, constantly guilty that she and her family had brought about this change in him.

She tried to be as loving as she could, while still feeling a certain restraint herself, never quite sure if she was going to be rebuffed or not. They shared the same bed, but because of her present temporary condition there was no question of their making love. And the nearer the time came to the advent of the new regime with the tutor, the more anxious she became.

'Why don't you tell me what's troubling you, Cherry?' he finally said in a low voice that night, aware of her uneven breathing as they lay together in the soft darkness.

She drew in her breath as she felt his hand steal over her breast and rest there lightly.

'I'm sorry,' he said, and removed it at once. At which point, she caught hold of it and replaced it with her hand over his.

'No, don't take it away. I like it there,' she whispered.

The pressure on her flesh increase a fraction, but he could tell there was no invitation in her voice and no physical response to his touch.

'Then tell me what's wrong. If I don't know, I can't help.'

It was so very tempting to tell him everything she knew about Josie's snide remark, and about Cook's reassurance, but if she did that, she would have to betray her knowledge that Cook and Gerard had decided it was best to let the kitchen staff know about her own background. Lance might be calm and gentle now, but she knew he would flare up into a rage in an instant, and two old retainers who had been with them for years might well be out of a job by morning, and she could never do that to them.

'It's silly, really. I suppose I'm being over-anxious that the children will get along with Mr Trelawney. It's the thought of how everything is changing.'

'When did such a thing ever bother a girl of your spirit? Worrying about changing times is for old women, not for my bright and beautiful Cherry-ripe!'

She caught her breath again as he folded her into him. This wasn't the time for passion and he knew it, but she couldn't fail to feel the hardness of his body as he cuddled her close.

'You see what you do to me?' he said in an amused voice. 'Some things never change, and even though I know I must bide my time for a few days yet, just keep that thought in mind, sweetheart!'

She smiled back in the darkness, thinking that, for these few sweet moments at least, he was so like the lover she had first known, the man who was the love of her life, and always would be.

'I do love you, Lance,' she whispered.

'No more than I love you, Cherry-ripe,' he said, and she was still held in the circle of his arms when she fell asleep.

The children were spruced up and ready when Monday morning came. Ethan was eager and excited to start the new lessons with Mr Trelawney now, having always scorned the idea of being taught by Nanny Green. Bella was haughtily unconcerned, at least on the surface, while Georgie was a little apprehensive.

'It will be all right, darling,' Cherry assured him. 'I'm sure Mr Trelawney won't make you do anything you're not capable of doing.'

'Do you think he'll let me have a ride in his car?' Georgie said.

'*I* wouldn't let you, so there's an end to it,' Cherry said firmly. 'Mr Trelawney is here as your tutor and nothing more.'

She ignored his small pout and left them to await Trelawney's arrival. She saw his car roar along the long driveway and stop outside the front of the house, and gave a frown. He should know his place and arrive at the side entrance, where there was access to the schoolroom, and she would make sure Gerard informed him of such. If she was asserting her position, she had every right to do so. She sought out Gerard during the morning and mentioned it.

'It's already done, my lady,' he said, to her satisfaction. 'The gentleman has already removed the motor car and won't be parking it there again.'

'Thank you, Gerard. I might have known you would be alert to it.'

He hesitated. 'And if I might be so bold, my lady – apropos of the conversation you never had with Cook the other day – may I assure you that the kitchen staff have been made aware in no uncertain terms about where their loyalties lie.'

'I see. Then I'm glad to know that we are in agreement over many things, Gerard, including imaginary conversations.'

She received a slight bow in return. Things had once been so starchy between them, when he had taken such umbrage at one of his own minions marrying the son and heir to Melchoir House and becoming his mistress. But, over the years, they had formed a more than mutual respect for one another, and Cherry would even go so far as to say he would always be her champion, if the need arose.

She breathed more easily, knowing that he and Cook would always keep their eagle eyes on the young maids, making sure there was no hanky-panky going on between them and any kitchen callers or tradesmen, and certainly no golden-haired tutors who were out of their class!

But she couldn't deny that she was anxious for this first school day to be over, and to see what the children had made of it. Trelawney had left by the time their tea was brought up to the schoolroom, and she was pleased to see that Lance had joined them. So he should, since it was his idea to engage the tutor, but she was never sure of his moods these days. Today, however, he was quite jovial.

'We're going for a nature walk tomorrow, Mummy,' Georgie shouted at her, the minute she entered the door. 'We're going to look for beetles and spiders, and Mr Trelawney is bringing a glass thing for us to see them much bigger.'

'He means a magnifying glass,' Ethan put in. 'We're going to take our sketch pads and sketch what we see, and then we're going to learn the background of whatever creatures we find.'

'How interesting,' Cherry said, taken aback by his sudden
enthusiasm – and by the way his shining eyes had the same
gleam of excitement in them that Brian's used to have when
he had some unsavoury scheme in mind. She turned to her
daughter quickly.

'What do you think, Bella?'

The girl screwed up her nose in a way that would have had
the Honourable Cynthia Hetherington's mama telling her that
she should stop doing it at once or it would spoil her pretty
looks . . .

'I think it all sounds disgusting. Nanny Green never made
us inspect horrible things like that.'

'I should think not,' the woman put in severely.

'It's not disgusting and horrible. It's nature,' Ethan snapped.
'I saw far worse things in the Bush. Everything has a right to
exist, and, for all you know, beetles and spiders might be just
as curious about us!'

'Now you're being plain stupid,' Bella snapped back.

'And you're just being a *girl*!'

Cherry was astonished to see that Lance was grinning widely
at this heated exchange going on now between them. If nothing
else, David Trelawney had certainly given them all something
to think about, and argue about, and become animated about,
and that couldn't be such a bad thing.

'Well, why don't we all forget about beetles and spiders for
the moment and have our tea?' she said, playing the peacemaker.
'I'm sure there will be many more interesting things that Mr
Trelawney will be teaching you in the days to come.'

It wasn't all for Ethan's benefit, of course, but he certainly
seemed to have come alive more than any of them. She was
glad. It couldn't have easy for the boy to try to settle into a
household of strangers, even if one of them was his aunt –
especially a household that hadn't wanted him here and made
no bones about showing it. And if *she* didn't feel defensive
about the boy from time to time, who else was going to?

'Well, today seems to have gone fairly well,' Lance said, when
they finally left the schoolroom, with the older ones still squabbling mildly, and Georgie becoming bored with it all and
reverting to his picture books. 'There's nothing wrong with a

healthy argument or two, and it shows that, whatever else Trelawney has done today, he's captured their interest.'

'Thank heavens,' Cherry murmured.

'It helps, of course, that he's a personable young man,' Lance went on. 'If he'd been one of the old dodderers I was taught by, he'd have frightened Georgie half to death and bored the other two. You saw the potential in him, didn't you?'

She gave a start. 'Potential? What do you mean?'

'My dear girl, I'm not blind and neither are you. A good-looking young man appears in our midst, and it's hardly surprising that it was a pleasant surprise, just as it was to that serving girl – what's her name? The one always flashing her eyes, I mean. She may need to be watched.'

'Josie, you mean?' Cherry said numbly. 'I don't think we'll have any trouble from her, Lance.'

He looked at her shrewdly.

'Well, if that means you've done your duty and had a few sharp words with her, so much the better. You know I leave that side of domestic affairs to you, sweetheart.'

And we wouldn't want any shenanigans going on, such as any of the upper classes mixing with the lower ones, would we?

As if he had read her mind, he walked over with a laugh to ruffle her hair and plant a kiss on the back of her neck.

'There's only room for one such union in this household, isn't there, Cherry-ripe?' he whispered seductively.

'Yes, Sir,' she replied demurely.

'It's amazing,' she told Paula two days later on Wednesday afternoon. 'I know I was dead against this tutor idea, but it seems to have relieved Lance of some of his constant irritation about Ethan. To the boy's credit, he's become far better behaved since Trelawney's been here. I know it's only been a couple of days, but the atmosphere between the children has already improved. They still argue, of course, because that's what children do, but it's what Lance calls healthy arguments.'

'Crikey, if the bloke's achieved that much already, he must be a saint!' Paula said.

'I wouldn't call him that. In fact, I think he's got wandering eyes.'

'Just as long as they're not wandering hands,' Paula said wickedly. 'So do you still fancy him now you've seen a bit more of him?'

Cherry laughed. 'I don't fancy him at all. Oh well, I thought he was handsome enough when I first saw him, but almost too much so, if you know what I mean. And doesn't he know it! I wouldn't go as far as to say he's started to give me the creeps now, but he's far too smooth when he's around anything in skirts. Thankfully, Bella's too young for all that nonsense, and Nanny Green's too old, and I think I've put the kibosh on any ideas that Josie might have had.'

'Well, thank goodness for that. You got me a bit worried last week, Cherry. About Josie, I mean.'

'Yes, well, I knew I had to do something, and it wouldn't stop nagging at me until I'd asked Cook outright if anything had been said. She admitted that she and Gerard had felt obliged to tell the maids about my past, or as little as they needed to know, in case Ethan began blabbing about it, and they made them swear on a Bible not to divulge a word of it or they'd be out of a job for good.'

'My God! And you trust them?'

Cherry shrugged. 'I don't need to remind you what Cook and Gerard can be like when they get going. We had to endure the rough end of their tongues enough times in the past, didn't we? The wrath of God was nothing compared to them! So as for trusting them – wouldn't you?'

Fifteen

It was noticeable to Cherry that Josie was more subdued and deferential than previously, so whatever the dressing-down she had had from Cook, it had certainly had the desired effect. It suited Cherry to continue exactly as before, and not to betray by a word or a glance that she had noticed anything different in the girl's manner.

Whether it bewildered her, or made her uneasy, or gave her added respect for Cherry, so much the better, but by now Cherry no longer cared.

She was far more concerned by the fact that although she and Lance were getting along better now, it was only marginally so. The barrier that Ethan O'Neill's presence and unwelcome reminders of his father had unwittingly created between them was still there, unspoken, but very real. That the boy was clearly responding to Trelawney's style of tutoring far better than Bella or Georgie should have pleased him, but, contrarily, it didn't.

She didn't know what he was afraid of. Was it that Ethan would turn out to have the brain of an Einstein, and put his own children to shame? Or was he simply furious that any son of Brian O'Neill should have any brains at all, when all of Brian's had been in his fists? Whatever it was, she felt as though she was walking on eggshells for much of the time, and her weekly meetings with Paula were the only respite.

As October merged into November, nothing had really changed, and there was a strange feeling of anxiety in Cherry's heart. She had never thought of herself as being particularly psychic, nor had she ever wanted to be, having no truck with ghosts and ghouls, but the sense of impending doom seemed to fill her head, night and day.

'You're letting it all get to you when there's no need,' Paula told her flatly. 'The kids are doing all right, and you don't get bothered too much by Lance, so I'd say you've just got too much time on your hands, girl. You don't have anything to do all day, so you just sit around imagining things that aren't there. You should try changing lives with me, forever polishing and cleaning and cooking, and then see if you've got time for daydreaming!'

She finished on a laugh, and Cherry joined in, knowing that Paula simply adored her house, and that she revelled in looking after Harold and Thomas. Polishing and cleaning and cooking were the very things she enjoyed most. It wasn't the same as skivvying for other people; it was now done lovingly, to keep her own little palace shining.

'You're really lucky, Paula,' she said without thinking.

'Good God, Cherry, buck up! You must be bloody hard to please if you don't count yourself the luckiest woman in town with all that you've got. My Harold will never have the where-withal to take me on a sea voyage, for a start, or buy me all the lovely clothes you wear. So stop your griping and be grateful for what you've got. It's a hell of a lot more than other people have.'

Cherry grinned, knowing when she was being lectured.

'You're right as usual, you irritating little burr! I am grateful and I shall stop griping right this minute, all right?'

'Well, thank the Lord for that. So apart from imagining things that aren't there, have you seen anything of Cynthia whatsit and her familiar lately?'

That was one way of describing Monica, Cherry supposed . . . not that she would ever call Cynthia a witch!

'We have the occasional card-playing evening at the Hetheringtons', which is always enjoyable enough. I've always liked Cyn, but I'll never take to the other one.'

Paula snorted. 'I wouldn't expect you to. Has she taken to smoking cigars yet, or is it a pipe that these chapesses prefer?'

Cherry burst out laughing at her words. 'You do say some daft things sometimes, Paula.'

'Oh well, as long as it made you laugh, who cares?' Paula said, going cross-eyed and pulling a comical face just to empha-size it all.

Cherry always felt better after an encounter with Paula, who could always bring her down to earth again. She inevitably walked home from Smithy's with a lighter step and approached Melchoir House with a new determination not to let herself wallow and worry over things that didn't exist.

As she walked through the gardens on that particular afternoon, she thought she caught the whiff of something unfamiliar, and she frowned, unable to identify it for a moment. And then she did. It was the pungent aroma that came from someone smoking a cigarette.

Lance had forbidden any of the servants to smoke inside the house, and he would be just as furious if he caught one of them smoking in the grounds. It would be prudent for Cherry to put a stop to it before he had the chance to do so himself. She followed the scent into one of the little arbours that had been her trysting place with Lance many years ago, and the memory didn't escape her now, although their meetings hadn't involved tobacco . . .

She stopped abruptly at the sight of David Trelawney lounging on one of the garden benches. He leapt up at the sight of her and removed the cigarette from his mouth at once, to stamp it out underfoot as his face reddened.

'What are you doing out here, Mr Trelawney? Lessons aren't over for the day yet,' Cherry said, annoyed with herself for being taken so unawares and probably handling this less like a lady than she should.

'I'm sorry, my lady, I didn't mean to startle you,' he said smoothly. 'I occasionally take a break from lessons to allow the children free rein in their art class. I find it inhibits them to have their tutor breathing down their necks, so I sometimes take ten minutes out here on my own.'

'I see.'

He was so very plausible, Cherry couldn't help thinking. He was the type who would have an answer for everything. Brian had been like that. Cook had always thought her daredevil brother with the dark hair and dancing gypsy eyes was a bright and breezy fellow, liked by everyone . . . except for his bare-knuckle opponents, of course, and eventually his debtors . . . and Lance . . .

She pulled herself up short from these unwelcome thoughts.

'Does it bother you, Lady Melchoir?' Trelawney said in a

softer voice. In any other circumstances, it could have been called seductive, but it was hardly appropriate here.

'What do you mean?' she asked.

'My being here. In the house or in the garden. Just my being here.'

It could have been no more than a concerned question because he had been caught somewhere he shouldn't have been, but Cherry knew immediately that it was something more. She wasn't born yesterday, and she also knew he had been well aware of that momentary spark between them on the day of his interview. She could see the echo of it in his eyes now, that arrogant, challenging sense of masculine power in those bluest of blue eyes. If it had briefly intrigued her then, it repulsed her now.

'I think you forget yourself, Mr Trelawney,' she said, in her most frigid voice. 'My husband has engaged you simply to tutor the children, and providing you do that to his satisfaction, then your presence here will be tolerated. I trust we understand one another.'

His eyes flashed anger then, and she guessed at once that he wasn't used to being simply tolerated, which was surely a total affront to his ego.

'Then please forgive me, my lady, if I seem too bold,' he said, just as coolly, and Cherry guessed that it wasn't often that his advances, whether subtle or blatant, were refused.

'It's of no consequence, Mr Trelawney, but I know that Lord Melchoir would prefer it if you would restrain your smoking habit until your working hours are at an end. I'll bid you good afternoon.'

She stared him out for a few seconds longer, and then turned away and walked purposefully towards the house.

Oh yes, my lad, I know all about types like you, she was thinking. *I had a brother once, who could charm the birds from the trees, and it would take more than a puffed-up, over-confident young oik to think he could flatter me and get away with it.*

She didn't know how the disparaging words to describe him came into her head, but they suited him very well. And if he thought the reference to his *smoking habit* was intended to be a rebuff, then he would be right. She was quite sure Lance would disapprove of the tutor returning indoors to the school-room with the smell of tobacco on his breath, to say nothing of Nanny Green's outrage.

She felt an odd little sense of triumph. Her earlier assessment of the tutor as a ladies' man would definitely seem to be justified, but she had let him know, in no uncertain terms, that this particular lady was far and away beyond the likes of him.

A swift memory of how Cynthia Hetherington had first helped her in her new role as Lance's wife brought a rueful smile to her lips. She may have had to play a part when she had married Lance, but the part came easily to her now, and, when it mattered, the play-acting was long since over.

If Paula was amused by the way Cherry related the small incident with Trelawney in the garden, she was also openly admiring.

'I always said you could squash anybody as flat as a flea with one flash of those eyes, let alone your superior lady-of-the-manor voice,' she said with a chuckle.

'Yes, well, thankfully I don't need to flaunt it constantly, but there are times when it's come in very useful,' Cherry admitted.

'Oh, come on, it's second nature to you now,' Paula said. 'Her perishing Lady Elspeth-ship would be really proud of the way you've turned out, Cherry. You're a real chip off the Melchoir block, I'd say.'

'I doubt that,' Cherry said dryly. 'But as long as Lance is happy, I really don't care.'

'And is he?'

Cherry stirred her tea thoughtfully. 'I don't know. Oh yes, of course he is. But sometimes I think he's disappointed in me.'

'Well, now you're being completely daft. He's always been mad about you, and after all the two of you have been through, it would take more than one little setback like Brian's kid to come between you.'

'Is that what you call him? One little setback?'

'It's what you need to call him,' Paula said severely. 'Otherwise, you really are going to let him come between you and Lance. And let's face it, the kid's not going to go away, is he?'

'Not without some other relative coming out from the

woodwork and claiming him,' Cherry said wryly, and then she
pulled a face. 'Lord, Paula, that would be a turn-up, wouldn't
it? Imagine if Brian and I had cousins we never knew about,
and one of them came looking for Ethan. We might end up
with a houseful of Brian lookalikes! That would really drive
Lance loopy!'

The thought of it started them giggling again as the ideas
got wilder, and by the time Cherry went home that day she
felt considerably calmer, the way she always did after seeing
Paula.

Trelawney was still encouraging the children to go on their
nature walks several times a week, no matter what the weather.
It was getting decidedly colder now, and even though the older
two were clearly enjoying being out of the schoolroom for a
time, Georgie was complaining.

'Then Nanny must be sure to wrap you up warmly, darling,'
Cherry told him encouragingly, not wanting to interfere with
the tutor's regime. 'Wear your hat and scarf and gloves and
you won't notice the cold.'

She was tucking him up in bed as usual, and the child
frowned, not prepared to let it go just yet.

'Mr Trelawney tells us what we have to look for while he
talks to the girls,' he said.

'Does he?' Cherry said evenly, ignoring the little jump of
her heart at the child's artless words. 'What girls are those?'

'The girls who are walking on the Downs. Bella says they're
working girls doing their errands.'

'Oh well, I daresay Mr Trelawney is only being polite in
passing the time of the day. Snuggle down now, Georgie, and
go to sleep.'

By the time she had kissed him goodnight and walked along
the corridor to Bella's room, she was seething. Bella wasn't
undressed yet, staring at herself in her dressing-table mirror
with a gloomy expression on her face.

'Do you think I look odd, Mummy? Ethan says I've got a
posh face, whatever that means. What do you think?'

'Ethan doesn't know what he's talking about. You're not
odd at all, you goose. You're a very pretty girl, and boys of

his age often scoff at girls, so don't take any notice of his nonsense. Anyway, I want to talk to you about something else for a moment, Bella.'

'Have I done something wrong?'

'Not at all. Come and sit down beside me on your bed.'

Bella did so obediently, looking at her mother with wary eyes, clearly expecting to hear about some misdemeanour.

'When you go for your nature walks with Mr Trelawney, does he sometimes leave you alone at any time?' Cherry asked, not quite knowing how else to say it.

Bella shrugged. 'Not really. We all wander off to search for whatever we're meant to be looking for, and then he often has a chat and a smoke with the laundry-girls.'

'What laundry-girls?'

A chat and a smoke? It was getting worse by the minute.

'There are three of them. I think they work in some laundry down by the docks. They're common girls, not our sort at all, Mummy, but they're always screeching when Mr Trelawney says something to make them laugh.'

'I see. And does this happen very often?'

'Whenever we go out. Am I going to get into trouble for telling you?' she said anxiously.

'Of course not, darling. Get ready for bed now, and I'll be back in a little while to say goodnight.'

First of all, she needed time to think. It incensed her to think that the children were wandering over the Downs while their tutor was chatting and smoking with common laundry-girls. What the devil did he think he was doing! She should go and inform Lance at once, but Lance had gone out to his club again and probably wouldn't be back until she was in bed and asleep.

It would have to wait until tomorrow, but wait any longer, it certainly would not. If Trelawney wanted to consort with common laundry-girls, then he could seek some other employment more suited to his tastes than looking after the children's education in a gentleman's house.

Of course, the irony of it didn't escape her. But what happened in the past couldn't be changed, and the present was all that mattered now. She had a position to uphold, and she couldn't bear the thought of any harm coming to the children while Trelawney was dallying.

She brooded on the situation until her head ached with it all. There was no doubt that Trelawney was an excellent tutor. He had brought out the best in the children in the time he had been here, and was far better qualified than Nanny Green. And Nanny Green had settled in to her lesser status in the house as general nurse factotum far better than anyone might have supposed. It was clear that she had found the teaching work arduous, particularly since Ethan's arrival, and was glad to hand it over to someone else.

To her own surprise, Cherry found her eyes softening a little as she thought of her nephew. The boy had mellowed considerably during these past weeks. It wasn't likely that he saw something of a father figure in Trelawney, but being without a father for so long, it was natural that he should look up to the man.

He certainly didn't find any such peace of mind when Lance was around. She would never have thought he could be so hard-hearted, so unable to forgive and forget what had happened in the past, with Ethan the ever-present embodiment of that past. Nothing could change the fact that he was her kin, and it saddened Cherry to know that Lance would never willingly accept it.

She was asleep by the time Lance came home that night, and he had risen and gone to the stables before she was properly awake, still with the nagging headache of the night before, and knowing that something important remained to be resolved. There was no chance of doing it imminently now, she thought crossly, since he obviously thought more of his precious Prince than he did of his family.

She wondered what he would do when he heard of Trelawney's escapades, which was the only way she could think of them now. She doubted that he would dismiss him, having acquired his services through excellent references and word of mouth, and being well satisfied with his qualifications. It would take a far greater sin than gossiping with laundry-girls to be rid of him, more's the pity.

She had had an invitation to go to one of Cynthia Hetherington's fund-raising coffee mornings that day. Cherry knew this would inevitably include Monica, among others. But she didn't like to refuse, and there had been no feasible excuse she could invent. Besides, it would look churlish to refuse, so she had instructed Dawkins to take her and she would be there at around eleven o'clock. Why not? She had nothing else to do. Lance would still be out, the children were at their lessons, so she might as well help to raise the coffers for Cyn's latest charity.

That morning, the young chauffeur was prepared to be talkative.

'Saw the children going off out with their new teacher a while ago, my lady,' he said. 'They seem to enjoy their lessons outside the schoolroom. All that fresh air must be good for them.'

'I'm sure it is, Dawkins,' Cherry murmured, for a ridiculous moment wishing that she had known of this before, and then she could have followed them, to see just what the tutor was up to in his nature walks.

Stalked them, you mean, she could almost hear Paula say . . . and yes, that was exactly what she did ruddy well mean. But there was no chance of that now, with the limousine drawing up outside the Hetheringtons' palatial mansion.

'I'll telephone you when I'm ready to leave, Dawkins,' she said automatically. And with any luck, it would be sooner rather than later . . .

'Very well, my lady,' he said, touching his cap and preparing to drive away. She watched him leave, and in a rare moment of introspection, despite all that had happened in recent months, she thought how easy life was for her nowadays. She only had to ask, and whatever she wanted, it would be done for her. The life of a skivvy was a world away from that of a lady. She brushed the thought aside, put a smile on her face, and rang the Hetheringtons' bell.

Lance Melchoir had always found that the best way to dispel any worries in his life was to ride his horse hard across the Downs. There was an excitement in feeling the power of the animal beneath his body and the exhilarating air in his lungs, as man and beast performed their exercise in perfect unison. It had been that way with his beloved horse Noble, long ago expired, and he had never thought he would find such mental and physical rapport with another animal, but in Prince he had certainly done so. Together with one or other of his equine fraternity, it was the best way he knew to keep troubles at bay.

That morning, the air was clear and fresh, the Downs relatively empty of walkers near the well-ridden horse trails. As the acknowledged leader in the race he and his contemporaries were engaged in, he was well ahead of the pack and was barely aware of any other people nearby. He certainly didn't notice his recently engaged tutor, lounging by the railings near the long drop to the Avon Gorge, or the children busy with their task of picking wild flowers.

The first thing he heard was the combined warning shouts of the few passers-by who had been admiring the gentlemen riders. He hardly had time to realize that the small figure racing across the grassy Downs towards him, delight in his chubby face, was his young son. His own shout of warning was lost in his throat as a second figure hurtled in Georgie's wake, pushing him aside just as Lance frantically reined in the wildly flailing hooves of his squealing horse.

By then, it seemed as if the previously quiet area was alive with people running their way, and as he still tried to quieten the frightened Prince, he saw one of his fellow riders sliding off his horse to gather up the quivering Georgie in his arms.

Only then was he able to drag his wits together to look down and see what the gasping and horrified folk gathering around him were seeing. In the midst of his shock at the speed of what had happened, and still unable to take it in exactly, he could hear their comments, shrill and angry and accusing, as though they came from somewhere very far away.

'That boy was a saint, saving the little'un like that.'

'Throwing hisself at the little kid, with no mind to what the danger was to hisself.'

''Twas the gent's fault, riding so fast and endangering God-fearing folk. The police should put a stop to it once and for all.'

Amid the shouts and babble going on all around him, Lance was finally able to still the terrified horse well enough to take in what had happened. When he did, his face went ashen, the long scar on his cheek startlingly livid by contrast, as he slid off Prince's back and knelt down beside the crumpled mass of the boy.

'My God, Ethan,' he whispered brokenly.

That the horse's hooves had struck the boy cruelly in the back of his head, there was no doubt from the bloody and pulpy mess that remained of it. Blood ran thickly from the wounds made by the lethal blows, and it was obvious to anyone that the child was dead.

Even as he tore off his riding jacket and covered Ethan with it, he found himself shouting hoarsely to anyone who would listen.

'Somebody send for an ambulance, for God's sake.'

He caught sight of Georgie, snivelling with fear and being comforted by one of Lance's fellow riders.

'Get my son away from here, Walters, and inform my wife what's happened,' he went on, still in that strange, hoarse voice that didn't seem to belong to him. 'And where is Bella – and that goddamned tutor? Why weren't these children being properly supervised?' he was finally able to roar.

They spotted the tutor breaking away from the people he was with as he saw the disturbance on the far side of the Downs, and he began to sprint towards them. By then, Bella had come screaming towards her father, and Walters had taken hold of her and was lifting her and Georgie on to the back of his horse and leading them away from the scene and towards Melchoir House.

Trelawney reached Lance, his eyes wild and distraught.

'*Christ Almighty*, what's happened, Sir? I swear I never took my eyes off them for more than a moment or two—'

One of the onlookers accused him immediately.

'Oh aye, long enough for you to dawdle with them laundry-girls as usual, I'd say, and long enough for this poor young boy to kill hisself!'

'Is this true?' Lance said harshly, almost beside himself as he waited for the ambulance to come and take Ethan away.

'I'm sorry,' Trelawney stammered. 'I swear I meant no harm by it. I kept my eyes on them at all times.'

Lance's guilt at his own treatment of Ethan O'Neill, and the realization that the boy he had so despised had saved his own small son from certain death, now made him scream with fury.

'Get out of my sight, man. You haven't heard the last of this by any means, but right now I can't bear to look at you.'

Trelawney fled, aware that the growing crowd was baying at him now, as they realized how he had been lacking in his duties. Lance continued to kneel by the side of the dead boy, cradling him as if he was his own and paying no heed to the blood and mess seeping over his fine clothes, until the police and ambulance men came and took the child away.

Only then, when he had given the briefest of statements to the police and they had made everyone disperse, did he remount Prince and trot him slowly towards Melchoir House. He could never have walked, for his legs seemed fit to crumble beneath him at any moment. One of his companions rode gently beside him, trying to offer him what little comfort he could. He was more wretched than he had ever felt in his life, consumed by guilt and remorse, and filled with the overwhelming dread of having to face his wife.

Sixteen

Cherry wondered just how soon she could get away from the fund-raising coffee morning at the Hetheringtons'. She was utterly bored, not so much by the worthy cause as by the people concerned. She disliked Monica intensely, and most of the other women were cronies of Cyn's, whom she didn't really know, and didn't particularly care to. They were all what Paula would call airy-fairies, with nothing much going on in their woolly heads except buying expensive clothes and jewellery and the hunt for a suitable man – or woman, as the case may be. That none of them made their preferences particularly blatant meant nothing. Anything seemed to go these days, and ever since Cyn had returned from Germany, the excesses had got worse.

And she was turning into a prize prude, Cherry admonished herself, as the funds far exceeded Cyn's expectations, and would do much good where they were needed. What did it matter if these people indulged themselves in ways that didn't appeal to her? They did a lot of good in other ways.

'Come and sit with me, Cherry,' Cyn said to her a while later, 'and tell me how the new tutor is getting on with the children. It's a good thing your lovely Bella isn't a few years older, since he's quite a looker, isn't he?'

'He might be, but he certainly doesn't appeal to me!' Cherry said.

'Well, nor to me, darling, but that's another matter, and there's no need to take the huff. You're a little touchy today, aren't you? Not quite yourself?'

Whatever Cherry might have answered to that was interrupted by the Hetheringtons' butler announcing that Dawkins had arrived to take Lady Melchoir home.

'He's rather taken it upon himself, hasn't he?' Cyn said in surprise. 'I thought you were going to ring for him.'

The butler cleared his throat and addressed Cherry directly.

'Forgive me, Lady Melchoir, but the chauffeur has arrived in some urgency, and requests that you join him immediately.'

'For heaven's sake,' Cyn said irritably, 'it's probably some little domestic matter that's got out of hand in the kitchen, but I suppose you had better go, Cherry, before war is done.'

Whatever the cause, Cherry said her goodbyes thankfully and went out to where Dawkins was waiting. The moment she sat inside the limousine, he burst out crying. It was so unexpected that, for a moment, Cherry simply stared at him blankly, before an icy feeling of presentiment crept over her from head to toe.

'What's happened, Dawkins? Tell me at once.'

He could hardly speak, and then he began snivelling and trembling uncontrollably until she pressed a hard hand on his shoulder and gave it a shake.

'*Tell* me, man!'

He was stuttering wildly now. 'Oh, my lady, my lady, I can't say the words, I can't. It's too terrible. You'll have to hear it from his lordship, and I'm to get you home as quickly as possible, so please don't ask me anything more.'

It was ridiculous. *He* was being ridiculous, but he was young and gauche, and whatever had happened, it was clear that she wasn't going to get anything more out of him. So she sat in the limousine, full of fear, as rigidly as if she was carved out of stone, not knowing what awaited her – only the certainty that something terrible had happened – and trying very hard not to imagine what she was going to find when she reached home.

The first thing Cherry noticed was the ominous sign that all the curtains at the windows at the front of the house had been drawn. Dawkins still didn't seem capable of coherent speech, and by now she was too afraid to ask him anything more. She almost leapt out of the limousine as it pulled up at the house, and the second thing she saw was Lance waiting for her at the open front door.

Her heart was beating so fast and so hard now that she thought she might faint, but she rushed towards him and grasped his arms tightly as he drew her inside.

'What's happened? Please tell me, Lance,' she gasped. 'Is it the children? Has something happened to them?'

'Bella and Georgie are perfectly safe, darling, although we've sent for the doctor to check Georgie for cuts and bruises after his tumble.'

His own words sounded pathetic to his ears. How could he diminish the terrible thing that had happened today as a mere tumble?

'Then, is it Ethan?' Cherry gasped again. 'Where is he? If he's been hurt, I must go to him at once.'

Her brain simply refused, in those first wild moments, to register that the drawn window curtains told a very different story to someone simply being hurt.

'Cherry darling, come to the drawing room and sit down,' Lance said gently, his voice unsteady as he tried to avert the moment when she had to know. But have to know she did, and he was the one who would have to tell her, however unpredictable her reaction was going to be. He had to tell her that he had been the one, however unintentionally, to cause her nephew's cruel death.

'Tell me *now*! Why is everyone creeping around me as if I'm a child? Dawkins was practically weeping, so I know it must be something dreadful. So *tell* me, Lance, for I swear I won't move from this spot until you do!'

He held her tightly. 'There was an accident, darling. A terrible accident, but thank God Georgie is safe, and Bella wasn't involved.'

'You've said that,' she almost screamed. 'So where is Ethan?'

'He's at the hospital, my love, and we shall go there as soon as you feel able to deal with what's happened.'

'Is he badly hurt?'

Lance closed his eyes for a moment, wishing he could spare her this, and wishing himself anywhere but here, causing her the pain that was to come.

'He's not hurting any more,' he said in a low voice.

She was shaking all over by now as the sense of what he was saying penetrated her brain, and, as if in the middle of a horrible dream, she caught sight of Gerard standing nearby, his face white, and she heard the scurrying footsteps of one of the maids and heard her whispering and weeping to one of the others. And then she collapsed and knew nothing more.

When she awoke, she found herself on one of the sofas in the drawing room, with no idea how she had got there. The pungent smell of smelling salts was in her nostrils, and the doctor was telling her gently to take it easily before moving. As memory rushed in, she was gasping again, unable to breathe properly, and she was urged to take deep breaths and not to try to sit up just yet.

'Ethan,' she croaked.

She was aware of Lance hovering nearby, looking shaken and as ashen as everyone else. She supposed she must look that way too, she thought almost dispassionately. A distraught Josie was standing by with a pot of hot sweet tea, the usual panacea for shock, and Lance told her to put the damn tray down and leave them. Cherry felt briefly sorry for the girl as she fled from the room, her hand stuffed against her mouth to stop herself from crying.

The doctor was talking to her now in measured tones, the way he might speak to someone demented, which Cherry felt very near to being.

'My dear Lady Melchoir, you have had a terrible shock, and it will take some time for you to come to terms with it. I will prescribe some sedatives for you, and I strongly recommend that you rest for a day or two and let others deal with the situation.'

Cherry stared at him for a moment, and then her voice seemed to come from nowhere. 'Are you completely stupid?' she snapped.

At his affronted look, she was hardly able to believe she was speaking in this way to this most stiff-necked of medical men, but she thundered on now, not caring a damn, not for him, nor for Lance's embarrassment as her normally controlled accent slipped a little.

'I've just been told the worst news about my nephew, but nobody has bothered to tell me how it happened, and you treat me like an imbecile and expect me to lie here and rest! I'm made of sterner stuff than that, Doctor! I will go and see my children, and then my husband will take me to the hospital to see my nephew for myself, once he's had the goodness to explain everything to me. If that's too much to ask, then I will bloody well go there under my own steam.'

She sat back exhausted once she had finished, and she was aware of Lance talking quietly to the doctor and asking Gerard to show him out. So what if she had let the side down? What did it matter? What did anything matter but that Ethan was dead?

The horror of it all swept over her like a giant wave. He was dead, and she still had no idea how or why or where. She seemed to be the only one still in the dark, the one who had cared about him the most, and she couldn't bear it. She stood up, swaying, and grasped Lance's hands.

'The truth now, please,' she grated. 'Or I swear I will do as I said, and walk out of here right now to go to him.'

He made her sit down again, took her in his arms, and told her, as gently as he could, all that had happened that day. She listened with rising hysteria, trying to take in all the tragic, horrible circumstances that had led to a boy's death.

'It was a terrible accident that nobody could have foreseen, my darling. It was nobody's fault, not Georgie's, not mine, and not poor Prince's.'

He knew it was a mistake as soon as he uttered the horse's name. Until then, she had been relatively still, but hearing how he was concerned about the trauma to his horse, she felt a kind of madness seize her. She was suddenly pummelling at his chest, hating him and all he stood for; hating the idyllic life that had stolen her identity from her, turning her into something she was not. At that moment, she longed to be plain Cherry O'Neill again, kitchen-maid, with no worries other than pleasing Cook and avoiding the swipe of her hand.

He was agonized by her reaction now. 'Cherry, sweetheart, please don't do this. I'm desperately sorry for what happened, and don't you think if I could turn back the clock, I've wished it a thousand times in these last hours?'

She sagged against him, weeping silently for long minutes, until at last the paroxysms ceased, and she wilted again. He spoke very guardedly then, unsure how she was going to react to his next words.

'Our children need their mother, Cherry.'

Her head jerked up. 'Where was Trelawney when all this was happening? I swear I will not allow that man anywhere near them again.'

'Trelawney's gone, and he won't be back. The police and my lawyer will deal with him, since he has much to answer for.'

Cherry took a deep, shuddering breath.

'Then I'm ready to see Bella and Georgie now,' she said.

He had to admire her dignity as she walked slowly out of the drawing room, supported by his arm. The schoolroom was at the rear of the house, where the curtains hadn't been drawn, so it was a relief to see it bright and normal, the children talking excitedly to Nanny Green and relating all that had happened. It seemed to have taken on the proportions of a huge adventure, at least in Georgie's eyes, and Cherry realized that they didn't yet know the truth of it. They didn't know what had happened to Ethan, even though Nanny Green obviously did and was doing her best to keep them occupied.

'We thought it best if we told them together,' Lance murmured in her ear.

Her heart baulked afresh at the task ahead. Bella was clearly uneasy, but Georgie was proudly showing off the multicoloured bruises on his arms and legs.

Cherry shuddered, realizing anew what fate could have befallen her baby if Ethan hadn't intervened.

'Would you leave us, please, Nanny Green?' she said. 'Please go and have some tea. I'm sure you could do with it, and have some food sent up for the children.' Her own tea was still in the drawing room, cold and unnoticed.

'Come and sit with us, my dears,' Lance said to the children as Cherry fell silent again. 'We have something to tell you.'

'It's about Ethan, isn't it?' Bella said at once. 'He had a nasty fall, Daddy, and he hasn't come back yet, so where is he?'

Georgie had come to sit on Cherry's lap now, and she cuddled him into her, his warm little body sending a brief comfort through her frozen limbs.

'I think he's gone to live with the angels,' he said, shocking her.

Bella cried out at once. 'Don't be so daft, Georgie. That's a wicked thing to say, isn't it, Mummy?'

The words threatened to clog Cherry's throat again, knowing she was forced to reply to her daughter's candid, worried plea. But Georgie's innocent words had given her the lead she needed.

'I'm very sad to say that Georgie's right, Bella, and he'll also be reunited with his own mummy and daddy again.'

Bella stared at her and then at Lance, her face going a furious, fiery red.

'That means he's dead, doesn't it? And Daddy's horse killed him!'

Lance intervened before Georgie went to pieces at her outburst.

'You didn't see exactly what happened, Bella, but it was a complete accident, and Ethan was very brave to do what he did. We should never forget that. He saw Georgie running across the Downs towards me and Prince, and he rushed over and pushed him out of the way just in time. He saved Georgie's life.'

Georgie was snivelling now, but his eyes were shining with pride.

'He was a hero, wasn't he, Daddy?'

'He certainly was,' Lance said quietly.

'I hate Mr Trelawney,' Bella said suddenly, her anger switching to the only place she could think of. 'He should have been looking after Georgie instead of flirting with those common girls. I don't want him back, Mummy.'

'He's not coming back, darling. I'm sure Nanny Green will take over the schoolroom duties again, if we ask her.'

They sat with them a while longer until Nanny Green returned with Josie, and a tray of tea and sandwiches and Cook's special pastries, which would be sure to take their minds off the trauma for a while. And as soon as they took their leave, there was only one place they had to go.

Dawkins drove them to the Infirmary in silence. Cherry and Lance sat in the rear seats, hands clasped tightly together, wrapped up in their own thoughts and emotions. It was a sombre journey. Outside the limousine, city life continued the way it had always done. Buses trundled by; people walked and talked and did their shopping; children squabbled and played football, dodging the traffic. All were oblivious to the fact that, inside the luxury vehicle, two people were mourning a tragedy and on their way to see the young boy who had left the house happy and cheerful that morning and who would never smile again.

As they walked inside the hospital and Lance gave their names, they received the expected deferential treatment. A doctor and head nurse came to greet them and offer their condolences, and then escorted them to the quiet side ward where Ethan lay.

Cherry walked the long corridors as if in a dream. She didn't want to believe where she was going, nor for what purpose. She didn't want to hear the doctor explaining to Lance the full extent of Ethan's injuries, or that he had died instantly and would not have suffered. It might be of some comfort to her at a later date. Right now, it was not. She was simply numbed by the knowledge of why she was here at all.

As if to block out the present, and to ward off the inevitable moment when she would have to enter the ward, her thoughts reverted to another time, long ago, when Lance had been missing after being badly beaten up and left for dead by her own brother after his failed blackmail attempt. Nobody knew where he was, but she had been the one to find him, here in the Infirmary, his memory gone, and only able to give the doctors the name of Noble.

They had called him Mr Noble then . . . but Cherry had known it was the name of his beloved horse that had been the last thing in his memory. And now another horse had been responsible for bringing Ethan here, in such terrible circumstances.

Her arm was threaded tightly through Lance's, and she felt him squeeze it even tighter.

'Other days, darling,' she heard him murmur, so softly that only she caught the words, but it was enough to know that he remembered too. It made her feel not quite so alone.

And then they reached the place, and the doctor and nurse left them for as long as they wished to have their private moments with the boy.

Cherry felt nervous and afraid, but Lance urged her gently forward until she was sitting on the chair beside Ethan. He could have been sleeping, except that it was all too obvious that he was not. He looked so small, devoid of colour, and so defenceless on the narrow hospital bed, the white sheet pulled up to his chin, so that only his face was visible. Around his head was a heavy bandage, disguising what was not for public viewing. Cherry was choked, just watching him, as if she was somehow intruding into his long slumber. At any moment, surely, he would open his eyes, those wicked eyes, so like his father's, laugh and joke and tell her it was all a mistake, and he wasn't dead after all . . .

There were so many different emotions milling around in Cherry's head in those moments. Sadness for a life that had ended so young, pity that he would never grow into manhood, regret for the loneliness he must have endured after losing both his parents, sorrow that he had never been as welcome in her family as he should have been, and, ultimately, tenderness bordering on love.

She gave a shuddering breath as the tears filled her eyes. This was her brother's son who had come to them for help when he had no one else, and she felt acutely guilty that she had never shown him the love she should have done, or could have done, if only Brian's shadow hadn't still been hanging over them.

'Come away, Cherry,' she heard Lance say, still in that awkward, low voice. 'There's nothing more we can do here.'

She nodded wordlessly, and then, after a moment, she leaned forward and kissed that cold, pale cheek. And then she stood up and turned away, her eyes blinded by tears now, as Lance ushered her out of the room.

The nurse was gentle and solicitous, offering to take her to another room and bring her a cup of tea. She wanted to say no, to be out of there and somewhere on her own, where she could allow her emotions to have full flow. But Lance urged her to do as she was asked, while he spoke to the doctor to consider was arrangements were to be made.

This should be her job, Cherry wanted to say. He was her nephew, and she should have some say in where the boy was

buried . . . but even as the word entered her mind, she flinched
and nodded again; letting Lance do what he had to do, letting
the nurse take her away, letting others take over . . .

Eventually, they left the Infirmary to take the sad drive back
to the house. Lance told her quietly that Ethan would be taken
to a chapel of rest, and from then on he would see the undertaker and all would be taken care of. Ethan would be buried
with his mother – if that was Cherry's wish.

So, finally, she had her say. But what was there to say? Lance
had taken care of everything, easing her out of her grief in
the only way he knew how, by quiet efficiency in an almost
military manner. So she agreed, adding her thanks, and feeling
the tight grip of his hand over hers as they reached home.

'I will go and speak to the staff, darling, so that they hear
the proper story, rather than rumours,' he told her next. 'And
then I must make some telephone calls. The official ones must
come first, and when all the arrangements are in place, our
friends must be informed. This has been a terrible shock for
all of us, Cherry, so I want you to go and rest, my love, and
leave everything to me.'

His compassion brought the tears to her eyes again, but she
dashed them back. He was being so kind, so understanding of
her grief, even though his own must be tinged with enormous
guilt. But, above all, he would be overwhelmingly thankful
that Georgie had been saved. If a life had to be sacrificed, then
how much more convenient was it all round, and especially
for Lord Melchoir, that it had been Ethan O'Neill's?

The shock of such wicked thoughts sent cold shivers running
through her. How could she think like that, even for a moment?
It was shameful, and she shamed Lance for letting the thought
into her head for a single instant. She kept her gaze low as
she went inside the house and Lance went below stairs to
inform the staff, glad of this respite to try to dispel those ugly
thoughts from her mind.

The telephone was ringing as she reached the drawing room.
She stared at it for a moment, its jangling note disturbing and
intrusive. Surely it wasn't someone already trying to offer their
condolences, when the news could hardly have got around the
town yet? She was tempted to let it ring, but then she thought

it might be someone from the hospital checking on arrangements, so she picked up the instrument and spoke as normally
as she could into the receiver.

'Oh Cherry, thank goodness you answered it and not Lord
snooty!' came Paula's excited voice. 'He'd probably have thought
I was going dippy – well, I'm sure he thinks I'm dippy anyway
– but I couldn't wait to tell you our news. You'll never guess
what it is, so I'll have to spill the beans. Harold's bought us a
little motor car! Not one of them posh ones like your Roller,
of course, nor like the Hon Cyn's lah-de-dah one, but big
enough for him to take me and Thomas out at weekends. I'm
dying for us to show it to you. So what do you think of that!'

Cherry couldn't speak. Any other time, she would have been
wild with excitement over Paula's announcement, knowing
what bit of status this would have brought to her. But right
now, anything she might have said was simply stuck in her
throat, and how could she get excited over a small family car,
when the next vehicle that Ethan would be in would be an
undertaker's hearse?

'Are you there, Cherry? Did you hear what I said, or have
you gone deaf?' Paula screeched. 'Bet you never thought I'd
come up in the world enough to have me own car, did you?
Well, mine and Harold's, of course.'

'It sounds wonderful, Paula,' Cherry said, finally dragging
out the words.

There was a momentary silence at the other end, and then,
knowing her too well, Paula's attitude changed completely.

'So what's wrong? What's happened? I can tell by your voice
that it's something bad, Cherry.'

Cherry stared at the wall ahead of her, not knowing how
to put it into words for the first time, and this would be the
first of many times.

'There's been a terrible accident,' she said, raw and hoarse.
'It's Ethan.'

'Oh my God. Is he hurt bad? How bad is it?' Paula persisted,
her voice rising in fear.

'He's dead, Paula. He's *dead*, and I can't talk any more. I'm
sorry.'

She slammed down the telephone and sank to the floor,

sobbing wildly. Paula had had more of a rapport with Ethan than she had. Paula had known how to get through that prickly barrier of his. Paula was far more of an aunt to him than Brian's uppity sister could ever have been . . . Guilt and shame rushed over her in equal measure, and when Lance came upstairs, he still found her there, huddled up on the floor. The next thing she knew, a glass of brandy was being forced between her cold lips and she swallowed without tasting it until the fiery liquid ran down her throat, making her gasp.

'I want you to go and lie down,' he told her next. 'You'll be no good to anyone like this, and your children need you to be strong, Cherry.'

'Ethan doesn't need me any more, does he? I failed him, Lance.'

She had said it now. All the pent-up rage in her soul had come bursting out in one bitter sentence. She had failed him.

Lance was rocking her like a baby now. 'You didn't fail him, darling. What would he have been without you? Where would he have gone after his mother died, if not to you? He was able to hold his head high, because of you. Now, do as I say and go and lie down while I make these phone calls.'

She obeyed, feeling like a leaf in the wind, but she knew she couldn't see the children right now without breaking down, and that wouldn't help them. She went to their bedroom and curled up right inside the covers exactly as she was, needing the comfort of being cocooned.

She must have fallen asleep from sheer exhaustion and the strain of the day, because she was suddenly aware of being woken by the bedroom door opening, and the sound of hushed words coming towards her.

'It's all right, Josie, I don't need to be ruddy well announced,' came the semi-irritated whisper of a voice she knew, and the next second Paula had rushed across the room and clasped her in her outstretched arms.

Seventeen

Lance had easily discovered where Sara O'Neill was buried, and Ethan would be buried with her in a week's time. Cherry learned the facts as though he was talking about somebody else. She couldn't seem to grasp it all, even now. People came and went, friends and strangers, offering their condolences, being kind, being quiet, and tiptoeing around her as if she was an invalid. She didn't want their sympathy cards or their awkward words that meant nothing.

Paula was the only one who understood. Paula came every day, letting her talk it out, or sob it out, or rage it out . . . and it was four days later, when Paula told her in no uncertain terms that enough was enough, that she began to come to her senses.

'Just look at the state of you,' Paula snapped. 'You've let yourself go, Cherry. Your hair looks like straw, you haven't dressed decently in days, and how Lance can fancy you like this, I'll never know.'

'I don't want him to fancy me right now,' Cherry said, flinching. 'It's not decent. Do you think I can think about anything like that at such a time?'

'Well, Lance might, if only to know that you're still alive and not blaming him for what's happened. You're *not*, are you?'

Cherry gave a helpless shrug, but she could no longer deny the way she was feeling. 'I don't know. I don't want to!'

'Then don't, or it will tear you apart, and after all you've been through, I'd hate to see it happen to my two favourite people. Well, to one of them, anyway,' she amended.

She saw the ghost of a smile on Cherry's lips at that remark.

'It's not only Lance I'm thinking about, anyway,' Paula went on determinedly. 'I've been in the schoolroom, and Bella's walking around like a little ghost, and Georgie's clinging to her as if he thinks she'll be the next one to leave him. They need their mother, Cherry, and Nanny Green's no blooming mother substitute, to put it mildly!'

'Georgie's clinging to Bella?' Cherry said slowly, as if she hadn't heard anything else.

'Well, if he hasn't got his mother to cling to, I suppose he thinks she's the next best thing, barring the old duck Nanny Green,' Paula said sharply. 'He wants to know where Ethan is, by the way.'

'He does know.'

'No, he doesn't. He's confused, Cherry, and you need to explain it to him properly. About the funeral and all.'

'I can't!' she said, aghast. 'I can't tell him that Ethan's going to be put in the ground. It will give him nightmares.'

'Better to know it than to imagine all sorts of things. We'll tell him together, if you like — if you're too chicken.'

Her eyes challenged Cherry's, and, after a moment or two, she saw at last an answering spark in them.

'No. This is my job. I'll do it now. You'll stay, though, won't you?'

'Your children don't need me around right now, but you're not going anywhere until you've changed your dress and brushed the knots out of your hair,' Paula said, still bullying her. 'Then I'm going down to have a gossip with Cook, but I'll come back upstairs in a little while.'

Like an automaton, Cherry did as she was told, finally giving in to her distress at having to talk about Ethan to the children, particularly to Georgie, who only half-understood what was going on. But he was remarkably open to all that she was saying, and Bella added her own words now and then, being so grown-up and considerate of her little brother, Cherry thought gratefully, in a way she would never have suspected of her precocious little daughter.

'We won't have to see him put in the ground, will we?' Georgie asked fearfully.

'No, darling. You and Bella will stay here and keep Nanny Green company. There will be people coming back to the house afterwards for something to eat and drink, and if Nanny Green agrees to it, I'm sure you can help Josie set it all out. That will be something you can do for Ethan, to remember him by. Even though he won't be there, we can think of it as a sort of party for him.'

She answered all his questions as honestly as she could, and he had cheered up considerably by the time she went back to the drawing room where Paula was waiting for her. She felt increasingly guilty that she had been wallowing in her own grief and hadn't had the sense to talk to the child before now.

'Never mind, you've done it now,' Paula said. 'Where's his snootyship today, by the way?'

Cherry bit her lip. 'I don't know. He's so wary of my mood these days that I think he prefers to keep out of my way.'

'Very wise,' Paula said.

Cherry hesitated. 'There's something else I have to do, Paula, and I've been putting it off. Will you come with me?'

'Of course. Whatever it is.'

'I haven't been inside Ethan's room since it happened.'

'Come on, then, old girl, let's get it over with,' Paula said briskly, before she could change her mind.

They went out of the drawing room arm in arm, just the way they used to do when they left their attic room in high spirits to go dancing all those years ago. Outside Ethan's bedroom, Cherry took a deep breath and opened the door.

It was just a room, she told herself. A room that had been cleaned and tidied by the maids, and showed no evidence of anyone sleeping here. The bed was pristine with fresh bedding, the pillow having no slight indent where a boy's head might have rested. It was poignant to see it this way, even though it was what she had expected.

The only personal thing in evidence was Ethan's small tin box on his dressing table, and she drew in her breath at the sight of it. It was what she had come to see, but now that the moment had come, she was afraid to open it.

'What's wrong?' Paula said sharply. 'You've broken the ice, but if it's too much for you, come back another time.'

Cherry shook her head. 'No, I'll do it now,' she said, and walked across and took the box in her hands. She sat down on the bed, and Paula sat beside her as she opened the lid.

'This was so precious to him,' she said. 'It was his whole life, really, all that he had left of his mother and his father.'

She took out the documents, one by one, and handed them to Paula for her to see. Paula didn't comment until it came to the last one, the poster with the laughing image of Cherry's brother looking up at them, the daredevil bare-knuckle fighter who had been so obviously the young boy's idol.

'He was always a handsome devil and none could deny it,' Paula said at last. 'No wonder Cook and everybody downstairs was so charmed by him. And his kid had certainly inherited some of that charm, once you got through the tough side of him.'

Cherry nodded, replaced everything carefully in the box and closed the lid.

'This will all be buried with him,' she said.

'So can we get out of here now?' Paula asked.

Cherry stood up. 'There's one more thing, but I hardly know how to ask you, Paula, or how you'll react.'

'For pity's sake, you should know by now that you can ask me anything.'

'Yes, but it's not just you. It's Harold and Thomas as well.'

'So are you going to ask me, dummy, or do I have to start asking twenty questions until I find out what you want?'

Cherry smiled uneasily. 'It's Ethan's clothes that you so kindly helped me choose for him. He was about the same size as Thomas, and I wondered – oh God, Paula, I can't ask you!'

'You're offering them to me for Thomas? And you think I'll refuse? Do you think I'm too proud to accept hand-me-downs that are given in the right spirit? Especially as half of them haven't even been worn, I bet.'

'They haven't. Ethan didn't really care for what he called the feel of all that new stuff. He always said they were too prissy for a Bush boy,' she added with a catch in her throat. 'I wanted to offer them to you for Thomas, but I was worried that Harold might object. So what do you think? At least help me sort through them sometime.'

'No time like the present! Let's do it before you get cold feet at coming in here again,' Paula said. 'I'll be honoured to take them off your hands for Thomas, and, as for Harold, you leave me to deal with him!'

Paula had left by the time Lance came home, wondering uneasily what mood Cherry was going to be in today. The tragedy was still new and still raw to her, and she was taking it very personally, and he understood that. He didn't blame her, but he simply didn't know how to cope with it. He was upset about the boy too, and horrified about the circumstances, but he had been brought up by parents who believed in showing a stiff upper lip and never giving way to emotions in private or in public, and never in front of servants. Having had the police in the house to answer questions was an added affront to his ordered and private way of life. Some might think it outmoded, but it was inbred in Lance, and impossible to shake off the shackles.

It was a surprise and a relief, therefore, when he found Cherry in a calmer state of mind than before, and looking decidedly less wild-eyed and dishevelled than when he left.

'Paula's been,' she said unnecessarily, since he knew it was a daily ritual now. 'We've been having some serious discussions.'

'What about?'

'I've given her most of Ethan's clothes, except for the ones I want him to be buried in. Of course, he must have his tin box buried with him as well, and I've had a talk with Bella and Georgie. Bella would have liked to come to the funeral, but I persuaded them that they should stay and look after Nanny Green, and then help her with setting out the food and drinks for when we all come back to the house. I told them they would be doing it for Ethan.'

Her eyes felt damp again, but she was determined to be strong and not let her feelings run away with her. In doing all that she had done today, she had realized it felt much better to be decisive and taking charge of things, than to let it all wash over her. She should have remembered the way life had been below stairs, when there was no time for being maudlin, when they just had to buckle up and get on with things, no matter what.

She felt Lance's arms go around her, and she tried not to stand too stiffly in his embrace, but she was simply unable to respond completely. It pained her to know it, but she couldn't help it. Maybe once the funeral was over . . .

'I'm proud of you, darling. These things had to be done, and it was better that you did them yourself, even though I would have taken care of it all, as you know, and Josie could have sorted out the boy's clothes.'

'No,' Cherry said sharply. 'Ethan wasn't Josie's nephew.'

She untangled herself from his arms and sat down on the sofa, angry that he still couldn't seem to say Ethan's name easily. He went to the sideboard and poured himself a drink, offering her one, which she refused. She didn't want spirits to lift her. She needed to feel the grief, knowing that inevitably it would lessen, and when it did, it would be as if Ethan had never existed. Not him, nor Brian, nor even his wife Sara, whom she had never known. She drew a deep breath. Three more days, she told herself; then it would be the ordeal of the funeral, and after that perhaps she wouldn't feel as if this house was stifling her.

She wondered briefly if, out of all the mourners at the grave, it would only be she and Paula who would really care. And perhaps Cook and Gerard, who had asked to be present, half in memory of her brother. The others would only be doing lip service out of respect for Lord Melchoir's family.

'Have you forgotten that Cyn and her parents are visiting tonight?' Lance went on quietly.

'No, I hadn't forgotten,' she said wearily. 'More people to sit around with long faces, trying to think of things to say, and wishing they were somewhere else, I suppose. Why can't people stay away instead of gawping at us?'

He slammed his glass down on a side table, his eyes flashing.

'For God's sake, Cherry, pull yourself together. These people are our friends, and they offer their support in any way they can. Wallowing in your own misery won't help anyone. Now I'm going to see the children, and show them at least one cheerful face in this house.'

He left the room angrily, leaving her biting her lip, knowing he was right, and not knowing how to deal with it. In the end, she joined him, listening with a forced smile to their son's important tale of how he and Bella were going to help Nanny Green and Josie get Ethan's party ready. It took so little to persuade Georgie that life went on, and Cherry knew she should try to take heed of a child's innocent thinking.

★   ★   ★

The day of the funeral arrived, and she was in a state of jitters all over again. But it was something that had to be done, and she would be letting Ethan down if she didn't behave with dignity. Even though the sight of the small coffin nearly blew all such sensible thoughts out of her mind, she struggled on, with Lance's hand held tightly in hers as she clung to his arm during the simple service, from where they led the procession to the churchyard.

Afterwards, she couldn't have said who was there. She knew there were dignitaries and Lance's business acquaintances, his lawyer, the Hetheringtons and other friends, and Paula and Harold, who kept as close to Cherry as they could without superseding these other fine folk.

Back at the house, though, with the curtains drawn back now to end the week of mourning, and Bella and Georgie being fussed over as the company ate and drank, Paula managed a few words with Cherry alone.

'Well done, old girl,' she breathed. 'I knew you had it in you. Old Lady Elspeth couldn't have done better.'

'I suppose that's a compliment of a sort,' Cherry said dryly.

'It's meant to be. You can hold your head up as high as any of these toffs, and that's a compliment too.'

She drifted away to join Harold, deep in conversation with Georgie now, and Cherry wondered just what her son was telling him. She managed to move through the mourners to hear the last of it. Georgie was excited, and she couldn't blame him, since he was being the centre of attention among many of the doting older mamas.

'Daddy's going to have a special stone made, with Ethan's name on it, so we won't forget him, and Nanny Green's going to take me and Bella to see Ethan's grave, so we can put flowers on it.'

Cherry blinked. She realized again that she had been so wrapped up in her own grief that she hadn't been aware of any of this.

'That's a very good thing to do,' Harold Farmer was saying. 'I think Thomas might like to join you for that as well. What do you think about it? As he was your cousin, I think you should decide, Georgie.'

He considered, putting his head on one side like a little old man, Cherry thought, with a rush of emotion. Then he nodded.

'All right. I think Bella would like it too if Thomas was there.'

Cherry met Harold's eyes above the child's head, and there was a perfect smile of understanding between them. How clever Harold was, she thought, speaking to him like an adult and letting him have the last say. It took more than a good education and family breeding to know how to talk to a child.

But, at last, everyone had left and the house was their own again. Because it was a special day, Lance had suggested that the children should join them for a simple dinner that evening.

'It will tire them out and offset any morbid thoughts,' he told Cherry, 'and it will be a good thing for us all to be together, on this night of all nights.'

She agreed, knowing he was doing everything in his power to please her, and she felt obliged to tell him what she had overheard about the stone he was arranging for Ethan's grave.

'I was waiting until the right moment to mention it, and I apologize for telling the children first,' he said awkwardly. 'We all have our own ways of helping, Cherry, and it gave them something positive to think about. But you must tell me the words you want on the stone in due course. Since he's with his mother now, her name should be included too, if you wish.'

She agreed, and there seemed nothing else to say until finally this interminable day was over. She lay in bed beside Lance, hearing his regular breathing as he slept, and wishing that she too could push the milling images out of her mind so easily. But, out of sheer exhaustion, sleep came at last.

It was impossible to remain in a state of grief for ever, especially with two lively children who demanded attention and love, and Cherry was learning ever more humbly how the innocent questions of children could start to heal the pain of loss. Two weeks later, when all the official floral tributes had been taken away, and only the small mound of earth was left to await the stonemason's work, she accompanied Nanny Green with Bella and Georgie to put some simple flowers on Ethan's grave.

Harold had driven Paula and Thomas in their new little car to meet them there, and as the three children stood talking together in their own way, Nanny Green and Harold stood respectfully to one side, and she and Paula clasped hands.

'Who ever thought we would be doing something like this?' Cherry murmured.

'Who ever thought life would take us in the direction it did?' Paula said, always the practical one. 'It doesn't stop, Cherry, and we have to go on.'

'I know,' Cherry said sadly. 'I'm trying, truly I am, but, in losing Ethan, Lance and I seem to have lost something between us as well, and I don't know how to get it back. I don't blame him for what happened, but I'm not sure he believes it.'

'Well, there are some things you can't force, and this is probably one of them. You'll just have to give it time, kid.'

Cherry gave a weak smile. 'Do you know, nobody else but you ever calls me kid?'

'Do you want me to stop, my lady?'

'God, no! It reminds me of who I am!'

'You mean Brian O'Neill's sister?' Paula said deliberately.

'Cruel, but true. We can't change our past, can we, Paula? And I don't want to. Now, for God's sake, let's stop getting so miserable and take all these kids, and Nanny Green, to Smithy's for a treat. And if any toffs think it's far too soon for Lady Melchoir to be out gallivanting after her nephew's death, nuts to them, I say.'

'Attagirl,' said Paula.

If time was supposed to be a great healer, Cherry couldn't deny that even more so was the presence of the children, with their steady acceptance of what had happened, and the eagerness with which they consulted both her and Lance on what Ethan's headstone would say. It would be in place before Christmas, Lance told Cherry, which seemed like a fitting memorial to Ethan.

November was already over, and the beginning of December was cold and grey. They had heard no more of David Trelawney, except that the lawyer could report that he had left his relatives' house in some disgrace and no one knew where he had gone.

Cherry didn't want to know. She had more important things to think about, and that was how to break through the barrier that still seemed to exist between herself and Lance. On the surface, everything was as it was before. She loved him and she knew he loved her with the same passion as ever, but something indefinable had been lost between them.

He spent more and more time at his club, or closeted in his study, and she knew that, like most people in the country, he was caught by the growing political crisis over the monarchy. Everyone knew of it, of course, for it was impossible to miss the importance of it any more, but in Cherry's opinion it would make no difference to their lives whether or not the king continued his association with the American divorcee, Mrs Simpson.

Wrongly or rightly, she couldn't share the fervour of those who took one side or the other. It would probably all blow over, since Edward VIII had been king for less than a year, even though the newspapers were already speculating wildly, but, according to Lance, they were clearly being blocked from how much they were able to reveal. And then, on December the eleventh, he arrived home in a great state of feverish anxiety, immediately switching on the wireless in the drawing room, and calling urgently to Gerard to do the same below stairs.

The stiff BBC voice was announcing solemnly that His Majesty was about to address the nation from Windsor Castle. Within a very short time, the whole country knew that King Edward VIII was abdicating for love of Mrs Wallis Simpson, and that they now had a new king in the shape of his brother, King George VI.

'So it's actually happened! I didn't believe it was going to come to this,' Cherry said, when the final words died away.

'Haven't I been telling you all along?' Lance said.

'Yes, but to give up a throne and everything that goes with it was not what I expected at all,' she said in bewilderment. 'What will he do now, do you suppose? And what of the new king and queen and the two little princesses? Their lives will be changed for ever, won't they?'

She tried to imagine the turmoil that must be going through all their minds now. Kings or commoners, they shared the same emotions, the same fears, hopes and dreams. And all because of love. Love had a great deal to answer for.

'I think we should drink a toast to the new king and a new future for us all,' Lance said, pouring them each a glass. 'You and I should look on all of this as a lucky omen, Cherry, even a retrospect one.'

'Well, I'm not sure even what that means.'

He didn't explain. He merely took her glass away from her and placed it on a table beside his, and then took her hands in his. She saw the special look in his eyes, so long absent in these last sad weeks, and she felt her heartbeats quicken.

'So you don't see any parallels in our former king's decision and ours?'

'I think I would prefer to hear you explain it to me,' she said.

'He was prepared to give up everything for the woman he loved, and so was I. I'm sure there are many men who dream of doing such a thing, but few who would actually go so far as to act on it, confident that it was the right and only thing to do.'

'So you think yourself equal to a king now, do you?' she said, half in teasing, since these moments were becoming far too charged for her to do otherwise.

But he was quite serious, and she could no longer doubt his sincerity.

'I think myself far more fortunate than any man alive, Cherry-ripe, because I have you, and if he finds half as much happiness in his decision as I did in mine, he will be a fortunate man indeed.'

And then she was held close in his arms where she belonged. His kiss was the sweetest she had ever known, and, in the end, love was all that mattered.